The
Madonnas of
Echo Park

A NOVEL

Brando Skyhorse

Free Press

NEW YORK   LONDON   TORONTO   SYDNEY

Free Press
A Division of Simon & Schuster, Inc.
1230 Avenue of the Americas
New York, NY 10020

First Free Press trade paperback edition February 2011
FREE PRESS and colophon are trademarks of Simon & Schuster, Inc. For information about special discounts for bulk purchases, please contact Simon & Schuster Special Sales at 1-866-506-1949 or business@simonandschuster.com.

The Simon & Schuster Speakers Bureau can bring authors to your live event. For more information or to book an event, contact the Simon & Schuster Speakers Bureau at 1-866-248-3049 or visit our website at www.simonspeakers.com.

Manufactured in the United States of America

3 5 7 9 10 8 6 4 2

The Library of Congress has cataloged the hardcover edition as follows:
Skyhorse, Brando.
The Madonnas of Echo Park : a novel / Brando Skyhorse.
p.   cm.
1. Mexican Americans—Fiction.   2. Echo Park (Los Angeles, Calif.)—Fiction.   3. Domestic fiction.   I. Title.
PS3619.K947A44   2010
813'.6-dc22   2009034403
ISBN 978-1-4391-7080-9
ISBN 978-1-4391-7084-7 (pbk)
ISBN 978-1-4391-7085-4 (ebook)

Here. I want you to have this.
It's an opening, and you're welcome.
It's a city, and in the palm of the city
is a lake. In the heart of the lake is a wing.
All the people, all the exhaust & sprawl:
it's perfect. Let them sleep in you
when you sleep. And wake with you,
that you might know them and their streets,
and the light that makes them fall in love,
the light that has always been your light.

—Jeff G. Lytle

Contents

They thought I was a Mexican, of course; and in a way I am.

    — Jack Kerouac, *On the Road*

I wish I was born Mexican, but it's too late for that now.

    —Morrissey

It's no fun to pick on Mexicans. You guys got a country.

    —Richard Pryor

Author's Note

This book was written because of a twelve-year-old girl named Aurora Esperanza. In the 1980s, before I knew I was Mexican, Aurora and I were in a sixth-grade class of American-born Mexicans and first-generation Vietnamese immigrants, both groups segregating themselves into clusters on opposite sides of the room. This was an awkward arrangement for me, because though I felt I belonged to neither group, my Mexican-ness would peek out every so often from under the shadow of my stepfather's last name when I rolled a vowel too long in my mouth, or grew coarse tufts of premature facial hair. Emphasizing my "in between" status, a desk chair shortage placed me alone at an oversize table with an obstructed view of the chalkboard and my back to the American flag.

There was a constant tension in the classroom, each group suspicious of the other for conspiratorial hushes peppered with strange, foreign-sounding words that shared jokes, kept secrets, plotted insurrections. We were, however, still kids, and our hunger for the latest fads led us to break ethnic ranks and whisper in a common language of desire. We wanted Garbage Pail Kids and Pac-Man sticker trading cards, packaged with sticks of bone-hard bubble gum you could rub against the pavement to write out your name in pink zigzagged letters, a scent of hot caramelized sugar lingering on the concrete. We wanted futuristic digital watches that blinked out the time in a blood-red neon LCD phosphorescence, as bright as a sparkler strapped to your wrist.

And, of course, *we wanted our MTV.*

It was the rare child in Echo Park whose family could afford something as frivolous as cable television. Most families had one or two parents working a spread of jobs to support both their kids and their in-laws living under one roof. My family had a different arrangement, but I was as astonished as any of my friends would have been when one afternoon I found MTV installed on my very own television in my room, a present for getting a part-time job as an after-school ESL tutor. I sat twelve inches away from the screen, transfixed for the next seven hours, leaving it on when I went to bed with the sound off like a night-light. The next morning, I spread its legend in Ms. O'Neill's class, watching the tale jump from Mexican to Vietnamese and from boy to girl, just as difficult a bridge to cross at our ages. You could watch music on television? *Yes,* and every song has a story, and every story has a happy ending. You could watch Michael Jackson dance whenever you wanted? *Yes,* and when he walks, each step he takes lights up the sidewalk. Here was a way you could see how the music on our cheap transistor radios *looked,* these popular songs that throbbed with glamour, desire, and plastic gratification—a reimagining of the American Dream in bright pastels. Our parents didn't comprehend the words and were fearful that the songs *they* had fallen in love with growing up would be attached to a language we'd never speak and a country we'd never see.

Right before lunch, Ms. O'Neill intercepted a note I'd written to a table of Mexican boys outlining everything on MTV the night before: girls in short skirts dancing down a street in a conga line; girls with shorter skirts dressed as cheerleaders forming a bright Day-Glo pyramid; girls in bikinis dancing by an open fire hydrant. Ms. O'Neill asked how many of us thought MTV was "cool," and thanks to my classroom gospel, everyone's hand shot up. MTV was now our mutual language.

The next day, Ms. O'Neill announced plans for an "MTV Dance Party" in our classroom on the Friday before spring break. There would be those expensive Soft Batch cookies that got gummy and elastic like rubber bands if you left them out for more than a day (making them an impractical purchase for most of us because junk food had to *last* in our houses), two-liter bottles of Coke and Pepsi (not the generic, white-label, noncarbonated sludge with SODA stamped on its side that we drank at home), and Domino's pizza. In a neighborhood where takeout was considered extravagant, this was the equivalent of a Roman bacchanal. There would also be music. Each of us was to bring in a record and play it. A number of hands shot up in confusion. What if we didn't have any records of our own? Borrow them from your brothers, sisters, or parents, Ms. O'Neill said. What if they didn't have records either? Buy a record you'd want to play. What if we can't afford to buy one? Buy a single, she suggested, they cost the same as two packs of those gross Garbage Pail sticker cards you're so fond of. All but one hand went down. Aurora Esperanza's pink fingernails sparkled as her white cotton blouse sleeve fell back down her arm and curled up against her bare shoulder.

"Will we be allowed to dance in the classroom?" she asked. "Will there be dancing?"

"It's a dance party," Ms. O'Neill said. "Yes, there will be dancing."

Dancing? The boys didn't like the sound of this. Were we expected to dance with *girls*? And were Mexican boys to dance with Vietnamese girls? What about Vietnamese boys—would they dance with Mexican girls? Then a more terrifying thought arose: Who would *I* dance with? By the end of class, I had formed a pact with two Vietnamese boys I had never spoken to before, not to dance with any girl, even if we were asked. There were many other treaties of convenience made that day, as boys and girls who had segregated themselves by race and language throughout the year became unexpected allies in an effort to outsmart our teacher, who was white. Who, we wondered, would *she* dance with?

* * *

In the short weeks between the announcement and the party, every classmate had seen or at least stolen a peek of MTV. Was this because I did the charitable thing and invited friends over to my house to watch? Hell, no. Part of the fun of being a kid comes from having things other kids don't have and lording it over them. On the playground, I recounted the videos' story lines with such relish, anyone overhearing me would have thought these on-screen adventures were my own experiences, and in a way, I felt they were. What I hadn't counted on was my classmates' determination to see these videos for themselves, no matter the cost or inconvenience. Distant and more prosperous Vietnamese relatives, who lived in actual houses (not one-room box apartments) as far away as El Monte, had their remote controls hijacked. Mexican girls took the bus together to the Valley, racing through the Glendale Galleria to the electronics section of JCPenney. With each passing Monday, the MTV circle widened, and with it my reign as the "MTV King" diminished until the day of the party, when the two poorest boys in the class, twin brothers who alternated their clothes in an effort to project a larger wardrobe (the stains gave them away) were what remained of my empire.

The bare turntable wobbled in slow circles like a drunk uncle at a *quinceañera* in search of a young girl's ass to grope. Hands rustled in peeling vinyl backpacks, plastic supermarket bags, and cheap store-brand three-ring binders, a *shassh* of ripped-open Velcro fasteners as 45 records poked out from snug butterfly folders. While I had agreed not to dance, I didn't want to fail an assignment, so I bought Michael Jackson's *Thriller*. Its $9.99 price tag embarrassed me, the large record sitting on my desk like an arrogant boast; many of the other students had brought ninety-nine-cent, seven-inch singles from *Thriller*, each priced with a distinctive blue El Tocadisco sticker. El Tocadisco was a local discount *barateria* that sold Spanish music but reserved a small section at the front of the store for American pop stars. (It had occurred to no one to bring in a Menudo album, or any other kind of music. There was a tacit understanding among Mexican and

Vietnamese kids alike that MTV music meant *American* music, and American music meant English men with keyboards, white women with big hair, or Michael Jackson.) *Thriller* had been out for over a year, but kids here didn't have a lot of disposable income, meaning pop culture filtered through in spurts. Our teacher grimaced as she collected copies of "Beat It" and "Billie Jean." The boys nodded to each other in smug conspiracy—there would be no dancing today.

When Ms. O'Neill asked Aurora where her record was, she pulled from a torn grocery store bag a rainbow-sequined vinyl record case. A velvet sash strung around a plastic rose clasped the top of the box, which flipped open to reveal an alphabetized selection of 45 singles. Ms. O'Neill unsheathed each record from its wax paper sleeve with delicate fingertips, the girls ooohhhing and aaahhhing over the case's delicate satin lining and the number of singles the case contained. Ms. O'Neill counted over fifty, plenty for an afternoon dance party. She asked the class to give Aurora a round of applause for sharing with us something so important to her. Girls both Mexican and Vietnamese burst into squealing chant-cheers, something you'd hear on the playground before a fight, while the boys smacked their hands together like we were trying to smother fires in our palms.

"Aurora," Ms. O'Neill said, "why don't you pick the first song?"

She walked across the room in an outfit that matched her record case—a tight red fringe blouse with poet's sleeves and a tie-string bow across her budding chest along with tapered black jeans that hugged her curved thighs (up to that point, girls had been stick figures, straight lines wrapped in corduroy) and matching black platform sandals. Her face had a thin dusting of powdered-donut-white foundation to cover her chicken pox scars; her eyelashes were etched into her face like fiery black sunsets. I was attracted to her, though I didn't know what attraction was yet, and because I could think of nothing we shared in common—not one friend on the playground, not a single family acquaintance who shopped or did laundry with an acquaintance of her family's—I hated this feeling.

When she approached the record player, the boys fire-drill sprang out of their chairs. The girls, sensing some sort of new, significant moment, skirted the edges of the classroom and formed a rigid semicircle, cutting off any chance of escape. My two coconspirators had sandwiched themselves with about ten other boys into a far corner, leaving nowhere for me to stand but right in front of a firing squad of giggling twelve-year-old girls.

Aurora slid a 45 out of her case and in one graceful motion popped a plastic yellow "spider" in the center of the record and threaded it onto the turntable's spindle. When you play a record, there's that brief anxious moment of silence when the needle crackles but the music hasn't started. This was the kind of silence you could tear apart by making an obscene noise, setting off a laughing seizure so uproarious that Ms. O'Neill would lose control of the class, or by doing something catastrophic like wetting your pants, but that meant you'd risk being the object of a ritualized humiliation so vicious, moving to the next grade level wouldn't stop it. The boys waited in anticipation of who would be brave enough to make that fart noise or trickle "fear piss" down his legs.

Madonna's "Borderline" began to play. This was a *new* song, Aurora bragged, which, along with her opulent record case, meant that her parents must have been as "rich" as my parents. (There was a real low bar for "rich" in Echo Park.) I recognized the song from MTV. Part of the video for the song had been filmed in the neighborhood, and because of its story line (Mexican break-dancers, Latin boyfriend, Madonna's girlfriends dressed in retro *chola* girl outfits complete with drape coats, baggy pants, and hairnet caps), I believed Madonna was a Mexican.

The girls swayed their hips to the soft, synthesized tinkle that opens the song, then nodded their heads an inch to the left, an inch to the right (the way the Muppets dance on TV) to the syncopated beat, before singing along with the chorus. The circle on the girls' side tightened in anticipation of the first dance. Ms. O'Neill leaned down to Aurora, and after a quick consultation both nodded their heads in agreement. Aurora strode across the circle and placed her hand on my shoulder.

"This is Madonna," she said. "Come and dance with me, Brando."

There was an audible gasp as her fingers traced a line down my shirtsleeve and clasped my hand. Was it too late for me to make an obscene noise or wet my pants? The girls leered with confidence; Aurora's boldness had made them aware for the first time how powerful a girl their own age could be. So much change was possible in so short a time. I looked to the boys for some sort of help, an intervention, one good idea to get me out of this. They stared back hypnotized in defeat, the way men look when they have played their last, failed excuse. I could sense the walls of the room sliding together, two sides of a V closing shut, our bodies interlocking, our differences now irrelevant. It was simple as following Aurora's lead.

I shrugged her hands off me.

"I can't dance with you," I said. "You're a Mexican." It was a moment I'd rehearsed with my mother, but the word *Mexican* caught on the roof of my mouth like a stutter. It was the hard *x*—the same consonant that degrades the word *sex*.

"What do you mean?" She laughed, her shy smile saying, *You cannot be serious.*

"You are *a Mexican*," I said, loud enough for the entire class this time. "I can't dance with you."

Aurora kept smiling, but her eyes focused on the chalkboard, evaporating me in a glance.

Madonna continued to play. Ms. O'Neill lunged at Aurora and pulled her into the circle. While they danced, the crowd relaxed and bunched into the segregated clusters we knew so well. My two useless cohorts emerged from the corner and patted me on the back. A couple of Vietnamese girls came with them, their satisfied smiles making me blush. They couldn't tell for sure whether Aurora, with her excellent command of English and British band names etched in ballpoint onto the cover of her denim blue three-ring binder, was a "real" Mexican (real as in a *chola*), but they *were* sure that Aurora's best friend, named Duchess, was. While we talked, a group of Mexican boys teased me in a singsong mock-Chinese. The boldest of the bunch asked Aurora to dance with him, which she did. I watched them in silent fury, like a lost man watches the horizon.

The school bell ended the party. Ms. O'Neill called me over to her desk and asked Aurora to stay after class. She was on the other side of the room, shoulders hunched, putting her records away as fast as she could.

"You did a terrible, terrible thing today, Brando," Ms. O'Neill said. "Why would you say something like that?"

"I don't know," I lied.

"Well, I think you owe Aurora an apology."

"Okay," I said.

We turned to see a door slamming the way it does in a vacuum. Ms. O'Neill raced out of the classroom, shouting "Aurora! Aurora!" until her voice cracked.

When Ms. O'Neill returned, she said, "You'll apologize first thing after break."

I spent vacation in my hot, airless bedroom in self-imposed exile, not leaving my house for fear of seeing Aurora at the bus stop or on my way to the supermarket or, worse, running into Duchess, who I believed was on the lookout to beat me to a bloody pulp (this being, at the time, the worst thing I thought a gang member could do to you). Playing on an endless loop on my bedroom television was MTV. I saw the "Borderline" video several times a day for a week. At some point in the video, there was a close-up of Madonna's face that would melt, time-lapsed, into Aurora's face, staring at me with that same hollow look I saw when I rejected her, betraying an emotion beyond disgust or contempt—it was a look that said I didn't exist. I'd recognize this look more and more as I grew older, in places both private and public, for reasons both explicit and unspoken, and once you've been *seen through* in this way—once you have been made *transparent*— no amount of physical pain matches the weight of invisibility.

When we returned from break, I told Ms. O'Neill that I hadn't forgotten about what I'd done at the dance and was ready to apologize to Aurora, even if I had to in front of the class. She said that wasn't necessary but was proud of how determined I seemed. The bell rang, and we took our seats in the castes we had arranged for ourselves and felt comfortable with. Aurora's chair was empty. Ms. O'Neill asked if anyone had seen her during the break. No one had.

A week later, her name was no longer called in roll. I asked Ms. O'Neill what had happened to her.

"Aurora won't be coming back," she said.

"Then how am I going to apologize?"

"You'll have to find another way to do it."

Twenty-five years later, I think I have found my way, in the book you're reading now. This is the story of Aurora Esperanza and why she disappeared, told through the people of Echo Park who ultimately led me back to her. And while I've changed some details to protect those who drifted in and through this project over the duration of its writing, these are their real voices. I want to add that everyone in this book insisted he or she was a proud American *first,* an American who happened to be Mexican, not the other way around. No one emphasized this more than Aurora. I *am* a Mexican, she said when I caught up with her, but *a Mexican* is not *all that I am.* To my surprise there were no hard feelings, and as we joked about that day ("I shouldn't have picked a Madonna song!"), she was gracious enough to ask about my mother's attempts to raise me as someone other than a Mexican in a curious rather than an accusatory way.

"I don't blame her," she said. "I must confess—and I guess this *is* a confession—why would anyone want to be a Mexican in *this* country at a time like this?" I understood what she meant. When writing this book, originally called *Amexicans*, there was such a vitriolic fever against illegal immigration (translation: Mexicans) that it made me grateful I had an Indian last name, and ashamed that I felt grateful.

Aurora, if you are reading this (it wasn't clear during our talk that you would), I have a confession of my own: I'm ready to dance with you. I'm ready to lace my still too-small-for-a-man fingers around your waist, ready to smell cotton-candy-scented shampoo in your long, black, curly hair as we sway our close but not touching hips to the beat of a song decades out of time. I won't offer an apology, because you didn't want one then, and I'm sure you have no need for one now.

I'm ready to dance with you, Aurora. I hope you understand why I need to say that to you here, in this way: because a work of fiction is an excellent place for a confession.

—B.S.

1

Bienvenidos

We slipped into this country like thieves, onto the land that once was ours. Those who'd never been here before could at last see the Promised Land in the darkness; those who'd been deported and come back, only a shadow of that promise. Before the sun rises on this famished desert, stretching from the fiercest undertow in the Pacific to the steepest flint-tipped crest in the San Gabriel Mountains, the temperature drops to an icy chill, the border disappears, and in a finger snap of a blink of an eye, we are running, carried on the breath of a morning frost into hot kitchens to cook your food, waltzing across miles of tile floor to clean your houses, settling like dew on shaggy front lawns to cut your grass. We run into this American dream with a determination to shed everything we know and love that weighs us down if we have any hope of survival. This is how we learn to navigate the terrain.

I measure the land not by what I have but by what I have lost, because the more you lose, the more American you can become. In the rolling jade valleys of Elysian Park, my family lost their home in Chavez Ravine to the cheers of *gringos* rooting for a baseball team they stole from another town. Down the hill in Echo Park, I lost my wife—and the woman I left her for—when I ran out of excuses and they ran out of forgiveness. Across town, in Hollywood, I lost my job of eighteen years when a restaurant that catered to fashion and fame found its last customers were those who had neither. And my daughters, they are both lost to me, somewhere in the blinding California sunshine.

What I thought I could not lose was my place in this country. How can you lose something that never belonged to you?

"Bienvenidos! You are all welcome here," announces David Tenant from the flatbed of his mushroom brown GMC pickup truck in the parking lot of the Do-It-Yourself Hardware store on Sunset Boulevard in Echo Park. He says this to the regulars, and to those who won't be back because the work is too hard or the pay too small or they will have been deported or they will have moved on, to Salinas, San Diego, Phoenix. There are hundreds of parking lots in Los Angeles like this one, and thousands of men like me standing in them, waiting for a good day's wages. That day doesn't come around too often now because construction jobs are in short supply, but today, the first dry, chilly morning to break through a week of rain, Tenant's looking for men, and if I'm lucky, I could make a hundred dollars for a ten-hour day.

A restless crowd of thirty to forty men undulate around Tenant's truck, our hunger for work an octopus's tentacles swallowing the vehicle into our mass of bodies. The younger men, punching buttons on their ancient cell phones, swarm the front, while the grandfathers are hunched over in devotion or exhaustion in the rear. Tenant leaps up on a set of crates, raises his arms as a conductor readies his orchestra to begin a symphony, and cocks a boot atop the tailgate.

"Who's here to work?" he shouts.

We raise our hands and yell, "Me, *señor!*"

He scythes the air with his palms, casting a line in the direction he wants men from and pulling them from the crowd into the flatbed. The chosen men stride past us, hoisting themselves into the pickup in ascension. Any man who fakes being picked is tossed back into the sea; any man who refuses to leave the flatbed has to deal with Tenant's son Adam, a squat, muscular former security guard and current aspiring actor who sits in the cab shouting into his cell phone until he's needed. He's been an extra in a number of horror films with Roman numerals in their titles and comes to help his father after the late-night shoots wired on meth and coming down on coffee, his thick biceps coated with what he says is real Hollywood movie blood.

Men materialize in the parking lot as fast as they disappear into the back of Tenant's truck. They come from a nearby alley, where they smoke weed and piss against the wall, or from the liquor store, fresh from checking their lottery numbers, or with forty-ouncers. Preachers have been here before to save us, but most of these men want the sermon that comes out of a bottle.

Tenant waves his arms in front of himself with a magician's swipe, his quota satisfied. *"No más!"* he shouts. "But we'll be back." The pickup jerks the dozen laughing and singing men in the back like bobble-head dolls as it speeds out of the parking lot and turns onto Sunset Boulevard.

We are left with our bodies coiled, smoldering, cursing our luck, waiting for the next pickup truck to approach, which could be anywhere from a few minutes to several hours. It's an erratic schedule better suited to a younger man, but when a boss like Tenant, who is in the business of supplying *trabajadores* to job sites throughout the city, says he's coming back, it's worth it to wait.

When I started as *un trabajador,* the bosses could tell I'd never done any outdoor work. And knowing English on top of that? I was lucky to last a day. They liked men fresh from the border, not a forty-plus-year-old man who'd worked most of his life in a restaurant but whose opportunities for a living wage had vanished, undercut by busboys pooled from the very men I now jostled alongside. They could mold these young *mojados,* push them harder and pay them cheaper. When the jobs dried up, though, my demeanor and reliability became assets.

The sun disappears behind a swath of clouds, darkening the street, when Diego arrives wearing a black Dodgers cap, smoking a cigarette, and holding a cup of coffee. He's many gray hairs away from forty, but we've been drawn together because he likes to talk and there's nothing else to do while waiting for a job except brag or listen. He drifted here from Mobile after a spree of murders targeting Mexicans in trailer parks. The murderers used baseball bats and, in some cases, machetes. Police blamed Colombians, though Diego insisted it was a meth-dealing white supremacist gang, and for that insistence he had to leave town fast. He sent his wife and four kids money working his way west, but by Albuquerque there was nothing left to send home. His expenses include smokes, whiskey, and underground taxi dancing bars where you can dance with women in lingerie or bikinis for ten bucks, grind on them against a wall for twenty, get a hand job for fifty, or take them home for three hundred (the term *women* is misleading; the girls at the bars we frequent in East L.A. are either teenagers with developing chests and acne dotting their cheekbones or haggard *abuelitas* with rubber tread marks around their flaccid bellies and breasts).

I never question the holes in Diego's story because he's honest company. He doesn't wolf-whistle, grope, or lunge at the Catholic schoolgirls when they walk by, doesn't brown-bag forties for breakfast, doesn't sell his drugs in front of me, and most important, he doesn't push, shove, or jostle to get chosen for a job. There's a civilized, dignified air in his approach to being *un trabajador,* and while he mentions no plans to change his day-to-day life, this is a condition he says—most of us say—is temporary. Ask any man why he's here, and you'll get the same answer: *What else can I do?*

An SUV with tinted windows creeps into the parking lot. Its stop-start approach marks them as first-timers. Nobody wants to take a job from a new boss. All the young men—those who have a choice—know it's not worthwhile. The pay's miserable (six or seven dollars an hour instead of the usual ten), and they think they've rented a slave instead of hired a housepainter. During the day, they're the ones ordered around. Out here, they get a taste of being in charge and get drunk on it. If you're not careful, a simple driveway paving job can turn into a landscaping job, a garbage collection job, a disposing of paint cans job, or a "suck my dick, *maricón*" job, and you'd better do it for the same fee you negotiated for one job because, really, who are you going to complain to? That's why you need to be smart about whose truck you get into. Get into the wrong one and you're broke, deported, or dead.

If you don't have a choice, like these men out here in their sixties who still wear cowboy-style straw hats with brims instead of baseball caps and long, dark dress slacks coupled with funeral dress shoes instead of jeans and sneakers, you risk what's left of your body. You know it's not worth much to a white man who needs a roofer, but it may be worth something to a Chinese lady who needs her lawn weeded. Slow and feeble, *"los hombres del país viejo"* can't be picky.

"Tenant pick up his first crew?" Diego asks.

"About a half hour ago."

"First sunny day we've had in a while."

"He said he'd be back."

"Man of his word," Diego says. "Bad trait in a *gringo*."

"I don't mind a man who's honest."

"Hate honest bosses. Honest men are bullies." He motions to the old men hunched around the SUV with his coffee. "Look at that," he says. "Why do they still come out here?"

"They're not that much older than I am," I say.

"You look young, though. You can lie about your age."

"Too many lies. I can't keep track."

"I'm lying less these days," Diego says, "but I don't want to make it a habit. When was the last time you got something for telling the truth?"

Tenant's pickup truck rattles into the parking lot. Diego taps my shoulder, and we walk (never run, Diego says, and never look too eager or out of breath) over to the gathering crowd, twice as large as before.

"Who's here to work?" Tenant shouts.

"Me, *señor*!" we shout back. It's a revival out here, and we let the spirit of potential employment move through us. The young men bounce up and down pogo-stick style while the older men wave their arms back and forth in the air, swooning as each man is chosen. Diego and I move to the front as Tenant picks his men. Both of us are careful not to jostle or ram up against the younger men, twenty-year-olds who will punch an old man in his remaining teeth if they think a boss will see them better, nor do we huddle with the older men, who cluster together to protect themselves from the more aggressive guys. Tenant picks Diego, and as I try to follow into the flatbed behind him, Tenant waves his arms and shouts, *"No más!"* As we shamble away, one of the twelve men in the pickup starts coughing. Diego mouths for me to wait. The man throws up on himself, coating his jeans and his shirt with a sticky pool of undigested alcohol and tendrils of bloody vomit.

Tenant leans over and pats him on the shoulder. "Can you stand up? Adam, come here and help this man out."

Adam hefts him out of the pickup. Tenant looks at the greasy pool and then down at me. "If you don't mind sitting in vomit . . ."

The site is a teardown in Angelino Heights, one of the oldest neighborhoods in Los Angeles, and overlooks Echo Park Lake. Rows of three- and four-story Victorian-era homes, restored to turn-of-the-century condition, have been selling for a couple million dollars each, while those houses that are too far gone are torn down and rebuilt from scratch to resemble "old" houses using a mix of new materials and relics salvaged from other gutted teardowns. Three historic Victorian mansions that could have fit thirty homeless families have been demolished for a new modern, Victorian-style house, a potential several months of steady work if the bank's financing doesn't fall through. Diego gathers this information for us piecemeal. Any of the men on the site could have passed on all the information, but no one here wants anyone else to know too much about a job site out of fear it could give them an advantage in getting attached as a regular.

Some of these men resent me sliding into another man's spot, though that spot's covered in vomit; they shift away or don't look at me. A couple of young boys who tell us they're from Jalisco say that they've never seen anyone get picked for a job like that before. It's a bad sign, and one of them crosses his chest, saying either the Virgin Mary or the Devil must be looking out for me. *"¡Tiene que ser la Virgen María!"* Diego shouts, *"Pucha, ¿qué hace sentado en su mierda?"* The rest of the men laugh until Adam's fist on the glass divider shuts us up.

We're ordered out of the truck at the dead end of a street that fetal-curls into a construction lot near a large Victorian house on the opposite corner, which will be dwarfed when, or if, this new house is finished. The lot pours onto a jagged hillside that men are excavating with pickaxes and shovels. Tenant talks to his black foreman, Adam lays out the tools, and we spend more time standing and waiting for others to make up their minds about where they want us, and for how long. Debris from the old houses has been hauled away, and we're sent to different parts of the new house's foundation outlines—prepping plywood, digging trench for pipes, mixing concrete—to begin.

I'm given rolls of nine-gauge chain-link fence to enclose the job site. I take some measurements, then gouge deep holes into the ground with a posthole digger, a mixture of what Tenant calls "soft" and "hard" work that allows me to float between Tenant's men and the *trabajadores,* earning me the nickname *malinchista*—traitor.

Diego leads off some teasing ("Mexicans are supposed to cut through fences, not build them!") that helps the men feel more comfortable about me being trusted with such a specialized (no heavy lifting) and suspicious job. It's a tricky thing to build a fence around a site of *trabajadores;* I make my calculations away from the other men—they hate anyone who uses pencils and clipboards—and when I set down the marking stakes and line posts, I stand on the inside of where the galvanized fence will be. It's more difficult this way, but I do it to demonstrate that we're working on the same side of the land.

The posthole digger slides in and out of the softened ground with ease. Diego, who's cutting sheets of plywood, jokes for me not to get a hard-on. The men laugh, and as Adam hovers around the different areas, tossing us tools like fastballs or rolling the command *"Rápido, mojados!"* off his tongue, we find the rhythms of an unusually cool summer's day. It's slower than restaurant work but much more exhausting, because the tasks here are repetitive without requiring the same sense of timing or orchestration with other men. A man working with you today could be arrested or deported or move on tomorrow. We work independent of each other, careful not to move too fast or too slow because no matter what our level of speed or competency, the wage is the same at the end of the day. Bosses like Tenant love a square deal, as long as all four sides of the square are theirs. If he has a deadline to meet, Tenant may bargain on a task-by-task basis. Finish off this stack of plywood before you leave and you get an extra ten dollars. Stay here until 8:00 P.M. and you get a twenty-dollar bill. There's a rumor that as a bonus Tenant takes the occasional man out to many rounds of drinks followed by a hearty dinner in a sit-down "American-style" restaurant where the plates are as big as hubcaps, but neither Diego nor I has had what Diego would call a *"una trampa de maricón."*

During the lunch break, Tenant calls me aside to do some additional calculations for a temporary path we're building up to the house's entrance. It's off-the-clock time, but I'm relieved for the task because I can't make a great lunch on my hot plate. That means I rely on whatever takeout's nearby, the "roach coaches" that troll job sites, Mexicans serving subgrade meat in slapped together tacos and burritos. I could cook meals in these trucks that would put these grill slappers (I won't call them cooks) to shame, but where would I get the money to buy a catering truck? How could I file for a license, permits, and insurance when I don't have a green card? And how could I apply for a green card without being deported? Or ask for help getting a green card without being scammed?

I don't know where to begin. What else can I do?

When I get to where I think the front door will be, I'm turned around at an awkward angle, away from the street, and I don't know whether I'm going in or coming out of the house. There are muddy paw prints on the ground, tufts of brown and white fur dancing with the wind, and a strong, musty dog odor. It makes my eyes water, a sour pungency that thrived in my first American apartment, where I decided to cheat on my wife and abandon my child.

She was the fourth prettiest Mexican girl in Echo Park, behind Silvia Morales, Liz Chacon, and Marisol Soto, but she was the only one you had a guarantee of seeing every day. All it'd cost you was a quart of milk. Or a stick of butter. Or a sack of flour. If you were a married man, you'd time your trips to Pilgrim's Supermarket so she'd be the first thing you'd see before breakfast and the last thing you'd see after dinner. Her winter's morning sky blue smock with a lace tie string cradled her breasts like newborns. Her black bob and ivory mestizo skin, her high cheekbones and pillowy Popsicle lips, and those fine patches of blond arm hair were such an attraction men would fistfight each other to cut in her line. And forget about buying ice cream—it'd be a sticky puddle by the time she rang you up.

Cristina Alarcon was a twenty-five-year-old checker when we met in 1972. I was eighteen, living with my wife, Felicia, our baby girl,

Aurora, and Felicia's dog in a one-room apartment with no furniture except a used bed and a folding card table from the church where we ate our meals, changed diapers, and kept our television set and her Bible. Cristina complimented me on being the rare husband ("So young and already a real man!") who accompanied his wife shopping and paid for the groceries while she told Felicia her secret for stretching a bushel of bananas when they changed color.

When we came home, I could hear the babysitter, our nine-year-old neighbor whose parents were never home, cooing words to our daughter, who screamed whenever the front door opened. Then that dog scent hit me. It was nauseating, oppressive. How could I be a "real man" if my life wouldn't have any more surprises or new opportunities, only a swelling of what was in front of me—more kids, more bills, more fat on Felicia's body? I'd memorized every stretch mark and lumpy ass-dimple. My life would be a series of a thousand more trips to the grocery store watching other pathetic husbands leer at Cristina and seeing the pictures forming in their heads: having wild sex (wild for a Mexican man is a woman on top) in an open field of white dandelions; seeing her breasts pop out of her bra for the first time. Then I got those pictures in *my* head. Before I'd finished putting away the groceries, I knew I was going to cheat on my wife.

I asked Felicia to change Aurora, then went back to the grocery store with a lightness that had vanished the day Felicia told me in church that she was pregnant. (She'd underlined a verse in her Bible and shoved it in my ribs: "If a man comes upon a maiden that is not betrothed, takes her and has relations with her, and their deed is discovered, the man who had relations with her shall pay the girl's father fifty silver shekels and take her as his wife, because he has deflowered her. Moreover, he may not divorce her as long as he lives"—Deuteronomy 22:28–29.)

In line with a cold beer I wasn't old enough to drink, I made a long list of reasons (call them lies) why what I was about to do was okay. When a man cheats on someone he's made a vow to love, honor, and obey for the rest of his life, that list protects him, gives him courage, helps him reach the one lie that makes all deceit possible: I *deserve* this. In bed with that new woman, you feel your head, and a sensation dangling between your legs, swell. This lasts until morning, when your sensation is the size of a flea and your only possessions are the lies you told to get into bed. You guard those lies with your life, because to admit the truth is to admit how weak you really are.

"You're not old enough to buy this beer," Cristina said.

"I have a wife and a child. Why can't I have a beer?"

"Don't be such a typical man."

"The beer's ruined. It got warm waiting in line. Now will you sell it to me?"

Cristina laughed. "Where's your wife?" she asked.

"I lost her," I said. Cristina smiled and nodded her head. "Have *you* lost something, too?" I asked.

"A fearless brown-skinned man," she said. "What I wouldn't give to have that back again for a while." She looked at the warm beer on the conveyor belt. "My icebox doesn't work. Can you fix it?"

We drank warm beer and made love on balmy Sunday mornings when I skipped church and long afternoons when Felicia took Aurora out in her stroller. Cristina's apartment was a young woman's home, full of mystery, thrift, and unblemished promise. We had bedspread picnics on cornflower china purchased with books of Blue Chip stamps. She taught me the names of famous people from a collection of black-and-white photos that hung on the walls in cheap frames, including someone named Louise Brooks whom Cristina modeled her hair on. "These are my saints," she whispered before we climbed into bed. "I pray to them to get me out of this shitty neighborhood." It was Cristina's idea for me to try my hand as a busboy or a back waiter in a fancy restaurant, perhaps in Hollywood, she said. "Maybe you'll return Ryan O'Neal's lost wallet for a reward or serve Robert Redford a meal he finds so wonderful he leaves a thousand-dollar tip."

Then came a pregnancy scare. It was time to go home to my own family, not start another one. I begged Felicia to take me back, thinking her silence over my blatant adultery meant a brief exile. For me, there was the practical matter of citizenship. Felicia was a citizen and I wasn't. You needed to be married to a citizen for two years before you could apply for residency; we hadn't reached our first anniversary. Felicia wouldn't dream of seeing me, the father of her child, deported, but what a man doesn't understand is that a woman has an infinite capacity for love and generosity no matter how long she's been debased and abused—until she decides she is out of love.

That's what happened with Felicia; I saw it in her eyes easier than she must have seen the lies in mine. I gave Felicia a list of the ways I'd change, and waited for her answer. And then the days without her answer kept coming, like leaves falling off a tree, too many to count in the strong breeze of our busy lives.

A gust of wind blows my marking sheet from my clipboard, across the skeleton of the foundation and over to the site's edge. I retrieve it and hand it to Tenant, who instructs me to finish the fence. The dog stench, which I smell everywhere, and an empty stomach leave me light-headed, but I grab my mallet and hammer in the final support posts. The light-headedness sways me back to a sense of satisfaction at a task completed and a day's wages earned. No matter how bad your job is, there is one brief moment when you are content—a joke someone makes at the site before the most grueling routine sets in; the way sunshine streaks across your face at a particular time of day; the satisfaction of unloading the last of a batch of heavy boxes; and for the young men here, the cleverness at finding out how little they can do and still avoid being scolded. We are at our best when we are at work.

I'm installing the fittings and tension bands on the final two fence posts at the far edge of the site when I hear a loud, gurgling hiccup. No one's around. I think it's a dog that's broken its legs falling into one of the excavation pits, a common sight. A mount juts out over the cliff a few yards from where I'm working. I peer over the edge, and there's a sound like someone punching a wad of dough. Heights make me sick, but I step out onto the mount to see what's making the sound.

My vision's hazy from the view and not eating lunch, but I think I see Adam swinging a bright-yellow-handled sledgehammer down on a hairy pumpkin lodged behind a mound of dirt. There's nobody else on the cliff. I edge out a couple inches farther, loosening some rain-dampened dirt clods under my feet. There is a man on the ground, the receiving end of Adam's sledgehammer. Next to him is a black Dodgers cap. The ground, a blood-orange clay, shifts and swallows the head, which makes a trilling, gasping sound, as if it's being deflated. Where is Diego? When I step back, several large clumps of dirt give way, rolling down the hill. Adam sees me before I run back to the fence.

The chain-link mesh is loose in several places and curls up, leaving a large hole someone could crawl or slide through. I struggle to attach the tension bands, but they fall from my shivering fingers. Behind me, heavy footsteps attack the hill and climb up over the ledge. Another pair of footsteps runs over to greet them. Somebody's fleshy face gets slapped, again and again. Work across the site stops in a rolling wave as everyone except me watches the exchange. Tenant shouts in an exasperated voice, "We've had an accident. The ground's too soft. I'm gonna let you go home a couple hours early, but you're gettin' paid for a full day. Thank the Virgin Mary for me tonight before you go to bed."

The men cheer and line up in front of Tenant to receive handfuls of twenty-dollar bills. I drop my tools, leaving the fence unfinished, and try to mingle with the last of the workers clearing off the job site. I decide to skip out on my money—a hundred dollars I need to pay off *last* month's rent, with still no idea how to pay *this* month's rent.

"Hang on a sec, Hector," Tenant says. "Let me buy you supper."

He offers me Adam's seat in the cab up front while Adam, who's holding a shovel, stays behind at the site to "clean up." It's dusk by the time we're loaded and ready to go. Tenant's uncomfortable as he drives, and I can tell he's distracted, sweating and muttering to himself, taking turns too fast, not looking in his mirrors as he changes lanes. Not paying attention to the traffic, Tenant runs a red light and almost collides with a fast-moving MTA bus that has to swerve out of our way. We both sigh with relief when we reach Taix on Sunset, a French restaurant that's been in Echo Park since the sixties. It's seen the whites leave, the Mexicans come, the Mexicans go, and now the whites come back.

There are no windows in the restaurant, no way to keep track of the time passing outside. The light in here is thick and dark like rye bread. We're seated at a booth and given oversize menus with gold tassels and the prices written in pen.

"Want a drink?" Tenant asks.

"No thank you, sir."

"Service can be a little slow in here," he says and walks to the bar. It's a short distance between our booth and the front door. If I were twenty years younger, I could run. I *would* run. Felicia said I'd made a pretty good life by running away. I could try my luck at a different parking lot, or another town, and leave this life behind. But where would I go? How would I get there? What else can I do?

A pair of brown hands sets a large basket of cold sourdough slices on the table, making me jump. I'm amazed because I didn't see the man approach, and because of how dark it is, I don't see him leave.

These are my hands, asking a guest with a simple gesture whether he is done with his meal. These hands stack the silverware and the bread plate atop the congealed demi-glace and uneaten vegetables on her dish, whisking them away with the swift, unobtrusive movements learned through years of steady repetition. These hands have bused tables of famous actors and actresses, producers and directors, mayors and councilmen, diplomats, and a former President of the United States. These hands collect fat wineglasses, red plastic drink stirrers, cocktail napkins with the restaurant's logo emblazoned in gold type, and produce a silver bread-crumb comb that with no more than four broad sweeps across a laundered tablecloth collects any remaining food—in under thirty seconds (these hands have been timed with a stopwatch). Then these hands disappear, leaving time for coffee, dessert, liqueur, or a relaxed after-dinner conversation, creating an illusion that the table was bused on its own by a set of unseen hands, invisible hands that mother a city of infants.

The Option was one of Hollywood's oldest and most prestigious eateries. I brought Aurora there on the bus every Christmas Day when she was a child. She hated that my hands smelled like offal and wasn't impressed with the grand, oak-and-glass-paneled front entrance where pen-and-ink caricatures of famous celebrities (my favorite was Rita Hayworth's) looked down at customers from either side of a long, haunted corridor that appeared to expand as you walked along it.

How I wished I could have eaten at a fancy American restaurant when I was a boy! The upholstered booths were as big as a Cadillac's backseat. The prime seating tables had thousand-dollar centerpieces, some of which, when their bloom and scent faded, I'd set outside Felicia's apartment, then, as the years passed and our separation grew longer and longer, on the front porch of the small house she bought with money she made as a cleaning lady. And the meal itself: big American-size portions of steak, potatoes, creamed spinach, and the house specialty, macaroni and cheese, an "off the menu" dish made one late evening a hundred seasons ago for a famished Humphrey Bogart and available to those "in the know" enough to ask for it (except those "in the know" had stopped coming years ago).

Did my daughter imagine that *every* staff member was granted special privileges? How could she know that the holiday dinner (which took place in two separate dining rooms—one near the bar for aging celebrities, friends, and relatives of the head staff, and a second for the Mexican junior staff in a musty storage area) was a perk for those management considered important men, men with responsibilities who were valued and appreciated, and whose input was sought and respected?

Aurora learned her lack of enthusiasm for my work from her mother. We had separated, but I'd hoped my dedication to a single job instead of a string of temporary, trashy new ones would impress her ("Your penis could learn a thing or two from your work ethic," Felicia said). I wanted Felicia to marvel at how my peers in the restaurant respected and admired me, yet she cared nothing for my job, thought nothing of me clearing drinks from the mayor of Los Angeles Tom Bradley's table, where he'd enjoyed the house's signature martini ("A real Mexican would have spit in it," she said). She had not one word of praise when I was promoted to head busboy because Aurora told her busboys are addressed by their first names, while waiters and senior staff are addressed with an honorific *Mr.* Aurora, who was tending to her own simmering cauldron of anger, didn't understand busboy was one step away from waiter, though The Option had never hired (and with its closing, never would) a Mexican waiter. How could I explain to someone who never worked in a restaurant that this fixed hierarchy was not a symptom of prejudice? From how I described my workday, Aurora found a hundred perceived slights a week I didn't have the pride to correct.

Rarer still were Felicia's visits to the restaurant. I made sure the busboys who reported to me were on their toes and showed me respect. She felt I mistook their obedience for loyalty, their briskness for a sense of purpose or direction ("I see where you get that from," she said). These men and my bosses, she said, were conspiring against me, ridiculing my imperceptible accent, shortchanging my fair share of tips, and loading my sommelier's tests (one could not become a waiter without passing one) with obscure European wines the restaurant didn't serve, relegating me to the restaurant's bottom caste. Of course she'd never *heard* anything terrible; neither had I. Whispers were extinguished whenever I turned a corner into the kitchen. But she believed the taste of some offensive conversation lingered in the air, dangling on the edge of a testy comment I recounted about the junior staff not "understanding clear instructions" or how any requests to amend a work schedule had to be made "in writing and in English." Her life, in which she had always believed in the transcendence of fury, set an example for her daughter to turn against her father, excommunicating me to a nether region of the living dead, a place where the deceased form new families, creating and inventing new histories and biographies, while the ones left behind announce their demise with the ripping of mailbox labels and pictures in two.

Then the building craze came and The Option lost its lease. The land was to be razed for a multimillion-dollar apartment complex and parking garage that was never built after the craze found its senses. Aurora, now a beautiful, angry young girl of nineteen, accepted my invite to our closing night party. My special job was to help garnish slices of a five-tier cake with caviar, costing seventeen thousand dollars. Our self-anointed sous chef (he received neither the title nor the money), Felix, had brought from home a boom box and set it in the kitchen. A wiry Central Valley–born Mexican, he turned it to a Spanish station for the Mexican junior staff, who weren't invited into the main dining room for the restaurant's senior-staff finale celebration.

The head sommelier came to supervise while I bent over the cake like a sinner doing penance. He asked the waiter and sous chef to lean close so he could share something with them. I couldn't make out most of their conversation, save the ending, where the sommelier said aloud, "Guess what *his* nickname is?" The group exploded in laughter, repeating that odd punch line as if they were speaking their own language in a room of foreigners. I was unperturbed, my hands placing spoonfuls of caviar in gentle dollops along the cake's ridges.

"They're talking about you," Aurora said. She was standing against a wall, arms folded, looking severe and disappointed—an identical image of her mother.

"I didn't hear anything," I said.

"You never do. Excuse me," she asked, "what is his nickname?"

The three men either ignored her or couldn't hear her over the radio, so she repeated her question.

"What are you asking?" the sommelier said.

"His nickname," she said. "My father. What *is* his nickname?"

"Oh, we weren't talking about him," the sommelier said.

"It was a restaurant joke, *chica*," Felix said. "You wouldn't understand."

"What is his nickname?" she asked again, louder.

"We don't have time for this," the waiter said. "They're waiting for the cake."

"Aurora," I said. "Don't."

"What *is his nickname!*" she demanded.

My hand felt the slap on her face before my brain did. The waiter rushed to wheel the cake out of the kitchen, followed by the sommelier, his head bent down in shame. Felix turned back to his station.

Aurora said nothing. She picked up the radio and carried it out of the kitchen. I watched her walk away, mesmerized, the boisterous *ranchera* music echoing through the tight corridors that led to the dining room.

Atop an unused busing station, amid a maze of tables garnished with fine silver and crystal, the rows of extravagant buffet trays and carving stations, the hundreds of guests (many of whose youthful and now almost unrecognizable caricatures graced the front entrance) talking, laughing, and reminiscing in various states of drunkenness, sat the boom box, playing *ranchera* music at top volume. Aurora was cutting through the crowd to the front door, the curls of her long black hair cascading down her back like steam. That was the last time I saw her.

Felix raced to turn off the music, yet the crush of revelers made a short trip across the room a series of complicated dips, elbowings, and double-backs. The Mexican staff filed out to watch him juggle his limbs through the dining room. Some of them laughed, craning their necks, but continued working in the kitchen. Others were bolder, wading out into the room as if they were entering the deep end of a pool.

I straddled some invisible line between the two. I debated whether to rush in and tackle the boom box or retreat into the kitchen, humiliated, and leave out the back door before I could be scolded and denied a reference for another restaurant. A decision had to be made. I stood fixed in my spot, paralyzed, and clasped my coarse hands together, wondering if they were strong enough for outdoor work. I hadn't noticed one of the busboys tapping me on the shoulder, asking, *"¿Porqué estas orando?"* (Why are you praying?)

Tenant sits down with a loud *plumph* and slides into the booth with a drink.

"Tough work out there today, wasn't it?" he says, not waiting for my answer. He drains his glass in two gulps. His face has deep but smooth crevasses, scrubbed free from guilt, fear, or shame. "You know that behind every American worker are a couple of Mexicans doing his job? Course, you can't see them because they're so goddamned short."

Tenant clinks the ice in his drink, eyeing me to see whether it's okay to laugh. It's strange he needs this permission.

"I'm sorry. That's a bad joke." He chuckles. "Came out an insult. You Mexicans are the new niggers in this country, which is a real shame 'cause nobody in this damn country realizes how hard all you guys work. No offense meant. I like you. I like you because I can trust you. In fact, I want to give you something."

He pulls five one-hundred-dollar bills from his wallet. "That's for today. That's for you."

"I get eighty-five dollars for the time I worked," I say.

"No, that's the pay for the other men. You're more of a manager. This is *manager* pay."

"I'm not a manager," I say.

"Sure you are. See, a work site is a dangerous place. Accidents happen every day. We almost had one on the way over here with that bus, right? That's why we need someone to manage things for us. You know what a manager does, don't you? He makes sure everything runs smooth, and if there's a problem, he takes care of it. We have a problem, and because I trust you, I want you to take care of it."

Adam walks into the restaurant and heads straight to our booth. He's changed clothes, and his arms and hands have been scrubbed with soap; there's not a sliver of dirt under his fingernails.

"Hec here's going to help 'manage' the problem you created earlier this afternoon," Tenant says.

"Fine with me," Adam says and motions a waiter I don't see for a drink. "As long as he knows how to keep his fucking spic mouth shut. One call to La Migra and he's headed back to Mexico."

I know this, and it terrifies me. It terrifies me because Mexico doesn't exist for me. I have no memory of it. I was a few months old when my mother brought us to Los Angeles from my birth home in Guanajuato. We settled in a Mexican neighborhood called Chavez Ravine but were evicted when the city took back the land to build Dodger Stadium. Mexico is as foreign to me as Mars, Paris, or Florida. I have no heartbreaking story of the journey here; the heartbreaking story *is* here, in this small couple of square miles of land called Echo Park. Running through the desert, trying to stay ahead of the border patrol or the Minutemen or the coyotes or the rats isn't the story. It isn't the *getting* here, it's the *staying* here.

"Accidents happen every day, don't they, Hector?" Tenant asks, sliding the money over to me. "Now let's have a few drinks, a nice meal, then you'll manage our problem and that will be that. Okay?" I pocket the money while Tenant and Adam discuss the Victorian job.

It's night outside when we're done eating. Tenant opens up one of the side compartments on the pickup truck.

"Your first managerial duty is to get rid of this thing," he says, looking at me from the corner of his eye. "The lake's right down the road. I'll leave the details up to you."

The sledgehammer lies atop a thick sheet of black tarp. Small clumps of black hair are matted to the hammer's tip with blood and a hardened, gelatinous membrane that looks like skin.

"Go ahead," Adam says. "Pick it up." I reach for the hammer and then pull my hands away.

"Do you have gloves?" I ask.

"Fuck you," Adam says. "Wipe it down before you ditch it."

While I tie the sledgehammer in the tarp with some frayed twine, Tenant whispers something into Adam's ear. They look at me and laugh.

"What did you say?" I ask.

"Don't worry," Tenant says. "Bad joke. You wouldn't understand."

A short walk down a hill from the restaurant is Echo Park Lake, where the annual Lotus Festival is being held this weekend. Every July, thousands of people from across the city sample Polynesian, Filipino, Malaysian, and Hawaiian foods, most of which are served grilled with pineapple and on wooden skewers, along with the assortment of offerings from Mexican taco stands and cotton candy, popcorn, and funnel cake stands. Wandering amid throngs of people flitting back and forth in front of me like fireflies, I see dozens of inconspicuous places I can leave the sledgehammer. A foul-smelling stall in the public men's room; a battalion of Dumpsters lined up near

Glendale Boulevard; any of a hundred trash piles collecting behind the food stalls. The most brazen approach would be to walk up to the lake, lay it on the ground, and kick it into the water. Yet whenever I think of leaving it somewhere, the conditions don't seem right. I catch someone talking on their cell phone looking at me strange, or I see several open spots in a trash pile—where someone could nose around and stumble across it.

I wander from the spinning buckets to the jerking buckets to the thrashing buckets to the Ferris wheel, whose neon lights sizzle and pop into brightness. Basking in this light is a young woman feeling her way through the crowd, like a blind person searching for her misplaced sight—lost but determined. She's about my daughter's age and has a sweaty, radiant glow, the kind you get from spending your day in the sun or being in the sudden presence of the miraculous. That's what I felt watching her. She could very well be what my daughter would look like now, bursting with courage, desire, and pain of her own instead of the hurt and longing she inherited from me. That day at The Option was fifteen years ago. What would she think of her father wandering around a park filled with happy families on a summer night, trying to dispose of a murder weapon? I had five hundred dollars in my pocket, enough to get me as far north as San Francisco, and I hadn't even made a pathetic attempt to run. Was I too exhausted to act a coward?

A cluster of fireworks explode in the sky, lighting my path to a large trailer serving as the LAPD's portable drunk tank. Several cops are standing on the trailer's steps enjoying the display. I stand with them and bask in the flickering lights until one of the cops notices me.

"What you got there, pops?" a Mexican cop asks.

"It's a murder weapon." He takes a step forward, unsure if I'm drunk, his hand falling to his holster. "I've been paid to dispose of it." I hand the sledgehammer over.

"Okay, why don't we come inside and talk about it?"

The drunk tank is lit with fluorescent lights, loud as hummingbirds. He scrapes a metal folding chair across the floor and sets it next to his desk.

"Okay. Are you a citizen? *¿Es usted ciudadano de los Estados Unidos de América?*"

"A citizen?"

"*Sí, Americano, de dónde eres.* You speak English okay, but I need to ask anyway."

Anyone who works on the street knows there's a rule in L.A. the cops have: Special Order 40, or what the *trabajadores* call *"santo cuarenta."* The cops can't stop you if they think you're an illegal, only if they think you're an illegal about to commit a crime. This is to encourage illegals to come forward if they have information about a crime. They also can't hold you for more than twenty-four hours if the one thing they've got on you is that you're an alien. It's tougher in L.A. for illegals now, meaning cops have to ask you where you're from no matter what. But as long as you lie and tell them you're from here, they won't check your background or report you to immigration. As long as you lie.

"*¿Es usted ciudadano de los Estados Unidos de América?*" he asks again.

As long as you lie.

"Hello? *¿Es usted ciudadano?*"

Everything I have earned in this life by lying, I have lost. By lying.

"Sir, I'm not going to ask you again. *¿Es usted ciudadano?*"

The cop took down the story, asked me to sign a written statement, then turned me over to central processing, where the facts of my illegal status were noted on a long sheet of ruled paper. I had no birth certificate, no proof my daughters were citizens, no legal paperwork, no official state ID cards, no passports, no check stubs or electric bills—nothing to establish that I'd been in this country for years. I had lived in that invisible space where people like me live, the place between darkness and blindness where you try to make a life and everything is paid for in cash and sweat.

A public defender tried to attach me as a material witness in an ongoing murder investigation to halt my deportation, but Tenant, Adam, and Diego's body couldn't be located, and aside from the bloody sledgehammer, my statement was the single piece of evidence they had. The case was declared inactive, and I could be deported to Mexico right away.

"Don't worry," my public defender said. "You can be back in Los Angeles by tomorrow night. We'll get you home." But where was home?

Before sunrise we were corralled, our wrists cuffed in plastic twist ties like the necks of garbage bags, and shuffled onto a long, olive green bus with iron mesh on its windows and a steel partition between us and the driver. The bus drove through Downtown, an abandoned area with plenty of room, until it reached a steep freeway overpass, which we had to speed up on to get to driving speed. It was the way an airplane must feel taking off—speed, force, and elevation—and I got that twisted knot in my stomach again, that feeling I had when, over the ledge, I saw Diego's body.

Laid out in front of the dawn like a rug made of jigsaw pieces was Los Angeles. Through the wire-mesh window screens, endless fly strips of houses, *homes,* and the skeletons of those yet to be built; naked mounds of land that would soon be smothered by new homes, built with the hands, and on the bones, of the old landlords, homes in such a starry multitude that I was confident there was one for me, and in that home there'd be enough space for my small life, and the hopes I'd bring back with me.

2

The Blossoms of Los Feliz

Spring is here and it makes my joints ache. All those jacaranda blossoms on the walk outside to sweep up. Jacaranda trees thrive in Los Angeles, like blondes and Mexicans. There's no getting away from them, not even in my dreams. They've haunted me from childhood, when I believed a jacaranda tree would save me. Can you imagine such a thing, a tree saving a life? A silly girl thought so once.

I'd been sent to my grandmother's home in Chavez Ravine by a mother whose face I didn't remember and whose cruelty Abuelita wouldn't let me forget. The dirt road outside my *abuelita*'s house led to an outdoor *mercado* and was covered with an amethyst sea of pulpy jacaranda that felt like old skin and calico under your bare feet. I'd collect sprays of young jacaranda, then run down the road with them, petals raining from my arms.

When the white men came to build a baseball stadium for playing their games, they smoothed the land out like a sheet of paper to bring in their trucks and bulldozers that would destroy our homes. But there was a problem. The land was uncooperative and petty, swallowing contractors' flatbed trucks and, I prayed, the workers themselves into sinkholes and collapsing earth atop surveyors' flags. The jacaranda trees gave them the most trouble. They felled the mightiest bulldozers, which couldn't tear them down without themselves being damaged. I thought that if I grew a jacaranda tree in my room, it would anchor our home to the land and we wouldn't have to leave.

I found a thin branch with several young sprays and set it in an old wooden *batea*. We had no running water, and the rainstorms that fled across the ravine didn't give the dry, cracked ground a chance to soak up what poured out of the sky, so at night I'd slip out of my window barefoot to steal water from a neighbor's well.

I planted the *batea* in our swept-smooth dirt floor and waited for the spray to bear seeds whose roots would burrow deep into our ground. Two of the buds matured, plopping atop the water's surface before they could open, but the rest weren't growing fast enough and the sounds of the bulldozers kept getting closer and closer. I poured heavy gulps of water into the *batea* to get the other buds to bloom. I didn't want to hurt them. I wanted to give them more of what I thought they needed.

That night, a bad dream crept to my bed like a relative with filthy thoughts. I was a jacaranda blossom struggling to stay alive but whose violet color was dripping off my petals into a standing pool of water. But I was also me, laughing as I held the dying blossom by its bud under the water. I reached up with as much strength as I pushed my body down, drowning both my selves. There was the *drop drop drop* of running water, then a hard patter, then a shrieking roar, a scream pouring out of my mouth as I awoke coughing strands of spit on the side of the bed I shared with my *abuelita*. It was a vivid nightmare, one that revisits me, a persistent yet incurable sickness.

Fumbling to the *batea* through the rough darkness, I saw that the other buds had shriveled up. Two jacaranda flowers were submerged underwater. I cradled them out of the vase to dry them, but their milk and seeds popped out as the flowers tore apart in my hands. My *abuelita* heard me crying and without asking where the water had come from told me that a drowning flower moves toward the water, not away from it. Its stem may be strong enough to stand on its own, but when its petals grow wet and heavy, they drag the flower back into the water and that causes it to die.

Aurora Salazar, the last woman evicted from Chavez Ravine, learned this lesson when she was dragged by her wrists and ankles like a shackled butterfly off her land. And I would learn that lesson many years later working for Mrs. Calhoun. This is what women do, when they have an ocean of dreams but no water to put them in.

Mrs. Calhoun lived in a large house on Avalon Street in Los Feliz with her husband, Rick, who had followed a story in the newspapers and on television about a drive-by shooting. In 1984, during my twelve-year-old daughter Aurora's spring break, she and I had been standing for a group photo (which all the papers published) on a street corner when a car opened fire near the crowd. Neither of us had been in any actual danger, but because of the attention, I lost my job cleaning the offices of a law firm where I'd worked for four years as a "temp."

Before Rick found me, I was looking for work on a street corner, 5th and San Pedro, near the Midnight Mission. Back then, my English was terrible and Skid Row was where, if you were a woman, needed work, and didn't speak English, you'd gather in a group for the *gabachos* to come and hire you. We all had our own corners on Skid Row back then. 6th and Los Angeles, by the Greyhound station, was for junkies. 5th and San Julian was the park where whores would sell their time: twenty dollars for twenty minutes in a flophouse, or ten dollars for ten minutes in a Porta Potti the city put out for the homeless. And 5th and Pedro was where you went to hire day laborers and cleaning ladies.

The women came from everywhere south, some as far away as

Uruguay, each with her own Spanish dialect. The men had their own corner, across the street from ours. They weren't there to defend us when we were harassed (or sometimes raped) by the bums who swarmed the area but to keep an eye on us while they drank, laughed, and wolf-whistled the gazelles, beanstalky white women in suits and sneakers who parked their cars in the cheap garages nearby. They turned those *pendejos'* heads like compass needles, as if those girls' tits and asses were magnetized. We had the dignity to wait in silence, yawning in the flat gray sharpness of dawn under a mist of milky amber streetlight. Standing in a straight line, arms folded across our chests like stop signs, we prepared ourselves for a long day of aching, mindless work by sharing a religious, rigorous, devotional quiet.

When men want relief they hire a whore. When women want relief they hire a cleaning lady. And they did it the same way—first they examined our bodies. Could we reach the high shelves with the lead crystal without a stepladder? Were we able to fit into a crawl space and fish out their children's toys? Were our *culos* big enough to cushion an accidental fall? They never looked us in the eye because they could see us performing those disgusting chores no decent woman would dream of asking another woman to do. Then they tried to negotiate the stingiest hourly rate, or tossed out a flat fee that always seemed too good to be true, and was; at their houses, you were asked in a polite but insistent voice to do "just one more" messy, humiliating job (digging through moist, rotten garbage for a missing earring they "thought" might have fallen in, or fishing a tampon out of a clogged toilet) before you earned your day's freedom. The men were more direct, pulling up in large white windowless vans and snapping their fingers—"I need two plump, stocky ones and two that can squeeze into tight corners!"—like buying live chickens.

I wasn't the only American-born woman on this corner who never learned English. In Los Angeles, you could rent an apartment, buy groceries, cash checks, and socialize, all in Spanish. I tried going to the movies to learn English; at the theaters Downtown, Mexicans could come only on certain days and were "restricted" to the balcony. I snuck in whenever I could because I wanted to be more "American," and I thought these movies—"The rain in Spain stays mainly in the plain!"—had the answer. Yet whatever English I pieced together dissolved when I walked into the harsh sunlight outside.

When something really stumped me—paying taxes, for example—I asked for help. More Mexicans speak English than you imagine and understand it better than they let on. That's how I met Hector, in church; he could already speak English but never had time to teach me. (I should have known a man who could speak two languages could live two different lives with two different women.) How could I find time to learn English, when I left my house at dusk like a vampire, working in empty, haunted offices all night? And some vampire I was, frightened by all those ghostly sounds in an office, like copy machines that powered on for no reason or phones that rang endlessly. Before sunrise, I scurried out the service entrance with a horseshoe back, clenched shoulders, callused feet, and skin reeking of ammonia.

That's why Rick's letter arriving when it did gave me faith we were not destined to live our lives as victims. The papers painted Aurora and me as tragic near-martyrs, symbols of a community the city had forgotten. Aurora couldn't face her classmates because of this and some incident at school that she started telling me about, then stopped when she told me I'd gotten the details wrong (someone called her "a dirty Mexican"). After the shooting, she stopped telling me anything, became a sour and sullen stranger in my home. She changed schools and talked to me even less, but she was still my translator and my negotiator when I went to meet Rick. Cards and letters flooded our mailbox, but Rick had written on the most handsome stationery that he was looking for a cleaning lady (or better yet, a houseboy), and if I wasn't interested, would I inquire in the neighborhood in exchange for a "finder's fee"?

We rode the bus a half hour to Los Feliz and met Rick on his front drive under a gang of aging palm trees. He led us around the grounds, which included a shady grotto and swimming pool carved out of a hillside shielded beneath a canopied jacaranda tree that had thin green sprouts and young, tender, but still unripe ivory buds peeking out from its branches.

"You have a swimming pool!" Aurora said.

"Do you have a boyfriend?" Rick asked her.

"Maybe." Aurora smiled a confident, gap-toothed grin that meant she was lying.

"You can have a pool party with your boyfriend anytime. If he has an older brother, he can come and bring his friends, too," he said.

When I asked her how much the job paid, she began a back-and-forth conversation until I agreed on a schedule of three times a week, six hours each day. Aurora negotiated thirty dollars per cleaning day, with Rick providing the cleaning supplies.

"My wife will keep everything fully stocked," Rick said. "She's inside."

In a living room that could fit my entire childhood Chavez Ravine home, Rick's wife sat curled on a fancy corduroy couch (a couch I'd come to know very well), her head draped over a glossy magazine. I couldn't tell whether she was asleep or awake. There was a booming, echoed silence, what you'd hear in a cathedral.

Aurora dove onto the couch. Startled, his wife jerked up, and Rick motioned stiffly for her to shake my hand.

"Hello, Mrs. Calhoun," I said.

She dragged her legs off the couch, adjusted her silk blouse, then pinched the waist of her trim, creased slacks. "This is Felicia, the woman from the newspaper," Rick said.

"Hello, Felicia," she said, standing the same height as me in stocking feet. *"Hola. Buenos días* and *hola,* Felicia." She hugged me at an angle, like she was using tongs.

"My wife was the one who spotted that photo in the paper," Rick said. She looked surprised to hear this.

"Oh, the photo. The one with your friends. *Amigos. Amigas?* I'm sorry my Spanish isn't better," she said.

I understood this, and said, in English, "It's okay. My English should be better. It's America, your country."

"Oh, I thought you were born here," she said.

"I was. But it's your country."

She showed Aurora and me out, saying she was running late for a medical appointment. We descended the sharp incline back to the bus stop at the bottom of the hill. There were no benches—only Mexicans rode the bus around here—so Aurora and I squatted on the curb, massaging our calves and keeping our feet at what we hoped was a safe distance from the sports cars and new "minivans" speeding down the boulevard. We waited under the shadows of manicured wall hedges and palm treetops whose dry, spiny fronds crackled in the breeze like a brushfire.

"I want a house like his," Aurora said. "I want to live here."

"It's very expensive," I said. "You need to stay in school."

"You don't need to go to school to be rich anymore. I want to have a pool party here," Aurora said.

"My job is to work here," I said. "Your job is to go to school."

"Rick said I could come and swim," she said. "You can't decide for both of us."

"That wasn't an invite to swim," I said. *"Era una invitación a trabajar."*

Cleaners must arrive early, before their bosses have had their morning coffee, newspaper, and can mess up their houses any further. To get to work on time, I walked to the bus stop when the moon was still out. No one was around except the *borrachos* swaggering back home to their wives' cold beds when the bars closed, or the crazy bag lady who wore winter coats year-round, prayed at my bus stop bench as if it were a pew, and talked about her "friend," the Virgin Mary, as if Our Lady of Guadalupe was going to show up on the Line 200 bus at five in the morning. I hated rising early then, so I learned the driver's name and acted friendly; in a few weeks, he'd wait an extra minute or two for me at my stop if I was running late, though I had to listen to his endless bragging about how he kept to his schedule and always followed the rules. Don't know what page of the rule book chatting up women passengers was on, but I knew what his game was. Women can see through a man in a way men will never realize. That's because men never change—they'll slow time down trying to get under your dress, then speed it up once they've done it. I was still recovering from Hector, my one attempt at true love. He turned out to be a yo-yo lover, a man who stings you more coming back than going away.

There were many cleaning ladies and maids riding that bus every morning, fanning out across Los Feliz. Working on traffic islands or mountainous front lawns were armies of gardeners who came in their own pickup trucks, their turtle-shell backs inching across unruly grass they sharpened into crisp right angles.

You could hear us coming by the sound of our plastic buckets, knocking what we carried inside them around: spray bottles with homemade cleaning solutions, collapsible mop handles and scouring pads, dried out sponges and boxes of rubber gloves (many owners of these houses, mine included, didn't supply their own cleaning supplies as promised; we'd eat the cost along with our complaints), and a symphony of jangling house keys. If you weren't trusted with keys, you'd better get used to the curb.

It took me a while during those first weeks to learn a different rhythm of doing my job. At the law firm, I had to let others know I was there. Figuring out the best ways to be heard but not seen is a crucial skill for a cleaning lady so I wouldn't surprise anyone staying late, or walk in on lawyers having sex or touching themselves. Turning on the vacuum cleaner when I didn't need to or making a lot of noise arranging my cleaning supplies were the best ways. One lawyer's hands dipped below his waist whenever I cleaned his office, so one night I whipped the vacuum cord at his crotch like a lion tamer. He kept his hands on his papers after that.

In Los Feliz, I needed to be invisible and inaudible. Mrs. Calhoun and I managed to communicate without ever saying a word to each other's face. The massive double front doors made a loud, drawbridge sound when I unlocked them, letting her know I'd arrived. I'd shout "Good morning" in English until Mrs. Calhoun responded with an echoed "Good morning," often from one of the bathrooms. That was my sign to start at the opposite side of the house. When I finished a room, Mrs. Calhoun stepped inside and read a magazine until I finished the next room. Like the arms on a clock, we moved together through six bathrooms, five bedrooms, the split kitchen, two "recreation" rooms (a name that confused me; I didn't have a room to create things in, let alone "re"-create them), and a living room as big as Aurora's school cafeteria. We could spend the day inches apart and never see each other.

Many cleaning ladies would be thrilled not to have someone's eyes raking your spine, correcting your every move, but I felt it was bad luck to spend a day in the same house with someone you never saw or talked to. Sometimes I'd ask Mrs. Calhoun a question but would get no reply. Later, I'd find a note on a large glass table by a pair of sliding doors overlooking the grotto, a place Mrs. Calhoun stared out at most of the day. With the help of an English-Spanish dictionary Rick gave me on my first day, I learned how to translate her replies. "Don't clean the green back bedroom today" meant she'd be shut in there, curtains drawn, for the six hours I was cleaning. "Please clean the oven" meant the charred remains of some grisly attempt at a meal would be lying in wait for me. "Out this afternoon" meant Rick would come in right before I left smelling of chewing gum and alcohol, bobbing and weaving across the freshly waxed floors.

If a dozen people lived there, all coming and going, six hours wouldn't have been enough time to clean the whole house. But these two people didn't really need a cleaning lady, which led me to wonder why they hired me to begin with. I dusted the tables, made the (his and hers) beds, wrestled with the impossible-to-clean reversible pleather/corduroy cushions on their couch, and packed away Styrofoam to-go cartons and pizza boxes into large garbage bags. In the kitchen, foil take-out pans and doggie bags were arranged like an eager student's piles of books in a library. Some stacks were scattered across a cutting block; others were crammed into a refrigerator the size of a bank vault until they went bad. Again, we communicated by note. Food boxes were color-coded with tiny "sticky" notes, telling me what to pack away and what to dispose of, uneaten, untouched. Unused dishes, glasses, copper pans, and silverware were cleaned and polished twice a week. Three of the five beds were never slept in, but I stripped and remade every one of them. The six bathrooms were the most trouble. Each had dried stalactites of vomit and blood around the rims and on the bases of the toilets. To get these clean you need to scrub and scratch with your fingertips while the rest of your body's crouched in a runner's starting hunch, motionless above.

When I finished my assigned chores, there was an hour or two left over that I didn't want to cheat the Calhouns out of. I sorted the stacks of unopened mail and the towers of unread, outdated magazines and catalogs stuffed into overflowing wicker baskets, arranged the dozens of small trinket boxes on shelves, dusted the unused candlesticks and china, and swept dust bunnies off the cool marble floors.

It was one of these extra jobs that led to our first conversation. It had been eight—maybe nine?—months since I started cleaning their house. It may have been as long as a year. I can't be sure, because when you spend your life waiting, time *no me importa*. (I know this word *waiting* has two meanings in English, and I mean it both ways. Either I am waiting *on* someone, serving them, or I am waiting *for* someone, to answer a question, to give me freedom, to love me.) Mrs. Calhoun came into the kitchen holding a magazine.

"Did you," she said and clenched the magazine into a rolled-up wand. "The magazines," she said, "some of them are . . . did you . . ."

"I don't understand," I said.

She slapped the flattened magazine in front of me. She pointed at it and grunted "Uh-huh." Then she pointed at the trash can and grunted "Uh-uh."

"Magazines, yes," she said, clutching it to her chest. "Trash, no. Understand?"

"Magazines yes, trash no?" I asked.

"Yes. Magazines, yes, trash no," she shouted.

"I'm sorry, Mrs. Calhoun. I thought you finish them."

"Oh, you, you understand," she stammered. "You knew what I was . . . I'm, I'm sorry." She tossed the magazine on the ground and ran out of the kitchen. I went through the rest of my cleaning routine on tiptoe until the day was over.

I wanted to apologize before going home, but I couldn't find Mrs. Calhoun. Then I heard a low whirring sound coming from a rear unused bedroom near the three-car garage. Mrs. Calhoun was lying in bed wearing a knee-length lavender bathrobe, open down the middle, with a large white baton between her legs. She moved her arm in broad circles, tossing her head back and flicking her blond hair against the headboard, the sound it made like rain lashing a window. This wasn't shocking to me; I'd done this many times since Hector left, with ribbed corncob holders, candles, and a special, hand-carved "happy stick" a *curandera* sold me, but never with anything mechanical. I was ashamed because I was stealing pleasure away from her, the pleasure she got from being alone. I backed out of the room but jerked the door too fast, slamming it shut. Halfway down the hall, I heard the noise stop and her bedroom door open. Her bathrobe was tied tight, her face flushed, her hair stringy and frazzled. She had balled her fists up as if to fight someone, but there was a weird, crooked smile on her face, ready to collapse into laughter at the silliness of two women being ashamed at sharing the secret of how unnecessary men are.

A handwritten note on the dining room table was waiting for me on my next cleaning day. It was too long to make sense of it on my own, so I asked Aurora to translate. She read the unsigned note in a slow, halting voice:

Felicia,

I am uncomfortable with having to say "good morning" every day when you arrive. I feel I can't start my morning routine until I say "good morning" to you in return.

My morning schedule works on a very specific timetable. I use an electric toothbrush, and it's set on a two-minute timer. I'll be brushing my teeth, and my mouth will be full of toothpaste, and I can't say anything to you when you say "good morning" because there's toothpaste in my mouth, but you keep saying "good morning" until I respond. If I interrupt that process, the toothbrush doesn't reset for another two minutes, and that wastes time.

I don't need to know you're here. Just start working.

"What are you doing over there?" Aurora asked. "Walking around and bothering Rick's wife like you do me?"

When I arrived the following cleaning day, Mrs. Calhoun was lying on a chaise that had been moved inside and set next to the sliding glass doors that looked out on the grotto. Jacaranda trees sprouting white, unripened buds shaded the water. I unfolded the sheet of paper I'd begged Aurora to write out for me and tried to remember how she pronounced the words, which she refused to do more than a couple times because she said I'd never learn otherwise.

"Mrs. Calhoun," I said, "this is my answer to your letter," though *answer* was the wrong word, because Mrs. Calhoun hadn't asked me a question. She didn't want a back-and-forth conversation. I used the slow, dramatic "give me one last chance" voice Hector used whenever he begged me to take him back.

"I'm sorry I walked in on you during your 'happy time,'" I said with difficulty, eyes focused on the paper. "I won't say 'good morning' to you anymore, but please no more lies about your teeth brushing. My daughter read your note, and I don't want her to think her mother isn't doing her job."

The words didn't sound angry like they would have in Spanish, didn't poke through the air with the same fire or conviction. I stood there, having emptied my paper but not my thoughts, shuddering with anger at being humiliated in front of my daughter and fearful that what I'd said sounded much worse to Mrs. Calhoun's ears than to mine.

When neither of us said anything, I started cleaning the kitchen, banging pots and slamming cabinets, working twice my normal speed throughout the house, expecting Mrs. Calhoun to march over at any moment and fire me. By the time I had stuffed the vacuum cleaner in the closet without wrapping up its cord, I couldn't tell whether she was even at home. When I grabbed my purse to dig out my bus pass, I found a slip of notepaper inside. Written in large letters, the words were easy for me to understand: "Would you have lunch with me?"

With uncharacteristic patience, Aurora prepped me for our lunch. She told me what questions she thought Mrs. Calhoun would ask, and what answers I should give in reply. "Whatever she asks," Aurora said, "lie. If she asks you how you're feeling, it's always 'I'm feeling great.' Americans are never honest at lunch or in the bedroom. I learned that on *Dynasty*," she said, a TV show about rich, catfighting white women she loved to memorize quotes from.

With a change of clothes on a wire hanger in a plastic bag, I came in the Calhouns' home without saying "good morning." It felt wrong to enter a house this way, *como una ladrona.* Is this how criminals and cheating men feel when they invade a home? Is this how Hector felt?

The sound of running water was coming from the bathroom next to the kitchen. Steam and heat poured out the door, and every surface was damp with condensation. The water was hitting something in the tub. Behind the shower curtain near the drain was a large mound of bright pink and yellow flesh the size of a baby, frothing under a stream of hot water.

What I remember next is a firm hand patting my face and rubbing my cheeks. The water had been turned off. Mrs. Calhoun was kneeling by my side, panic-breathing as she tried to revive me.

"What happened?" I asked.

"You saw the turkey and passed out," she said.

"Turkey?"

"I'm so embarrassed," she said and lifted me up onto the toilet seat. "I bought a big frozen turkey. A turkey," she repeated louder, pointing to the tub. Americans always think you will understand them if they talk loud enough. Through the curtains I saw the pale, wrinkled yellow skin, smelled the undercooked meat.

"I put it in the fridge to thaw it out. But it didn't thaw. I thought if I ran the turkey under hot water, it would thaw out. This was supposed to be our lunch," she said.

"For us?" I asked. "Big, too big, Mrs. Calhoun. This is for ten people, not two."

"I ruined all this food," she cried. "What do I do?"

"I can cook," I said. "I will make the food."

"No, you can't cook," she said.

Offended, I said, "I'm a good cook, Mrs. Calhoun."

"I mean you can't cook when I invited you to lunch," she said.

"There may be some leftovers," I said. "In your boxes, in the kitchen."

"I can't serve you leftovers. But we could order something in," she said, dabbing at her eyes. "Order in? You know, delivery? We call," she said, motioning with her fingers on an imaginary phone, "and they bring the food to us. I have menus. Lots and lots of menus."

Mrs. Calhoun leapt to her feet and ran to the kitchen. She rummaged through a utensil drawer and spread out on the counter dozens of glossy, colorful take-out menus. "Whatever meal you want," she said, "we can get it here. Thai, Greek, Mexican . . . um, maybe not Mexican."

She pointed to the menus and suggested different dishes, most of whose names I didn't understand. I nodded when she said "pizza," and she circled a couple of items from a yellow-and-black checkerboard menu.

"My address is on the back," she said. "Their number's at the top of the menu."

"Number?" I asked.

"Yes, to call, to order. Order?" she said and made the same dialing motion with her hand.

"Oh, no, I make a mistake," I said.

"It's easy," she said. "I circled what we're going to eat. Say your name, the address, and give them the numbers. It's easy."

"You should call," I said. "I make a mistake."

"Felicia," she said, and her mood blackened in an instant. "If we are going to have lunch, you are going to have to call. You have to learn how to ask for what you want in English, too." She left me in the kitchen to dial the phone in private.

An annoyed woman took my order and told me how much the meal would cost (twenty dollars for two people—an incredible expense). I changed into my lunch outfit—a simple long-sleeve blouse with an ankle-length skirt—and went to help Mrs. Calhoun set the table.

"You're dressed for church!" She laughed. "This wasn't going to be anything fancy."

"I see. I can change back."

"No, I mean you didn't have to go to any trouble. God, no wonder I hate talking." She finished setting the paper plates and utensils on a rectangular white dining room table next to the sliding glass doors overlooking the grotto. "Let's have a drink while we wait for the food." She poured white wine into two etched glasses from the china cabinet and handed me one.

"Isn't Los Angeles beautiful?" she asked, pointing outside, from behind the glass.

"Yes," I said. "Maybe we eat outside? It's a warm day, very beautiful outside."

"Too hot," she said. "I don't enjoy going out there. Better indoors with the air conditioner. Keeps us cool," she said, rubbing her forearms.

"What about your pool?" I asked.

"No, no," she murmured. "If I got in that pool, I'd never want to come out of it." She paused. "How was calling in the order?" she asked, dialing her imaginary phone.

"Yes, easy," I said. "Too expensive, though, too expensive. I am fine with a sandwich."

"How about a turkey sandwich? We have a lot of that," she said, and we laughed. "See how easy that call was?" she asked.

"I like to speak English," I said. "But it's hard to learn."

"We have the opposite problems. I hate to talk, no matter what the language is. I can get you English lessons on cassette tape," she said and sipped her wine, a big gulp. "You can learn English while you clean."

"That would be very nice," I said and figured it was okay to sip my wine, too. The drink made my cheeks flushed, and I felt hot. There was a pause in our conversation, and we both glanced at each other and the pool many times, while I waited for her to speak.

"You need a Walkman. You have Walkman?" she asked, putting her hands over her ears and bobbing her head up and down.

"Oh yes, my daughter, she has Walkman."

"How old is your daughter?" she asked.

"Twelve," I said. "Straight A student, speaks English very good. Too good. She forgets her Spanish. Her English is much better than mine. But she doesn't help me practice."

"Why not?"

"We do not talk a lot."

"Well, she's at that age. Isn't she? Don't girls go through a 'phase'?"

"We used to talk, like friends."

"I don't think I ever left that phase. Talking's overrated. Silence is better. Silence can bring people together."

"Silence with my daughter is good?"

Mrs. Calhoun stared out at the grotto. "What you don't say can mean more than what you *do* say. Look at us. You have a hard time with English and I don't know any Spanish. But we get along great. Appreciate the silence between you and your daughter. She's angry, but in time . . ."

"She has no reason," I said. "No reason to be angry."

"Maybe she's upset over that shooting. It sounded like a terrifying moment," Mrs. Calhoun said. "That poor girl who was killed."

"My daughter was never in danger. Never."

"How about you?" Mrs. Calhoun asked. "How did you feel about what happened?"

"How did I feel?"

"Yes, how do you feel now?"

I remembered what Aurora told me. "I'm feeling great."

Mrs. Calhoun had a strange, confused grimace on her face, and I wasn't sure if I'd communicated what I meant to say.

The doorbell rang, and she slid over two twenty-dollar bills. "One for the meal, one for the tip."

"Twenty-dollar tip? No, too much."

"It's fine, Felicia. Answer the door," she said and gazed back out at the grotto. The jacaranda tree's blossoms were almost in bloom, and a breeze was swaying its branches over the water. When I returned with two small pizza boxes, Mrs. Calhoun hadn't moved. Inside each box was a pizza the size of a flour tortilla. How did white people get away with charging so much for so little? I slid the pizzas from their cardboard boxes to paper plates and sat across from Mrs. Calhoun.

I don't remember how much time passed or how much more wine I sipped before I asked, "Mrs. Calhoun, why do you not like to talk?"

We sat by the sliding glass windows in silence, watching the dangling white baby bell blossoms shudder on the boughs of the tree.

The next cleaning day, a Walkman and a box of *¡Inglés Ahora!* tapes were on the dining room table along with an open invitation to lunch. My routine gave me time to listen and memorize the tapes; the lunches, time to practice. My improving English led to longer and more interesting conversations, but they didn't grow more personal. I was no better able to ask about her troubles, or share troubles of my own. Our chats were mirages, appearing to offer a kind of connection or friendship if I answered things correctly, then yanked away as she ran to another part of the house to retch behind a closed door or curl up on a bed and not move for hours or retreat to a bedroom when the doorbell rang.

What we did best together was share space. While I scoured the counters or washed windows, she'd sit nearby, often on that corduroy couch dressed in nothing more than her lavender bathrobe, and watch MTV with the sound off. Sometimes I'd watch along with her while I cleaned and saw music videos with ladies wearing nothing but underwear. These videos also had unbelievable stories to explain why the ladies were in their underwear. I laughed at most of them but would stop and watch whenever they played the video for a song called "Borderline" by Madonna. I didn't understand what the words in the song meant, but the video was a little movie about a Mexican woman not forgetting where she came from. I liked that.

Mrs. Calhoun seemed afraid to be alone. And I think I felt all this silence wasn't healthy for her. Rick was never around, and whenever I tried talking to Mrs. Calhoun to break her silences, I'd be left standing there flushed and aggravated, unable to find the words I needed to have a real conversation with her. It was life with my ex-husband again, where silence was as close to honesty as you got.

Mrs. Calhoun was in the bedroom with a direct view of the grotto when I came in to practice another conversation with her. She was sitting on the bed in a stiff, upright Barbie doll pose, staring out the window.

"Mrs. Calhoun," I said. "I would like to have a talk with you."

"Your English has improved," she said. "Do you know that?"

"No," I said. "I try to listen more than I talk, but thank you."

"Do you know what day it is today, Felicia?" she asked.

"Wednesday, Mrs. Calhoun."

"It's the last day of spring."

"Yes, I see. But I would like to have a talk with you."

"I know what the reason is," she said. "My husband promised your daughter a pool party." She stared out the window again. "You can't start summer without a pool party."

"I would like to talk about another thing."

"We'll have it this weekend. Have Aurora invite all her friends. My husband will be there to make sure everyone has fun." Where would Mrs. Calhoun be, I wondered, since I'd never seen her leave the house once.

"Mrs. Calhoun," I said, "no, you don't understand me."

"We can talk at the party," she said and lay down on a pillow.

"No," I said, and again, the English words failed me. In Spanish, I could make a man tremble, force a woman to bite her tongue. But not in English. ¡Inglés Ahora! didn't have those kinds of exercises. "No," I said, "no, give me one minute, please."

"I want quiet right now," she said.

"No," I whispered, because she said she wanted quiet. And I left in silence because silence was what I thought she needed.

*   *   *

Aurora invited an even mix of boy and girl friends to take the bus with her on a warm Saturday up to Los Feliz, spoiling them with the promise of pizza *and* bus fare to and from the party. I was furious and insisted she had to use her piggy bank money to get everyone there. The driver who flirted with me was working that Saturday, and I asked if he could give Aurora a deal on the bus fare for twelve kids. He said they could ride for free if I went out on a date with him. Aurora overheard me refuse and called me a bitch as she dumped her piggy bank into the fare box.

When we arrived, Rick shook my hand, patted Aurora on the head, and after asking if any older boys were coming, pointed the children to a pool house for them to change. Aurora huddled with her best friend, Duchess, who wasn't swimming and didn't seem to enjoy the surroundings, while the other children took turns diving into the pool. Water splashed on the jacaranda tree's green fronds overhead, dampening the bright violet blossoms that peeked out from its branches.

Mrs. Calhoun watched the party from behind the sliding glass doors. "Come outside," I said through the glass. "Beautiful day." She smiled and waved her hands no, as if swatting away a fly.

"Can't overprotect her," Rick said, putting his hand on my shoulder. "Nobody can make her live a life."

"You are her husband," I said. "You can help her find a different life."

"I thought I did that when I married her." Rick laughed. "Listen, I want to ask you. I'm getting into the club business and need men who want to work. Where can I find some young, strong Mexican men?"

"You are asking me?" I snorted. "When you find one, let me know. I have a daughter that needs raising."

Around lunchtime, a young Mexican arrived hefting six "real" pizzas (not flour tortilla size) wrapped in a plastic tie strap atop his shoulders as though he was a pack mule. Rick led him over by the pool, instructing him to drop the boxes amid a ring of deck chairs. I thought I saw Mrs. Calhoun say something, but the sliding doors were closed and there was no one inside for her to talk to.

Fat drops of sweat plopped on the pizza boxes while the delivery boy set up paper plate and napkin place settings. Rick shadowed him, touching his forearms while he leaned over a table to grab a stack of napkins, whispering in his ear before he went back to the van for the rest of the food. When he returned, the delivery boy pointed at his watch.

"This guy needs to get going, Felicia," Rick said. "I think I left my wallet in my swim trunks. Finish setting the food out, will you?"

The delivery boy dumped a stack of Styrofoam boxes in front of me on the table and was walking with Rick to the pool house when the sliding glass doors opened.

"No!" Mrs. Calhoun shouted.

The kids stopped laughing and playing. She took two small steps outside.

"Don't touch a thing, Felicia. *He*," she said, pointing at either Rick or the delivery boy, who were standing side by side, "is to finish what he started."

She went back inside and slammed the glass door shut, disappearing into the house. Rick ran to the pool house for his wallet while the delivery boy sulked by the table. He counted up Rick's money and stormed off to his van with that arrogant postargument strut my husband used whenever he knew he was wrong. I called the kids over to eat and brought two slices to Mrs. Calhoun's room.

Outside her window, the blossoms fell, a steady rain into the pool. Mrs. Calhoun was lying in a curled ball on her bed with her shoes on.

"Good morning," I said and walked over to her nightstand, where I placed the pizza.

"Good morning," I said and took off her shoes.

"Good morning," I said and knelt by her side.

Mrs. Calhoun smiled. "Good morning," she said.

"Would you have lunch with me?" I asked.

"Yes, I will," Mrs. Calhoun said. We ate together as the sounds of a dozen children and my daughter's laughter, something I hadn't heard since the shooting, echoed through the house.

Alma Guerrero was a three-year-old girl who lived with her mother in a rough part of Echo Park, on East Edgeware Road. It was in the heart of a patchwork of hills blistered with junkyards and tin shacks made from leftover metal sheared off from the remains of disassembled World War II aircraft. This area belonged, at any one moment, to the street gangs White Fence, 18th Street, 13th Street, Diamond Street, Echo Park *Locos*, and perhaps the most terrifying gang in East Los Angeles, the Department of Urban Reclamation for the City of Los Angeles, which had marked off the land for a multimillion-dollar super high school/shopping mall/condominium complex that took years to construct and, a month after its inauguration, was condemned for being built atop a toxic stew of cancerous sludge that had steeped underground for years.

Alma used to dance with her mother outside El Guanaco, a *mercado* near Angelino Heights that sold rock-hard Twinkies, Colt 45s, and homemade tacos and burritos in the back. She and a half dozen other girls and their mothers gathered there on the corner spontaneously, then every Friday afternoon, when I recognized El Guanaco in Madonna's music video for "Borderline." In the video, Madonna, dressed as a classic "Low Rider" *chola* in a forties-style hair bonnet, white wife-beater, long drape coat, and baggy pants that came up past her waist, had been kicked out of her *gringo* photographer boyfriend's fancy loft for spray-painting a streak on his sports car. Out on "her" streets again, Madonna walks past El Guanaco and is welcomed into the arms of her *cholas* hanging outside, who realize she has not abandoned her *chicas* or her 'hood. They walk into the *mercado,* and after a selection at the jukebox, Madonna dances into the arms of her former boyfriend, a young Mexican guy who has pined for her throughout the video and represents the Mexican roots, the Mexican *life* she cannot turn her back on.

It started when I invited Ana Gomez from church to a *tienda descuenta* that had MTV inside to attract business, to try on new two-dollar dresses. When the video came on, I saw El Guanaco and pointed it out to Ana. It was visible on-screen for a few seconds, but she was as delighted as I was to see a place we walked by every day on television. There was something magical about it, a place in our neighborhood worthy of being on TV, and not because someone had been shot or killed. We agreed it would be fun to bring our daughters there, like a free tourist attraction we didn't have to travel hours on the bus to see. Aurora wouldn't come, but Ana's daughter did. Two mothers became three, then four. One sweltering Friday afternoon in April, seven mothers—the biggest gathering yet—met on the street corner outside El Guanaco with their daughters. I dragged Aurora there that day; being the oldest, she towered over the other girls dressed in their own Madonna-style outfits. Mothers and girls chatted together on a street corner in what was considered a dangerous part of town day or night, in loud, sassy conversations, both groups wearing acid-washed skirts, see-through mesh tank tops, traffic cone orange spandex tights, aquamarine ankle-high socks, tangerine pumps, shiny silver crucifixes, lace gloves, and black rubber bangle bracelets that were called "promise bracelets" because of the way the bangles were made to crisscross in the shape of a heart across the wrist.

A portable cassette deck was balanced atop a mailbox, playing songs taped off the radio. Beer bottle shards were kicked into the street by unsteady pairs of high heels, and the girls made a runway out of the curb, jumping, singing, and dancing around a streetlight as if it was a maypole. Their mothers stood around them in a circle on the sidewalk and on the street, clapping their hands to the beat and encouraging each girl to outdance the others *Soul Train* style. Alma wore an adult-size white T-shirt with Madonna's face on it and a pair of hot-pink tights. Her mother had wrapped a black leather belt with a silver hoop buckle around Alma's waist, turning the bottom half of the shirt into a skirt. Alma waved her arms and jumped in place on platform heels until her mother picked her up and swung her around the streetlight in short, ballerina-style arcs.

Over the hills, the smog above East Los Angeles reduced across the sky like skin on a boiling pot of milk. It was sunset, and the mothers decided it was time to go home. I wanted a picture—who would come to a tourist spot without one?—so I unwrapped a cheap Kodak Instamatic camera from its foil wrapper, lined everyone up against El Guanaco's graffitied walls, then dragged over a flirty old *abuelito* in a straw hat who had been sitting on his front porch stoop to take the picture. It'd only take a minute, I promised.

A chorus line of Mexican Madonna daughters knelt in front of their mothers wearing fierce, take-no-shit smiles, except Aurora, who resented being there and resented kneeling in front of me. The idea to come to the corner was mine, to get her out of her room on her spring break and stop her sulking about something that had happened at school, something about a young boy calling her a dirty Mexican and refusing to dance with her at a party.

Come with me, I said. I'll dance with you. There's this place where all the girls dance like Madonna, I said.

Dance on a street corner, Aurora scoffed. Oh, Momma, you don't understand, she said.

On the corner, I asked Aurora, *"Siéntate delante de tu madre, por favor,"* right next to Alma, so she would be the same height as the rest of the girls. Even in her flat sneakers, Aurora would have blocked me out.

"I don't want to," she said in English. "I'm too old to kneel with the little kids. I can stand with the women."

"No eres tan viejo para ser una mujer," I said.

"I'm not a little girl anymore," she said.

There was a "hot and cold" argument between us. I shouted *en español,* Aurora snapped back in English. The mothers grew impatient and demanded the *abuelito* snap the photo.

A short distance away we heard the sounds of sirens and gunfire. In the choppy, rolling valleys of Echo Park, noise boomerangs in many directions. An ambulance siren sounding like it was on the next block could really be half a mile away, or a gunfight could be sending stray bullets right through your front screen door while your ears told you it was somewhere up in the hills. (You could die around here making these mistakes.) While the *abuelito* fumbled with the shutter button, two pairs of headlights approached over the horizon, as if the setting sun had broken into large marbles. Five loud gunshots in quick succession, not firecrackers or popping corn but deep hammer thrusts, cut the fleshy air. The mothers screamed, their voices angry, then terrified as they dragged their girls' baby high heels across the sidewalk to hide. Broken glass splashed across the street like ocean spray.

The mothers threw themselves everywhere, curled up into tight armadillo balls. I tried to throw myself on Aurora, but she squirmed out from under me. Madonna played on the undisturbed tape deck as we rose off the ground. The sound of her voice outdoors, in the wake of the gasp-for-air silence that follows gunfire, and the music box with a synthesized dance beat melody—it was like hearing a beautiful, off-key hymn sung by a child in an empty church.

As we rose off the ground, one mother joked her husband must be starving for dinner to resort to a drive-by shooting to get her to come home. We laughed while plucking flakes of glass off our bodies. No drive-by shooting was going to ruin *our* day out.

Alma was lying on the ground. We all thought she'd fallen and scraped her knee, or was playing dead the way little children do all the time in the *barrio.* When her mother turned her on her side, blood poured out a small hole in the front of her neck, collecting on the Madonna T-shirt draped across her limp body. She knelt beside her daughter and tried to revive her by breathing into her mouth. Bubbles fizzled out of the wound. Alma's mother ripped off the bottom half of Alma's shirt with Madonna's face and wrapped it around her neck to stop the bleeding.

Crowds gathered on the porches and stoops of the surrounding houses, watching and pointing fingers, their words blending into a long, animated parade of shouts, exclamations, and laughter. Kids ran around in circles and danced to the sound of Madonna's "Borderline" on patches of dirt and weeds that made up their front lawns, oblivious to the dying girl on the sidewalk across the street.

"She doesn't move," Alma's mother said. "The music plays but she doesn't move."

The next day, the *Los Angeles Herald Examiner* ran a front-page picture of Alma in a torn Madonna T-shirt that covered her like a bloody shroud with the banner headline BABY MADONNA MURDERED BY HEARTLESS THUGS. This corner was the place, the story said, where "little Mexican Madonna-wannabes gathered and danced with carefree hearts," and "if there was a more vicious crime perpetrated in Los Angeles this year," the *Herald* couldn't think of it. Police sweeps followed, netting dozens of suspects, though never the actual killer; not one of the fifteen witnesses "saw" a thing, and none of their stories matched anyway. Little girls made pilgrimages to the corner where Baby Madonna was shot. They left candles, rosaries, pictures of the Virgin Mary, little bangle bracelets, and as the story spread and girls who lived in big houses from neighborhoods near the ocean came to pay their respects, big pink teddy bears and Madonna albums and posters—things a baby Madonna fan would want in heaven. While these gifts were stripped by covetous mothers at night, picking up the choicest relics for their own daughters—who in turn thought that their offerings had been taken up to heaven with Alma—for a period of several days the shrine was, according to Mayor Tom Bradley, "a spontaneous outpouring of generosity from the City of Angels."

Over two thousand parishioners stood in line to pay their final respects at La Placita, the oldest Catholic church in Los Angeles. A prominent *mariachi* group donated their services for the procession to Forest Lawn Cemetery in Glendale, and rumor had it that Madonna herself had donated Alma's hot pink with rhinestone trim coffin, along with the plot of land she would be buried in. Baby Madonna was a celebrity whose fame grew after her death, and as a testament to her memory, a mural was commissioned on the side of a building facing the Hollywood Freeway. A girl in a midriff-baring tank top rose out of a *barrio* in flames, carried aloft on a golden musical staff that snaked across the wall until it reached the gates of a pastel pink heaven with smiling clouds and characters from My Little Pony and Care Bears scampering about on a clean and spacious playground with angel wings attached to their backs.

The police report later verified that a stray bullet had ricocheted off a streetlight and severed Alma's spinal cord. The argument between Aurora and me was recalled by many of the other mothers at the scene, and the question was asked: Would the bullet have struck Aurora instead of Alma? Did Aurora kneel before the picture was taken, or was she trying to stand? One angry mother who wanted to cash in on the notoriety the story had built in the press suggested *la limpiadora* (she wouldn't call me by name) threw her girl in the bullet's path in an attempt to save herself. The accusation, if true, could have resulted in child endangerment charges. Aurora and I were called in as witnesses to Parker Center, but our versions of what transpired were so different, our statements were deemed unusable and the case was thrown out. Still the damage was done.

When the *abuelito*'s picture was developed, it was examined by several officers connected with the case. Because the camera was jerked at the time of the exposure, the image was jumpy, and no two investigators could agree on what they saw. Aurora was either being pulled down by me to kneel or pulling away from me to stand up.

What those policemen couldn't find, though, was something I could already see—a mother and daughter in a strangled embrace, looking for the space our faith had left next to each other to fill.

I'd never get the chance to quit; Rick gave me my two weeks' notice after the pool party. The young Mexican boy who delivered the pizza would do my job for less money. Mrs. Calhoun asked her husband to pass along to me a list of his friends and associates who were looking for housecleaners, and in no time I had work lined up every day of the week. There were many bosses to practice my English on, and while I'd never command the language the way my daughter would, I could speak it as well as a man making a promise—that is, with equal doses of earnestness and desperation, along with enough wiggle room to escape out of a commitment by feigning a misunderstanding ("Three days a week? I'm sorry; I thought you said three hours a week. We will need to renegotiate my fee").

Cleaning other people's houses—their cherished possessions in both good and bad taste, the chipped dishes they eat off of, the ratty sofas they make love on, the unlevel, puckering floors they shed curly hairs on—is the most intimate relationship you can have with them. Yet every boss I've worked for wants that relationship to be unobtrusive to the point of being invisible. I have done my best to live my life in between those two places, intimacy and invisibility. Over the years I've absolved the remains of a thousand indiscretions without judgment, and have learned not to ask questions. Men staying over, friends moving in, children moving out; none of this is my concern. If my job is done right, what you find when you get home is a comforting antiseptic, fresh Band-Aid smell, spotless floors, and no evidence another human being, a cleaning lady, was ever there.

Cleaning lady? A hell of a term. There's nothing ladylike about it. To be a good cleaning lady, you must learn to act like a man.

On my last cleaning day, I arrived to find a note from Mrs. Calhoun on the dining room table. I couldn't read it because blinds had been installed on the sliding glass doors and the house was coated in blackness. Opening the blinds for sunlight, I squinted to read the faint handwriting.

"Take the day off," it said. "You deserve it."

On the opposite side, "For Felicia," and a list of her personal items, including the corduroy couch. Confused, I wanted to ask Mrs. Calhoun to explain, but the house was quiet, save for what sounded like rain pelting the sliding glass doors, *drop drop drop*. Through the blinds, I saw the jacaranda tree raining crisp, dazzling violet blossoms from its branches atop a floating body in a lavender bathrobe, its legs together, its arms outstretched as if reaching for something.

I plunged into the cold water, wading through the thick swamp of jacaranda until I reached Mrs. Calhoun's feet. The flowers pounded our bodies, *drop drop drop*, with a sudden violence that blanketed us. Mrs. Calhoun's bathrobe was heavy and her body rigid. My head bobbed for air as I struggled to stay afloat; I was drowning. All around me was the loud roar of water, a sound that still wakes me up in the middle of the night, screaming. I could not carry us both back to the rim of the pool. When I surrendered her body, it floated out to the center of the pool and slid under the thick carpet of fallen flowers.

Beneath a raining jacaranda tree, the blossoms shuddered and fell.

3

Our Lady of the Lost Angels

Isn't a miracle something we see every day but ignore? Then I, too, am a miracle, but I want to be seen, and be heard. The telling is the most dangerous part of my story. And though we've just met, I can tell you have time to listen. I can tell we are going to be friends.

Evil is everywhere. The Devil is looking for lost angels; on the streets you wander, in your neighbors' hearts, which you peek into when gossip chirps in your ears, even under the bed you lie on. Do you know about the Devil's Toe? If you feet dangle over the bottom edge of the mattress, the Devil reaches up from Hell, touches your big toe, and controls what direction you walk in when you wake, steering you into bad luck, pain, misery, and death. I was nine when I overheard my mother scold my father Ruben's younger brother, Archie, for falling asleep in a bed too small for his body.

God sees where the Devil leads you, she said, and nodded at the room where my two sisters and I slept.

Mother could pretend unpleasant events weren't happening, but she would store away memories of them from which some future argument could be heated up and served without any advance notice necessary—call them emotional leftovers. Archie laughed and told her as long as we lived in his house she had better things to do than to worry over his soul. Had Ruben heard this, he'd have beaten Archie's soul right out of him.

Archie was a sniveling cur, but Ruben strutted like a man who crosses the street against the light, a defiant sneer in his canter, daring a car to strike him. You feared more for the chrome on those wide bumpers than for his legs. In the Zoot Suit Riots of '43, he tackled five sailors armed with baseball bats who were beating a poor spade they'd stripped of his drapes. Ruben fought them off as if that colored man was one of his own. My father believed in fairness for everyone. Well, except for women; he left my mother for a whore fresh off the *coyotes'* teats, a fifteen-year-old girl from Nayarit named Blanca. She bore him a bastard son, Jesús, who trains pit bulls for dogfighting in a brush-strewn lot somewhere around here. *En el Viejo Echo Park,* he could live across the street or cross my daily path and I'd never know who he was.

With Ruben gone, Archie's Devil's Toe stumbled him into my sisters' tiny beds, his thick, jaundice-yellow toenails, curved like horseshoes, poking out from under the delicate handmade quilts our *abuelita* made when Mother was pregnant. She listened to my mother's belly in a twilit den to see whether a boy or girl was coming, then sewed a quilt she felt best suited what that baby's personality would be. My eldest sister, Aracely, had roses dipped in a pool of fire on hers, Patricia a pink ribbon swirled in a bow around a cloud. Mine was a pale black wolf howling at a turquoise sunset, made for the son who didn't come. I cringed under that bedspread at night, chewing the top of it until it was damp, terrified the Devil that possessed my uncle's toes, along with every body part below his waist, would steer him into my bed next. My grandmother would come to the side of my bed wearing her favorite turquoise handmade puebla dress embroidered with pink lotus flowers and try to rub away the chilled goose bumps on my arms.

"Who haunted you, *nieta*?" she'd say.

"*Abuelita,* why didn't you make me a new *manta* when you saw I was a girl?"

"Thirty-seven years I've been listening to women's bellies. Thirty-seven years I've never been wrong. I thought you were a boy but you came out a girl. That means you have the soul of a man somewhere inside you. You're a fighter, you're my baby *lobo,*" she'd say. "You're strong, *fuerte,* a wolf."

"I don't want to be a wolf," I'd pout.

"The wolf is the strongest of all animals. Nobody can hurt him except himself. Do you know what happens when a wolf gets caught in a fence?"

"No," I'd lie. Her wrinkles would crease into smiles, and I would hear her tell my favorite story once more.

"If he goes under, he loses his back paws and will have to drag himself everywhere he goes, lame and of no use to anyone. If he goes back, he loses his front paws and his courage to try to return. If he doesn't move, he will die from thirst and starvation. There is no easy way forward, no easy way back, and no easy way to sit still."

"What does he do, *Abuelita*?"

"Why, he stands up. He stands up and walks around the fence."

"Wolves can't stand up!"

"*Si no lo crees, m'hija,*" she'd say, "*no lo puedes hacer.*" If you don't believe it, you can't do it.

Then my night with Archie came. This would be a fight between good and evil, between God's ears and the Devil's Toes. My sisters had fought with tears and cries out to God to stop. Did they not stand up tall enough for God to hear them? Perhaps a woman asking God for help needed a stronger voice. But how could I stand up lying on my back?

If I learned anything from my grandma's story, it was that pain brings clarity. I closed my eyes, loosened my grip across the top of my blanket, and let him slide into bed next to me, his toenails scratching the tops of my feet as my uncle's hardness crept up my thighs and brushed against the mousetrap I'd set under my legs.

His castrato shrieking was fit for the choir at St. Vibiana's Cathedral. His Devil's Toes hopped him out the front door and into the street. This was the confirmation I needed that God hears the screams of a man better than those of a woman. From that day, God kept my uncle out of our beds, but he also stripped us of a place to live. Archie threw us out of the house. My mother and sisters blamed me, and I was sent to a convent, where I tried to fend off the *monjas'* beatings and bed hoppings with my prayers and my fists. Prayers were weaker than mousetraps; my fists got God's attention.

Since then, I have come to understand that God is the fear that motivates you to protect yourself from evil. God cannot be everywhere at once, and it is up to each of us to use our own faith in Him to protect ourselves. My husband, Gabriel Esperanza, taught me this. His father was one of the few *Californios* to hold on to his land when the *gringos* came. They drew a line in the desert and said, Your property belongs to us now. When writs and warrants didn't scare him, a mob of drunken *gringos* came with a hangman's noose to "reposses" his land. Gabriel's father, an educated man of prominent civic standing, repelled them armed with nothing more than a Bible and a shotgun. When his father died, Gabriel kept up the vigil, leaving enough of a parcel for his own estate, then selling much of the land to the city at a handsome profit. That land became Angelino Heights, the first suburb in the City of the Angels. Can you imagine that? A *Mexican* created our first suburbia, a place built on the fundamental notion of keeping people you think aren't as good as you believe yourself to be—out.

Gabriel was rugged and dashing, and I considered myself fortunate that a sixteen-year-old would be married off by the convent to their fifty-six-year-old benefactor. God and a fistful of spiny, pink cactus needles sewed into a throw pillow kept him out of my bed until I turned eighteen, but Gabriel was a decent man, or as decent as a man who bought a girl from a convent could be, and while I never bore him a son (there was one daughter, Felicia, whom I sent away when she was four because Gabriel had no interest in raising a daughter, and I had no interest in being a single parent), he was content to live a life apart from me, listening to his Lucha Reyes records on a separate floor while I lived a life on my own floor of his turn-of-the-century Victorian mansion in Angelino Heights. It was a house he'd bought from a silent film mogul who was shot by a jealous mistress. The bullet didn't kill the mogul, but her thirty-seven stab wounds to his abdomen with a poisoned stiletto letter opener did, an excess that befitted the style in which he'd decorated the mansion's seventeen rooms—burgundy velvet wallpaper, gold candelabras, and an actual waterfall built into the stairwell's balustrade.

When Gabriel died, my faith would no longer endorse his often profligate spending: the Mexican maids he hired to "service" him when I wasn't in the mood to be ridden like a cow and his extravagant donations to the convent. A pair of white nuns came out in a fancy automobile and, in *my* house, had the audacity to say that, without Gabriel's contributions, they couldn't afford to keep the convent open.

"Sell your car and give the money to the poor," I said. Luke 12:33. The church is too rich anyway.

Then my sisters, Aracely and Patricia, begged to move into *my* house. There was more than enough room for us, they said, including my mother, who with age had grown slow, senile, and nearing death's hands, desperate for reconciliation.

Where's *Abuelita*? I asked. Where was my *real* mother?

She drowned herself in Echo Park Lake, my mother said, because Archie wouldn't let us back into his house. That's where I will die if you don't give me a roof to put over my head.

I told her: "And above all things have fervent charity among your-selves, for charity shall cover the multitude of sins"—1 Peter 4:8. Find the paths that don't cross mine, I said. That was my charity to them.

Thanks to me they found their way. Within a year, my mother was living a happy life with my daughter, Felicia, in a tin shack in Chavez Ravine; my sisters had left America and moved south, to a small Mexican village in Guadalajara, where they belonged; and the convent had been converted to a high school, St. Gottschalk's. I believed this was a better use for the community, but a foulmouthed miscreant—their running coach—now blasphemes the Lord's name by teaching his charges profane chants, which they bellow on their morning jogs throughout the neighborhood. Thank God I still have the strength to walk to the curb every morning with a garden hose and a hose end insecticide sprayer filled with holy water.

Do you now see how much of my industriousness has been devoted to Him? "Let your good deeds shine out for all to see, so that everyone will praise your heavenly Father"—Matthew 5:16. I am a pious woman and have lived a righteous life, never once strayed in my path of conviction.

This is why God sent the Virgin Mary to me.

Ah, you see now why telling you this story is dangerous! You've heard what happens to those who claim they've seen Our Lady. They are ridiculed and ostracized by disbelievers, hounded and persecuted by believers yearning to be healed, either in body or in spirit. But Mary didn't "appear" out of thin air; she had to earn my belief, as you have had to earn my confidence to hear this story.

There was an old Italian woman—a beggar—with a fake black wig, a cane, and ankles as sturdy as a nursemaid's who used to hobble across a hectic intersection in Echo Park every morning without cross-ing at the light. I made the mistake one time of helping her. Then, whenever she saw me, she'd motion me to help her across without so much as asking. Do once, and be prepared to do again and again, I say. Why should I help an old woman take a shortcut? Who has ever helped me across the street? The day I need help to cross the street is the day I learn how to find what I need on *this* side of the street.

When I saw her flailing that cane in the air, I walked to the bus shelter on Sunset Boulevard in front of Pilgrim's Supermarket (it's now some kind of convenience store that isn't convenient if you are poor or an old woman like me). There in the doorway of a block-long ninety-nine-cent store stood a shiny-faced teenage girl in ankle-length blue slacks and a matching blue coat spotted with a constellation of translucent stars, flat nurse's shoes, a red scarf wrapped around her head in the shape of a circlet to protect her fair skin from the sun, and a white lamb's-wool sweater with a fraying ring of delicate gold thread across her chest. There was nothing remarkable about her clothes—you'd find them at *las tiendas descuentas* up and down the block—but a young woman wearing such an old lady's outfit? Even back then, most of the girls went to church like *putas* in miniskirts and thongs, with their faces made up like *payasos*. It's worse today with that *chisme* coming out of their *telefonitos*! Who could be more important to talk to in a church than God? *Tus novios? Tus amigas? Tus chulos?* Disgraceful.

Her clothes seemed to float atop her body. Plus it was a Tuesday—*nobody's* idea of a holy day. When I turned to look, she was walking alongside me, a beatific smile on her face, one that for a moment made me forget my wariness of strangers, the only people I mistrust more than my relatives.

"*Ay, m'hija,* my feet are so tired today," she said.

There was no one else on the street. My shoulders tensed, and I began to think of what I could say to scare her away should she prove to be crazy or, worse, a panhandler.

"How have you been, *m'hija*? Did you hear about my son?" she asked. "Arrested him in the thick of night. Turned in by one of his best friends, *ay.* What am I going to do?"

"I don't have any money," I said. "Leave me alone."

"Don't be afraid, *m'hija*," she said. "There's nothing I want from you, Beatriz. What you have in abundance I want none of."

How did she know my name? Or that I was afraid?

"Go away," I said and quickened my pace. The woman kept up stride by stride without visibly moving her legs. She drifted alongside me as if carried on a breeze. There was a bus picking up passengers at the shelter, and I started to run; it wasn't my intention to board it—I had nowhere outside Echo Park to go—but I needed the security of a crowd.

"Beatriz, please." She laughed. "Why are you running to be alone?"

The bus pulled away before I could reach it. I sat down on the bench in the shelter to catch my breath. The woman hovered next to a garbage can, her ashen glow visible in the shelter's advertisement glass display. "If you stay on this path you're on, you'll get to where you are going whether you run or walk."

"How dare you speak to an elder this way!" I shouted. "Leave me alone!"

"*Ay*, don't be so rude!" she said. "You are not talking to your daughter!"

Not another soul living today knew about Felicia. "I don't have a daughter," I lied. "And I don't know who you are. I've never seen you before," I said, defiant. Her eyes were two pinhead flames of rose quartz, and I was unable to move, transfixed out of either anger or fear.

"You know me and have seen me, *m'hija*. I am the mother of all children, and of my son Christ, our Lord," she said.

"Your Son, *Jesús*?" I scoffed. "This is silly. Everything you say is false. Get away from me and beg from someone else." I turned my back on her, hoping she'd understand how degrading her behavior was for both of us, two women strangers arguing in public.

"You will be tougher than I thought." She wafted down on the bench next to me like a fog moving onshore. The street noise, its traffic and people, disappeared. A strange feeling of warmth poured over my skin. Imagine the weight of your many years that you carry on your shoulders disappearing in one single, immense, breathtaking moment. Your humiliation dissolved, your hurts healed, your griev- ances redressed, your bitterness crystallized into acceptance; every- thing that has been done wrong to you has now been done right, as if an enormous switch deep inside your soul has been flipped, reversing the flow of years of anger and hatred and animosity and grief, turning it into love and compassion. You never want to say another word in anger again. You have no memory of your mother beating you with a hairbrush, no guilt over watching your sisters being molested by your uncle behind a fetid apple tree and doing nothing, saying nothing. The desperation and hopelessness that you tried to rid yourself of but couldn't, because it left you exposed, floats away, leaving behind a body and a soul that feel transparent and blemish-free, like newborn skin.

She rose from the bench, and the weight of my hurt came crash- ing back onto my shoulders. The street roared back to life with cars, noise, and people. I strained my eyes to look at her bright face. "I will return when you are ready to hear what I have to say," she said.

"You didn't say anything. Wait," I said. She floated behind the bus shelter and disappeared. On the bench was a trail of rose petals that led to the garbage can, where a rosebush—not a bouquet but an entire bush—was blooming.

I smelled roses everywhere on my way back to my house—in the garbage, by Echo Park Lake, and in the dust kicked up by small chil- dren running home. I fell into a deep sleep at four in the afternoon, not waking for fourteen hours. In my dreams I wandered through a field of burning weeds wearing a coat made of rain. The coat envel- oped me with the sensation of both drowning and breathing, its chill warding off the incredible heat around me. I was searching for my daughter, now a grown woman, who was sitting on an island of blooming jacaranda trees surrounded by a brimstone lake. Her adult face, which I've never seen but knew intimately in the dream, floated out of reach. Then I awoke.

At the bus stop the next day, the petals and the rosebush were gone. The smell, though, was stronger than before, and when it entered my nostrils, I started crying. Tears that smelled of roses plopped on my hands and feet. I held out my hand to catch them, and brought up a palm brimming with rose petals.

Every day for six days, I made my pilgrimage to the bus shelter. The Virgin Mary didn't return as she'd promised. Every night for six nights, I had the same dream. I'd made no effort to tell people about my experience for fear I'd be branded one of those old, crazy women who mutter to themselves on the street. What I needed was a man used to the lunacy of the extraordinary. What I needed was a man of God.

Father Alemencio at St. Gotteschalk's had gained a reputation as a "street priest," a rare member of the church capable of offering both compassion and practical advice. He'd brokered truces between several gangs, was a discreet bearer of condoms to newlyweds, and offered a free literacy and job-training program for ex-cons. We met late one afternoon in his office, bright with fluorescence yet somehow dark as a tavern.

"Your husband was a great man," Father Alemencio said. "His generosity will be remembered for a long time."

"Why? If I hadn't ended his spendthrift ways, you and your school wouldn't be here."

"Your devotion has only assumed a different form, the same way as all of our own faiths take different forms as we get older," he said. "What do you want to discuss with me, Beatriz?"

"I am having complicated dreams," I said.

"I understand." He smiled. "I've had this talk with everyone from old women concerned that if they die in their sleep they'll die in real life to young boys ashamed about . . . well, Catholicism gives everyone something to feel ashamed about. Dreams, recurring fantasies, nightmares—they're quite normal. What happens in your dream?"

"There is this burning field, and I'm walking through it wearing an overcoat made of rain," I said. I didn't mention the part about my daughter.

"Something to keep the heat off your shoulders." He laughed. "When did you start having this dream?"

"After seeing the Virgin Mary," I said.

"Ah, Our Lady of Guadalupe. She has visited the dreams of many a Mexican woman. You should consider yourself blessed, Beatriz. Our Lady's strength and—"

"No, I've *seen* her," I blurted out. "She appeared to me. In real life."

"Appeared to you?" He leaned forward on a squeaky pivot in his chair. "I see. How did you know it was Our Lady of Guadalupe?"

"She told me she was the mother of all children."

"Our Lady spoke to you?"

"I had a conversation with her."

"You spoke with the Virgin Mary?" he asked, not a trace of disbelief or suspicion in his voice. "Can you describe her?"

"She had on a blue coat with stars on it, a red scarf over her head, a white sweater, and flat nurse's shoes."

"Nurse's shoes."

"Yes, it was a very basic outfit, nothing like the pictures in the murals around the neighborhood. Pressed, thick polyester. Almost like a pantsuit."

"A pantsuit," he said. "I see. And where did this 'meeting' take place?"

"At a bus stop on Sunset Boulevard. That's where she spoke to me."

"What else did she say?"

"She told me I didn't have to run along the solitary path I was on. And that'd she be back when I was ready to hear more of what she had to say. For being the mother of God, she was very testy."

"Our Lady was testy," he said. "I see. Did she say anything else?"

"No, but when she disappeared, there was a rosebush in a garbage can next to where she stood."

"There were roses in the can?"

"No, Father, an actual rosebush growing out of the garbage can. This was before she changed my tears to rose petals."

"The roses gave you tears?"

"My tears *became* rose petals," I said, exasperated.

"I see," he said. His expression never faltered, never betrayed an ounce of incredulousness. "And what question do you have for me?"

"Well, I've *seen* the Virgin Mary," I scoffed. Wasn't my question obvious? "I want to know what I should *do* about it."

He squeaked his chair back on that same rusty pivot, his brows furrowed together in a wrinkled clench. I half-expected its tightness would pop an answer right out of him.

"Beatriz, the Catholic Church has no standard response to Marian apparitions," he said. "But I should also tell you my *abuelita* used to see Our Lady everywhere—when she was cleaning the house, making the coffee, at night when she put the *perros* out. I don't think I've met an *abuelita* yet who hasn't seen Mary at one point or another. I've never heard of Mary appearing in a pantsuit at a bus stop on Sunset Boulevard before. That's a new one. Often, our mother appears in a long, flowing gown, saying very general, universal things. This is a personal vision."

"Is that why I keep having the same dream?"

"Sure," he said. "The overcoat could symbolize a desire for protection, for sanctuary, and no one offers more of both than Our Lady."

"What should I do?" I asked.

"If it's been a few days and she hasn't visited you again, you may be out of the woods. Chalk it up to some bad *frijoles* and too much sun."

"And what about the tears?"

He paused to clear his throat. "About that, I cannot discuss anything further with you."

"Why? What I experienced was a miracle."

"A miracle *if* it happened . . ."

"It *did* happen," I said.

"People don't understand miracles," he said. "They expect too much from them. Sometimes, a miracle is best when it is you that sees, and God that knows."

Father Alemencio rose from his chair and walked me to his office door. "If you see Mary again," he said, "take her advice: don't walk a solitary path. There are people out there who love you. I've met them. I know you will make the right decision."

He returned to his desk, leaving the door open behind him. In the quiet stained-glass-lined vestibule, a gust of wind blew through the front doors of the church and wrapped itself around my skin like a cloak. I was covered in goose bumps, and in that moment, I could hear my grandmother ask me: *Who haunted you?*

Father Alemencio said he had met those who loved me. I hadn't mentioned my daughter. What did he mean? This was a question whose answer I now felt I needed to hear. When I returned to his office, his door was locked, and I couldn't tell if it was he or the wind that closed it on me.

There are mornings in your life when you wake up earlier than your routine dictates, feel your body acting in a different way, and decide for an inexplicable reason you need to do something, a particular *thing*, to satisfy an innate desire for change. On the morning after I visited Father Alemencio, every inch of my skin was damp and clammy.

Who haunted you?

In a daze, I walked—it felt as if I floated—to the bottom step of my front porch, where a bundled newspaper had been delivered to me by mistake. It was a copy of that day's *Herald Examiner,* with a front-page picture of a group of Mexican women and children dressed like harlots, standing on a street corner not too far from my house. I thought it was a story about a prostitution ring, but the headline next to the photo read: CASE DROPPED AGAINST MOTHER IN "BABY MADONNA" SHOOTING.

A young girl named Alma Guerrero had been shot and killed on this street corner at an informal gathering of mothers and daughters. This happened on the very same day, I noted, that I saw the Virgin Mary. One of the mothers was accused of throwing her daughter into the path of the bullet. The girl ducked, and the bullet struck and killed Alma. I'd heard nothing about this case—gang shootings happened every day back then—but a photo had been taken right before the bullet struck this child. The police examined the accompanying picture to see if this mother had indeed endangered her daughter, but they could reach no conclusion. The paper ran a caption that asked: PUSHED OR PULLED? DECIDE FOR YOURSELF. The photo was blurry and printed on newsprint, but I could make out the two women in question. They appeared locked in a tussle that left a strange and awkward space between them.

In between them, in that small space, was the Virgin Mary, dressed in the same outfit, staring at me with a benevolent expression of happiness and joy. There was no mistaking her.

I threw the paper to the ground. It was a warm, sunny morning, yet my arms were covered with fields of goose pimples. I grabbed the first overcoat I could find. When that proved insufficient to keep the chill off, I threw on another. Then two more, and in my slippers, pajamas, and four housecoats raced through the street to the corner where Alma had been shot.

There was a shrine set up next to a weathered steel utility box. It resembled a tombstone with ALMA spray-painted in red across its side and hundreds of homemade cards, drawings, stuffed animals, and lit novena candles lined up against the curb where a galaxy of dark blood-red dollops drank the gray out of the concrete.

The candles flickered and burned themselves out. I didn't have to turn around to know who was standing beside me.

"Why did you bring me here?" I asked over my shoulder.

"This is what loss does to a heart," she said, touching the utility box. "The blood that runs through your veins should have been on this street, not Alma's."

"That's absurd. You're the Virgin Mary. You're not supposed to say cruel things!"

"I speak in the words that are the easiest for you to hear me with," she said and smiled.

"Are you saying I *want* you to blame me for that poor child's death? If it was her time, it was her time. She was dressed like a *puta* on a street corner!" I yelled.

"You speak to me like I am *tu niña*," she said. "You talk too much."

"Who are you to lecture me? You were sent here to protect me from evil, not chastise me!"

"I embrace those who embrace me but scorn those who profess to know my motives," she said, rolling her eyes. "Don't you know this? What kind of Catholic are you, *m'hija*? And why so many coats?" she asked.

"I'm freezing. But I'm sweating the old woman's sweats," I said. "I've been through menopause once. You can't curse me with that again. Do you know what's wrong with me?"

"Without love, you are cold," she said. "Without a heart, you are lost. *Tú sabes?*"

"No. You speak in riddles. I want answers. What about my dream? What about my daughter?" I asked.

The Virgin Mary smiled and shook her head. "Your daughter has been found," she said. "It is you, *m'hija,* who are lost. I thought you were ready to hear what I had to say. But it was a mistake to appear to you. That happens sometimes; it's blasphemy to think I am perfect.

Another messenger will come to you. They will give you something that means nothing to them but everything to you without question or expectation. Then I will come and find you."

"When? When will this happen, Mary? Please, tell me. Please," I said. "I cannot apologize to you. It is not my way, but . . ." And I wept without reason, understanding, or shame.

"*M'hija*"—she smiled—"you have much more crying to do before I find you again."

She was gone, and a thick blanket of fresh rose petals covered the spot where she'd stood. I swept my hands through the petals in a panic, desperate to find some other clue or message, and cut my palms on glass pebble shards from the shooting. On the corner was a *mercado* called El Guanaco. I told the owner my tale. He saw my bloody hands and laughed. "Of course you saw Our Lady," he said, "everyone's seen her out there on the utility box."

On Sunset Boulevard, I begged sinners and devils alike to please listen to my story, come with me to the shrine to see what I'd seen. People brushed past, mocked me, pushed me aside; the chill on my skin grew worse. At a *tienda descuenta* there was a sale on two-dollar smoke-damaged peacoats. A day later, those coats were worthless; they no longer kept me warm. I purchased several more at the May Company downtown on Hill Street. Those coats lasted an hour or two before they no longer kept the chill away. With each passing week, month, and year since, too many to count, I have amassed a collection of coats whose warmth dissipates like cheap perfume. Sometimes it takes days, sometimes hours, but the warmth the coat gives me, the comfort it provides, vanishes, leaving behind another coat to add to an endless collection, stored in a large anteroom in case any one of them regains its ability to keep me warm.

Do you know how it feels to be burdened with a thousand coats and a fierce, numbing, camphoraceous chill running through your veins every waking moment? Each new coat holds promise, relief, then disappointment, frustration, much the same way each stranger

I meet holds the promise of being Our Lady's messenger, then reveals himself as someone humoring an old woman.

Some would call that kindness. I call it cruelty.

And now it's time for you to go.

I must stay here, in this very bus shelter where Our Lady appeared to me over twenty-five years ago, kneel on this weathered bench, rest my folded hands over the bench's back, and pray for her messengers' protection and guidance. They will have a difficult path, because evil watches your steps when you don't.

Your bus is coming, to take you out of Echo Park. But I am waiting, because that's what you're supposed to do when you're lost. You stay in the same place to make it easier to be found. And I know God is looking for me; when He finds a lost soul, he turns it into a miracle. How can I not wait, then, when miracles are everywhere?

4

Rules of the Road

Last name, Mendoza, first name, Efren, operator number 00781. Position: bus operator (BDOF) for the Los Angeles County Metropolitan Transit Authority, twenty-seven years. Metro is the third-largest public transportation system in America, with more than 4,400 bus and rail operators moving one and a half million riders a day. I drive two four-and-a-half-hour shifts a day, five days a week, and carry anywhere from 1,000 to 1,200 passengers daily on my route, Line 200. My first shift begins at 4:41 A.M.; last shift ends 7:53 P.M. Part of the Metro "Local" bus line, 200 starts in Echo Park, a Mexican neighborhood, skirts along the edge of Los Feliz, an area for rich and famous whites, down a sharp turn onto Western Avenue, back across on Wilshire, through MacArthur Park, down Alvarado, and ends fifty-four minutes later in Exposition Park, a black part of town on the outskirts of South Central.

Aside from that short stretch through Los Feliz, Line 200 is an urban route with ninety-nine-cent stores, fast-food restaurants, and oases of crowded parking lots. There are 2,500 glass bus shelters throughout the city that cover passengers by day, the homeless and crazies at night. Stops are marked every few blocks and at four major locations: St. Vincent Medical Center, MacArthur Park, USC, and the Coliseum slash old sports arena. The areas around St. Vincent and MacArthur Park are Latino; Mexican, some Salvadoran. A new influx of Koreans hit the area several years ago, but there aren't enough of them yet for tension.

The base fare is $1.25 *(no* transfers) and nonnegotiable; nobody boards—no matter how tragic his sob story—without paying the full fare. I follow the rules. That ensures your safety and mine. I do not talk or text on a cell phone during my shift, make unexpected stops to accommodate passengers who try to board a half block away from the bus stop or at the stoplight, engage any of the riders in chitchat, or police any potential troublemakers onboard, though you'll find many bus drivers who do those things I've listed. I also do not deviate from predesignated routes, preapproved loading and unloading areas, prep checklists for prepull-out inspection at the division yard, rules for merging and turning, and most important, schedule times. My salary of $21.27 an hour relies on my punctuality (I carry a back-up watch; you are penalized if you are one minute late for your shift). It's a fair wage, one we had to go on several strikes—five during my time—to protect. Those socialist Che-worshiping *Reconquistadoras* complained these strikes hurt poor Mexican workers who cannot afford a car the most. You're a Mexican, they say, trying to bond with me by speaking Spanish. How can you turn against your own kind? they say. But they aren't my kind. They're not Americans. They're illegals, and the benefits to law-abiding Americans like me outweigh whatever inconveniences these people face breaking our laws.

Bus operators are not paid to be heroes, nor are we paid to absorb your abuse. We are paid to get you from point A to point B. That's my job. We have procedures that cover every kind of accident or incident you can imagine. There's no screen or enclosure protecting me from aggressive or out-of-control passengers; if there's a situation, I stop the bus and wait for the police to arrive. I've done this dozens of times with everyone from frothing smackheads to rabid crackheads and until the night of the twelfth never had a problem.

That's because the quality of my passengers' ride is as important as following the rules. This means a well-maintained bus that's on time and clean. No butts, no beverages, no trash left behind. There are drivers who feel it's not their responsibility to take pride in their work space. They wait for the custodial staff at the division yard to hose the buses down with pressurized hot water; the problem is that "situations" are often missed by the cleaning crews (on purpose, if you ask me). I don't need to enumerate those human functions that can leave a residue or footprint behind on a bus, but this doesn't bother me; cleaning up shit is part of any job.

My father, Manny Sr., was in the street gang Echo Park Locos and got my spoiled older brother, Manny Jr., to drop out of sixth grade to join. I was never into gangs. Running around the streets at night didn't interest me. I liked books and school, learning English, being educated. I knew more at twelve than Manny Sr. did at forty. When I turned fourteen, Manny Jr. tried to "jump" me into the gang by pretending he had Dodgers tickets then beating the shit out of me in a blind alley. "You're one of us now, *cabrón,*" he said. Manny Sr. took Junior's side, so I left home and moved into an abandoned house (Echo Park had plenty back then). I'm glad I ran off when I did. Living on my own taught me my sense of responsibility. I found work at a burrito stand in Lincoln Heights where I hauled bags of garbage, emptied the grease traps, and cleaned out the toilets. You know any fourteen-year-olds today who'd clean toilets at a burrito stand?

"Man, these sixteen-hour days are tough on a kid," I'd say to any customer who would listen. I wanted someone, *anyone,* to sympathize.

"Gotta start somewhere," they'd say back, because who'd sympathize with a fourteen-year-old know-nothing? To our customers, sixteen-hour workdays were the rule, not the exception. My boss, overhearing, would rap me on the head with his knuckles and finish the customer's thought: "Somewhere's better than nowhere."

Today, I work fewer hours than I did then, and make a take-home salary of $53,000 a year. That's generous money for a man who didn't go to college. I live in a clean one-bedroom apartment in Boyle Heights not too far from the house I grew up in, no kids, relatives (that I acknowledge), or wife/ex-wife. Most of the other operators are men who have lots of mouths to feed. I don't say "men" to be sexist; four out of five bus operators are men, and if you aren't a single mother or divorced, there's no reason to take such a physically demanding job. By the end of my shift, my arms throb, the film on my eyeballs peels like an onion, my ass feels stuffed with novocaine, and my lower back is in such excruciating pain, I have no energy for anything in my bed except sleep. Sex is the last thing on my mind.

That said, when a single female bus operator appears, she gets snapped up quick. I dated a bus operator named Carol—nice white girl, stocky build; large, healthy bottom; divorced with two children—until I discovered she brought her children along with her on her route. This was dangerous, but more important, it was against the rules. Perverts and pedophiles ride the buses (some days it seems nothing but) looking for children to grab or molest. There's a Mexican guy on my route, a regular, who wears these pants with a hole cut out in his crotch. He exposes himself to little girls and Oriental women. One time, he tried it on this little Chinese girl who screamed until he fled the bus at the next stop. The passengers gave her a round of applause, and I congratulated her. "He does that every night," I said. "Good for you." For some reason, she became hysterical. "Why don't *you* do something?" she screamed. "Why do you let him on?"

Discriminating against specific riders whom I haven't witnessed committing an actual crime firsthand (I have to see something happen right in front of me), along with direct confrontation of an assumed criminal, is a violation of Metro policy. I *can't* get involved. The same applied for Carol bringing her children on her route. I'd have forgotten the incident if it had been once or twice, but she admitted she was "sticking" Metro—to say nothing of the safety of both her children and her passengers—several days a week. Why not, she said, when Metro wasted millions of dollars on their new head-quarters Downtown (the *L.A. Times* called it the "Taj Mahal"), and her child-care benefits were shit? Besides, she said with a hint of pride at her resourcefulness, it was easier and cheaper than finding a regular babysitter.

How ungrateful can you get? She had a good job, with good benefits that at her age and skill set she'd never be able to find elsewhere. I could never get involved with, let alone marry, someone that reckless and irresponsible. When I dumped her, I made sure to tip off her supervisor, which led to her dismissal. Look, I'm not a *pinche jota*. A woman can be a beautiful thing at arm's length, but get too close and you find they are distractions, there to manipulate men who have succumbed to accepting mediocrity and need someone to share it with.

Passengers aren't any better. The women I've tried to court had a different idea of what their men should be—loud, drunk, jailhouse tats, deliberate facial hair. Working day in, day out for a living isn't as glamorous as dealing drugs or "smokin' homies"; you can't see the results right away. How can a guy who drives a bus for a living compete with a baller who rolls around in a jet-black Cadillac with wine velour upholstery? The girls hop in and take a ride, then get taken for a ride, right back to the bus stop, boarding with their hands covering their puffy black eyes, ashamed to be seen on the "Ghetto Express" (though not ashamed, of course, that a hardwork-ing American has to drive them around; to them I'm no better than a chauffeur). Then, a few months later, they waddle up the stairs onto the bus, hands cradling their large bellies, their eyes imploring me for sympathy. Those same hands will soon be dragging a chain of screaming children, yanking them along like a tangle of broken kites. If they look at me, which they do not, they'd say, *"What else can I do?"* I say, they made their choices, and there's no reason to feel sympathy for someone who wants nothing out of her life and gets what she aims for.

Now on occasion, in the past, I've been fooled by women who I believed were ambitious and uninterested in blaming whites for all their problems. I courted this cleaning lady when I started driving; I wasn't breaking the rules because *she* made the effort to befriend *me*. This was back when I spoke Spanish to the passengers (I refuse to speak it to them now), and I could tell my speaking Spanish made her feel more comfortable. She initiated the small talk, inquired about my day, gave me a warm good-bye at her stop on Vermont and Los Feliz. These were clear signals that she was interested in me, so I didn't mind waiting an extra minute or two at her stop in Echo Park if she was running late. When she told me the house she cleaned was on Avalon Street, about three long L.A. blocks (a twenty-minute walk) from her stop on Vermont, I didn't mind stopping at Avalon every Thursday, since it crossed Los Feliz Boulevard anyway. And when she told me about her ex-husband, this was a very clear signal that she wanted me to ask her out.

When she boarded with a group of kids she was taking to a pool party and had the nerve to ask for a discount, I figured that was as good a time as any to set up a date. She said no, and she wasn't nice about it either. That's when I realized she'd been using me to get special treatment, her own bus stop and extra time in the mornings. Not only did I refuse a discount but I didn't tell her that a couple of children in the group, the younger brothers and sisters dragged along by their reluctant older siblings, could have ridden for free because they were with a paying adult. I don't like to be cheated, and cheating her let me get something back that had been stolen from me. From then on, whatever satisfaction I got from this job would be earned through a series of small, trivial victories. I'm damn proud to say I have won more of these battles than I've lost.

I've made sacrifices in my own life to keep this job as long as I have, but overall it's provided me with a better standard of living than I would've had if I'd stayed with my father. When people on my bus say they're "trapped in the ghetto," trapped in their lives—and they say this a lot; my passengers *love* to shout into their expensive fucking cell phones—I'm the proof that escape is possible. The American Dream is there for the taking if you aren't lazy and have no qualms about the kind of work you do.

These new wetbacks don't see it that way. They're picky about what jobs they'll do and how much money they'll accept for the "privilege" to come and do half-assed work at your house. A lot of my riders are *mojados* going to MacArthur Park to buy fake IDs, passports, and birth certificates with forged birth dates. Papers in hand, they assemble in fixed meeting areas around the park—in front of the police, who won't touch them—to be picked out for odd jobs and day labor across the city. These aren't Mexicans who've lived in this country for years, looking to legitimize a life they've worked hard to build here. They aren't even Mexicans who, from what I've learned about the Mendoza name in libraries, became Americans when the border flipped on us, vanishing years of Mexican heritage with a quill stroke, turning rich landowners into migrant settlers in a new and hostile country. No, these are country hicks, *mojados* who've made no effort to assimilate, learn English, and do the hard work to become a part of American society the way I did. If I had time off from work, I'd be right out there with those Minutemen on the border, bullhorn in hand, screaming at the top of my lungs. These men looking to take our jobs, and their women who pop off babies for free health care, want schooling for their bastards and welfare from my taxes—they're freeloaders who focus unwanted attention on us legitimate Mexicans, who had to learn the rules and suffer the stings of becoming Americans. Get Mexico to take care of fucking Mexicans for a change.

You don't need to go to MacArthur Park to find *mojados*. These men are everywhere—loud, boisterous, and macho when they're in packs hanging on corners. But here on my bus? They sit near the front (away from the blacks who ironically like sitting in back), meek little church mice punching numbers or text messages into their cell phones.

General conversation is not permitted between me and my passengers; however, if I see a wetback staying on past MacArthur Park, I have been known to ask him—in English—if he knows he's heading into the black part of town. If a wetback doesn't *habla inglés,* I punch my hand and fist together and point straight ahead. *Mojados* caught past Washington Boulevard are taking a big chance, whether it's day or night, but they go where the work takes them. When I speak English to them, they look disappointed and offended. Can you imagine that? They're angry at *me* that I don't speak Spanish in *my* country? They've played the fucking *habla español* card from fucking Jalisco to here—that's *how* they get here so easy—and when they meet a Mexican who won't play that game with them, they have the nerve to challenge me on *my* fucking Mexican-ness!

Of course, I don't spend a lot of time getting worked up over this. That's how things are and I accept it.

See, even if conversation were permitted, this isn't the kind of route where I have regular passengers I could strike up conversations with. I had them on other routes, but here my riders don't set their schedules to mine; their work isn't regular, it drifts from region to region. They're itinerant, hostile (or both), and speak either no English or that Ebonics shit, which is worse than Spanish. I try to warn these *mojados* what they're in for because a large part of my job is communicating where the bus stops are so people will get off in the neighborhood they belong in and not wander into the wrong part of the city. Spend a few minutes driving down here and you'll see the blacks are angrier at these Mexicans than I am. You can hear it in the voices of the old men who lived through the Watts riots. "Every block," they say, "you'd point to the houses and go, 'That's where the Johnsons live,' 'That's where the Franklins live.' Now it's 'That's where the Gonzaleses live,' and 'That's where the Sanchezes live.'" Blacks kill each other up and down these streets I drive every day, but they cannot stand the thought of being threatened by fuck-ing *wetbacks*.

Moving down Alvarado to Hoover Street, the streets get resi-dential again; unlike in Los Feliz, here are long, straight lines of single-tract houses that must have been charming in the forties and fifties but have iron bars on the windows and front doors; Armenian and Arab-owned liquor stores; and Popeyes, KFCs, and Chicken-to-Go stands. The riders are loud black teenagers who want an air-conditioned trip down to the USC area to hang out (there's no way these thugs are college students). They wear white ghost-sheet shirts down to their knees, sagging denim shorts that fall to their ankles, diamond studs in their ears, and are outfitted with the latest technological gadgets—iPhones, iPods, iDicks—things they hook into their ears to make them oblivious to what's going on around them. They can't hear a thing and explode in profane rages if you disturb them from the bubble they've created to ask them for a bus pass that hasn't expired or to remind them—*no* free transfers to or from other buses. These teens carry a couple thousand dollars' worth of toys on them, money I never could have earned from working a straight job at their age, and they want a free transfer! Why do these kids' mothers (their fathers can't do much from prison) let their children walk around with expensive things that'll provoke a con-frontation ending in a robbery or a homicide? How many times have I run behind schedule because of a shooting along this stretch of boulevard? They close down one lane of traffic for emergency vehi-cles, and as we slow to a bumper-to-bumper crawl, these black kids run up to the bus windows with their cell phone cameras to see if they can take pictures of the dead body, the three-hundred-dollar sneakers poking out from under the sheet a giveaway of how old these corpses are.

I repeat: for a bus line that services different ethnic groups that don't enjoy each other's company, I've never had a major problem—that is, one that I couldn't handle on my own—until the one on the thirteenth. Or was it the twelfth? It's the twelfth or the thirteenth; you have the fucking report in front of you. Bus routes are not drawn up with any particular attention paid to where the different races live. It's impossible for a bus operator in Los Angeles to drive a route that doesn't cross at least two, if not more, ethnic parts of the city. Thus, it is up to the operators to keep their passengers aware of their surroundings. I've prevented dozens of fights, and maybe saved a few lives, by advising Mexicans and blacks about which stops are safe for them to get off. Judging from the coverage you've seen on TV about the "incident" aboard my bus, you'd never know this. Sure, there have been occasions (how many is impossible to say) where I've been honked at on the road in standstill traffic, by black drivers in those fucking pimped-out bitch wagons with the cannon-loud bass. I honk right back, to remind them *I'm* driving the two-ton bus. Or the balding white assholes in fucking convertible BMWs, slicing across two or three lanes of traffic to race onto a freeway entrance. What, you get to be in a hurry because you're rich, white, and on cocaine? What gives you the fucking right to cut me fucking off? Fuck *you*, you fucking *FUCKS*!

Not that I say anything. I'm a professional, and I take my job seriously.

I've seen what's been reported in the news. There's been protests, church convocations, and neighborhood meetings with Latino speakers and black leaders, with everyone from the NAACP to Al Sharpton (and what the fuck does Al Sharpton know about Los Angeles?). They're not debating what took place but discussing "community awareness issues" and "racial sensitivity" and "appealing for calm" and a dozen other bullshit things that have nothing to do with the actual facts of that night. I hate it when people get their facts wrong and act as if you have the problem when you try to correct them. For instance, it was a mistake on my birth certificate that wound up listing me in the police report as being three years older than my real age, which is *right there* on my Class C license. I didn't lie about my age. I don't lie, period. I *follow the rules.* And I never meant to leave that kid facedown, in his own blood, at that bus stop.

You want to hear what happened.

It was dusk. I can't recall the exact time, but the time line isn't as essential to my story as the news would lead you to believe. What's important is that dusk is the most dangerous time to drive. Any operator will tell you this. The sun drops out of the sky in Los Angeles like someone who's been standing next to you talking your ear off and then, *poof,* gone, and then the sky's on fire and the glare from that fire blinds you and you're alone.

For a long time, Washington Boulevard's been the official Mexican/black border. Everything north above Washington is Mexican; everything south below it is black. A sixteen-year-old kid got on at Washington. He was in uniform: Kobe basketball jersey that went to his knees, denim shorts sagging down his ass, and bright toothpaste-white high-tops. The black kid flashed his bus pass and shoved his way past a *mojado* in his uniform: baggy, untucked T-shirt, blue jeans, and a baseball cap. He was better put together than the average wetback, though. Gold chains dangled from his neck and wrist, and I remember how callused his tattooed knuckles were as he counted his change into the fare box. The black kid pulled a box of Skittles packs out of his backpack and tried to sell them.

There's a strict no solicitation policy on MTA buses and trains, one I enforce no matter what color or age the salesman is. On this route, it's black kids selling candy bars with a rehearsed speech in rapid-fire nonghetto English. They never look at you, though. On other routes, though, it could be Mexican kids selling plastic key chains with an intense stare. They shove their plastic Chinese-made trinkets in front of you but don't say a word. And God help you—literally—if you get one of those Korean Christians raising money for a pilgrimage of mercy to the Middle East; they stand there like some lost retards, with cards in the palms of their hands that ask you to give them a dollar in the name of Christ until you shoo them away or drop some change in their cups.

This black kid was so loud selling these Skittle packs I didn't hear the *mojado* at first. No one's ever been stupid enough to start anything with a black past Washington.

"Hey, you," he said. "You, buddy, with the candies. You pushed into me." Out of my peripheral vision, I could see his muscles tense. The *mojado* followed the black kid to the back of the bus. A glance in my cabin rearview—and remember I'm driving—put the kid about halfway between the front and the rear exit doors.

"Hey, asshole! You pushed me!"

"No cursing on the bus!" I shouted.

There aren't any specific regulations about passengers using profanity, but one curse word between two races is enough to start a fight. In the same way, I thought a shout from me would be enough to calm the ruckus. Most confrontations flicker out and die on their own, or a passenger takes the initiative and resolves the dispute himself. I can't drive and referee. Not in the job description either.

"I'm fuckin' talking to you, *maricón*!" the *mojado* shouted. The kid had no idea someone was shouting at him—I think he had one of those earpiece cell phones—when the *mojado* punched him in the back of his head.

He stumbled out of his unlaced high-top sneakers and fell back on a row of bucket seats, spilling the candy pouches. My eyes were on the road—that's my job—but in my memory I can hear every Skittle pack hit the rubber floor. The kid popped up off the seats, smacked the *mojado* to the floor, and then started throwing punches. The *mojado* punched back in the kid's ribs.

The passengers were shouting and screaming, and that's when somebody must have started recording with his camera phone. With a police call and the police reports, I was going to be put behind schedule, and lose time off the clock I wasn't going to get paid for.

Who needed this aggravation? Why not toss both of them off and let them duke it out in the street?

I pulled over at the next bus stop and turned on my flashers. At this point, I'm sure I radioed for police dispatch per regulations, but why no record of my call exists, I can't explain.

I grabbed the black kid's jersey and pried him off the *mojado.* "You're off my bus," I remember saying.

"Why you kicking me off?" the kid shouted. "He started it!"

You're wondering the same thing. Why him? There were eighteen Mexicans onboard, a late-night zombie army of classroom cleaners headed to USC, and about two or three blacks. Easy choice.

"Off," I said and shoved him to the door. "Off the fucking bus!"

"Fuck you! You wetbacks are all the same!"

Try, if you can, to pretend you haven't seen the video. I won't deny being called a wetback infuriated me, but the "kick" off the stairs and onto the street wasn't a kick. The kid used most of his strength to fling himself off the bus. I popped the doors closed and shouted something at the *mojado.* The video says I said, *"Vuelva a donde usted vino, pinche mojado!"* but I don't remember saying that. What I wanted was to get out of there.

The kid ran alongside the bus, slamming and kicking it as I drove away. He was right in my blind spot when I drove for an intersection. There's no footage of this, but I had the green light. I had the right of way. That truck, whose description I've given a hundred times and will give again here—late-model GMC pickup truck, mushroom brown, white guy driving and a Mexican seated next to him in the cab—ran straight through a red light, cutting me off. I had two seconds to decide whether to plow into the truck, risking my and my passengers' lives, or swerve to the right to miss it.

There was a loud thump, followed by the dull, thudding sound of what could have been a heavy sack dropping from a roof.

Leaning out the front door, I could see the kid had smacked into the bus's sideboards and was propelled forward about thirty feet, cracking his neck against the curb. I've seen enough bodies spread out on the pavement to know he was dead.

What was I feeling? Nothing. I wanted to deal with the situation in a quick and professional manner, the way I'd been trained. I turned on the hazards, alternating light on, then off, then on, over his crumpled body. It was dark by then. Nights here are sudden, like an accident.

I'm confident I radioed for help when I reboarded the bus. I have no explanation why the call came in eleven minutes after those first 911 calls came from my passengers. Standard procedure is to keep everyone onboard until the police arrive to prevent witnesses fleeing the scene. Following regulations for hitting a pedestrian, I asked if anyone onboard was hurt, but there was too much noise and screaming for me to hear their answers.

Under the baseboard in a storage box was a thick sheet of canvas. I exited the bus and covered the body. A group of blacks from an apartment complex across the street pooled out in front, watching the scene.

I lit several flares while the crowd across the street whooped and hollered and drank beer. Then they shouted and pointed before they bolted over. A small crowd grew into a large one, forming a rowdy semicircle around the body. That's when one of the blacks on the bus pushed open the front door and shouted, "He killed him! The Mexican threw the brother off the bus and killed him! I got it on video!"

A small group clustered around the light of his cell phone, their pinched, illuminated faces carved out from the night behind them. It was a short clip, maybe fifteen seconds, but I could see the light flickering in an endless loop, hear my voice repeating itself, the crowd's conviction and anger rising with each replay.

"You killed him, motherfucker!" a man shouted, followed by a chorus of *yeah*s!

"He ran alongside the bus in the street," I said. "It was an accident."

"Fuck accident!" another man shouted. "You ain't even from here!"

"I didn't see him."

"Oh, you didn't see him!" a third voice shouted. "'Cause it's night and he's black you didn't see him?"

"No, no," I stammered. "That's not what I meant. He was in my blind spot."

"The fucker who started it's on the bus!" the black with the camera phone said. "He grabbed the brother! Get him, too!"

The crowd had heard enough. A group of them—shirtless, tatted thugs—stormed up the open front doors and onto the bus.

"We got him!" somebody screamed from inside. "We got the motherfucker!"

A Mexican guy—not the one who started the fight—was thrown off the bus and corralled into the semicircle with me and the dead body.

"What you got to say for yourself?" a voice shouted.

I didn't answer. The Mexican was trembling. He whispered *"No sé"* under his breath.

"Fucking *cholos* go hunt for black people! You wetbacks been trying to kill us up and down these streets!"

"Say something!" one of the crowd shouted.

A large hand smacked him in the face before he could. Then a solid punch, and he went down. He screamed for help in Spanish, which made the crowd rabid. Someone lunged at me, and I scrambled up the stairwell, kicking back at the hands trying to grab my legs. I slapped a hydraulic button to lock the doors. The mob threw the Mexican up against them.

"Habre la puerta!" he screamed. *"Dios mío, habre la puerta!"*

The man pounded his fists against the glass doors. His face was bloodied and bruised. There was a short moment where the crowd outside sounded worn out. Inside the bus was screaming, shouts of *"Sácanos de aqui!"*

I started up the bus, hoping the roar of the engine would scare the crowd outside into thinking I might barrel into them and back off. Instead, they threw the Mexican back into the doors, his face a bruised sunset, then down onto the sidewalk with an audible *crack*.

It's a violation of Metro policy to leave the scene of an accident. But I had the safety of my passengers to consider. Nobody mentions that, by driving away, I saved those other Mexicans' lives. In the rearview, the silhouettes chasing us receded, swallowed into the dark. I switched the lighted marquee to OUT OF SERVICE—HAVE A NICE DAY! and sped down Hoover, missing all the stops. On the corner of Hoover and Jefferson, I pulled over at a Denny's, radioed dispatch my new location, and opened the passenger doors.

Everything I did up to this point, I think you'd agree, a reasonable man would have done the same way. The Mexican who started the fight ran off. A few others followed him. I told everyone to wait either inside the restaurant or across the street on the USC campus.

I was shaken and wanted to clear my head, grab a bite to eat, some coffee maybe, something to settle me down. With no police car in sight, I drove east, then north, up Figueroa back to my division yard, off Mission Road, in Boyle Heights, behind the 5/10 interchange. At the corner of Figueroa and the point where César Chávez turns into Sunset Boulevard (the one spot in Los Angeles where a Mexican name changes into an American one), instead of turning right down Chávez to the yard, I turned left on Sunset and kept driving.

Why? I don't know. There are specific rules that cover off-route trips, but I couldn't recall what they were. I'd never seen the streets that deserted before. The city lights shimmered like a pinwheel on a child's grave, hard, gray beams cut up and spun in a dozen fingered directions. In front of me was this long straight line of blue-green diamond streetlights stretching out in a fluid purple blackness, like blood in an artery. And a silence to rival any national park, any mountainous abyss, a silence you'd think impossible in a city of millions.

Daybreak was washing the night away off the sides of the horizon.

I parked in front of a gas station, shut down the bus, and rested my head on the wheel. I don't know how long I was out for, but the sound of someone pounding to get inside woke me up. The man kept knocking and didn't seem to care about the blood smeared on the doors.

When I opened them, he climbed the steps and emptied his pockets into the fare box before I got a word out.

"I'm out of service," I said. I could see why he didn't notice the doors. He was bruised and bloodied himself, had been in one hell of a fight.

"I am too," he said. "But here we are."

"No, this bus is out of service."

"Okay," he said. "When you going to be ready to roll?"

"No, mister, the bus, totally out of service." I wasn't sure he understood English, and I was too exhausted to stand by my principles. *"¿Comprendes? Tienes que coger otro autobús."*

"I understood you the first time," he said.

"Then why are you still here?" I asked.

"I have somewhere to go and no other way to get there."

"Why is that my problem?"

"Because that's your job, right?"

He held himself with a swagger but had this faraway stare in his eyes, that look you get when you've had enough pain for one day and aren't sure whether you'll be able to take on any more tomorrow. And he was right; it *was* my job. It didn't take me long to decide what to do.

"You're right," I said and glanced at the fare box. "You put in too much."

"That's okay, man," he said. "It's a first for me."

Yes, I know many of the facts as I've remembered them don't match the numerous eyewitness reports on file, and *yes,* they never located the truck that caused me to swerve into that kid. And nobody's been able to find this guy, this "Freddy" I picked up, the last passenger of the night, and maybe of my career, but I'm telling you this *did* happen.

"How do we get to where you're going?" I asked.

"I don't know."

"How far away is it?"

"I'm not sure."

"How will you know when we've arrived?"

"I'll know."

"Okay," I said. "I will get you there."

He took a seat about halfway back in the empty bus, picked something off the floor I couldn't see, and rested his head against a window. It was several long blocks on Sunset before we hit our first red light, one of those lights that take forever to change, but I could wait. I would get him where he needed to go no matter how long it took me. I would learn a new set of rules. I would find another way home.

5

Yo Soy el Army

We used to own these streets. From Echo Park Lake, up Echo Park Avenue, and into the green hills and avocado trees of Elysian Park, home to the Los Angeles Police Academy, up to Dodger Stadium (built in the 1950s on top of the 'hood that used to be Chavez Ravine), down to the whites' six-lane escape route to the San Fernando Valley, Glendale Boulevard, under and through the freeway interchanges downtown, across the big Victorian mansions of Angelino Heights, then back to Sunset Boulevard—this whole part of Rampart belonged to the Echo Park Locos. I'd been a Loco since I was fourteen; my father, Manny Mendoza, Sr., before me a legendary Loco who'd taken on nine members from 18th Street who dared cross out of their territory on a Friday night. Or was it eight members from 13th Street on a Saturday night? I never could be sure how true those stories my father told me were.

Most of the gangs around here didn't take the Locos seriously before my old man. My *abuelita* was a Zooter in White Fence, and even she didn't respect the Locos. "Why don't you join a gang *con huevos?*" she asked and laughed at my dad. We were considered teeny-boppers before he did shit that made us legit in the eyes of bigger and harder gangs. He was the most respected *veterano* the Locos had; even during his final bedridden year, when he had to wear a diaper, homeboys from as far as Temple Street held their noses and came to *"el maestro"* for counsel. In a respectful voice he never used with me or my pussy brother Efren, who ran off because he loved his faggot books more than his own *sangre,* Dad broke it down for the younger *vatos.* How you use rubbers, the right way to "jump" someone into the gang (never kick the head or the balls— you don't want to be stuck with a brain-damaged *maricón*), and the trick to taking apart a Chevy Impala carburetor. Manny called it *"cholo* school." (This was back when *cholos* still cared what us OGs had to pass down.) There were lessons on how to handle fights with junkies and drunkards, when to fuck or be fucked in the joint, the best place on your body to hide shanks, where to go after you've shot someone (not your mama's or your bitch's house, *pendejo*), and what to do if some *puta negra* gave you what my old man died from at forty-seven, "permanent pneumonia" (AIDS)—these were the perils of our streets.

Turns out we didn't own these streets at all. One by one, the houses on my block of Laveta Terrace sprouted For Sale signs on their front lawns like tombstones, each one taking away a friend or an enemy, but neighbors all, cashing out homes that had been in their families for decades for hundreds of thousands of dollars, taking with them *veteranos* and future *veteranos* alike. There's a handful of OGs left in the neighborhood. You can spot 'em by their tattoos, etched black letters spelling LOCOS across their knuckles and crosses in the soft spots on their hands where their pointer fingers and thumbs meet, not these bullshit white-boy rock-star tattoos of make-believe tribal bracelets on their forearms or random Chino characters on their lower backs. Our tattoos weren't fashion statements. They were marks of fidelity, to our streets, our homeboys, and our allegiance to hate those born on the other side of town. Now they were bitter reminders of a war neither won nor lost but redeclared, with new opponents who carried not knives, guns, and family grudges but hammers, contracts, and measuring tape. There is no elegy for those who have been dispossessed of their anger—what remains is a future carved out of banality instead of blood.

"Do you want bean sprouts, sir?"

A girl with dyed cotton-candy pink hair and metal spikes decorating her collarbone jabbed an impatient finger at my paper plate. "Bean sprouts or kettle chips?" she asked.

"Bean sprouts," I croaked, ashamed I'd reached a point in my life where I had to make decisions like choosing between bean sprouts or potato chips (and then going with fucking bean sprouts!). They were a side dish for my lunch, a grilled cheese and soy bacon sandwich, made on seven-grain bread with organic, grass-fed, raw-milk cheddar and, at my request, heart-healthy mayonnaise.

Somewhere I thought I smelled, wafting into Membo's Coffee Shop on Sunset Boulevard, an outdoor hibachi cooking thick steaks and ribs slathered with honeysweet barbecue sauce. I paid for my sandwich with a ten-dollar bill and received a handful of nickels and pennies. My son Juan, holding a miniature coffee cup and saucer, claimed two chairs under a canvas umbrella amid a cluster of streetside outdoor dining tables.

"We were lucky to get these," Juan said.

"It's hot out here," I said, sinking down into a cushioned patio chair made for pampered *jotas*. "Don't understand why everyone wants to sit outside. Tables are right next to the street. Eat a mouthful of dust and exhaust when the lights change and a bus roars by."

"What'd you get?" Juan asked.

"The one thing they had with fake meat," I said.

"You have to watch that because of your . . . ," Juan said, pointing to my chest.

"I asked for the good mayo."

"Good," Juan said. "And stay away from these, too," he said, raising his cup. "These espressos are addictive."

I took a small bite from my sandwich, leaned back in the chair, and wiped my mouth with a coarse brown napkin made from recycled paper.

"I don't know why we keep coming here," I said.

"It's in the neighborhood," Juan said.

"I don't know anybody here," I said. "Nobody who works here, nobody who sits and eats here."

"They don't know you either, Dad," Juan said. "Give it time."

"I should have gotten a beer."

"It's not a restaurant anymore," Juan said, sipping from his cup. "I keep reminding you they don't serve beer here."

"Won't be a problem where you're going," I said, biting into my sandwich. Juan nodded, sipped from his cup. "How much more you need to get done?"

Juan set down his cup on the saucer. "Got my clothes, gym bag, towels, toothbrush, toothpaste, floss, shower shoes—everything at Target. I need to make copies of my birth certificate and papers."

"You got a mailing address yet?" I asked.

"No, Dad, not until I've been processed."

"So you're not official yet?"

"Dad, we've been through this."

"Have you signed anything?"

"Dad . . ."

"You don't have to do anything if you haven't signed anything. Have you signed anything?"

"Yes, I've signed something."

I thought about this, pushed my sandwich away. "Aw, signed papers don't mean shit. I signed a bunch a parole papers in my day. Never followed up and nothing ever happened to me."

"Okay, Dad. My mistake."

"I'm glad you admitted you were wrong. You're ready for married life," I said, and we both laughed. "Mom would have liked Angie."

Juan nodded and lowered his eyes. If Ofelia had been here, she'd've been equal parts thrilled that Juan was marrying a Mexican and not an Oriental girl (he went through a phase) and furious he'd enlisted in the Army. *"Yo soy el Army?"* she'd've screamed. If she'd been here, she'd have figured a way to make him stay.

"Mom would have *loved* Angie." Juan smiled and took another sip from his cup.

In the gang, I treated women like unexpected gusts of cool air on a hot, dry day, a soft westward breeze (westward because the sun sets and disappears in the west, where all women head to sooner or later). Then I moved on. Ofelia was different from the start. We met in the parking lot of what used to be Chief's Auto Repair in the first mini-mall on this stretch of Sunset. She was picking up a replacement battery for her Volkswagen bug but had no idea how to install it. Man, she was beautiful; had a mouth so smart it had a Ph.D. in insulting your ass. Her body didn't move so much as it cut through air that didn't have time to get out of her way.

I ended up with acid residue that ate through the knees in my pants, and her phone number. The first time we made love, after her special high school graduation dinner with her folks at El Cholo, her hands brushed the nape of my bare neck, caressing a gentle swirl that spelled out my name with the tips of her press-on fingernails. No one had touched me that way before. She told me later she was spelling out a rumor she'd heard about me: *tú eres maricón.*

"It's just for money," I said, "not for love. *Tu sabes?"*

She went to L.A. City College in the fall, a firebrand majoring in Chicano studies and an intent to help *"La Raza."* We continued dating, but it took her longer to return my calls. On the phone, I spoke picking up right where we left off, the way guys do when their feelings for a girl haven't changed but they don't realize that their girls' have. There was something cold growing in her voice, brutal, monotone in its inflection. What had been warm and comforting in her personality had hardened into something that resembled pity but was closer to indifference. When spring came, she told me that being in a gang was "detrimental to our people" and that she couldn't have anything more to do with me.

Six weeks later, she called me with news of her pregnancy and, being a good Catholic, the date for our upcoming wedding. I'm not sure how she felt about our child derailing her plans for *La Raza,* but she was a great mother, a much better mother than a wife. She spoiled Juan, read to him from the time he was a baby, and tried from an early age to indoctrinate him with that Mexican pride bullshit. Whenever I got hauled down to the Glass House for some piece of shit violation, she'd have him memorizing *La Raza* catchphrases and slogans, the only things Brown Power groups and MEChA were good at if you ask me. Her plan to raise the next César Chávez didn't pan out, but she converted plenty in the neighborhood.

Ofelia lectured the Mexican women in her supermarket shopping circle on the latest real estate gossip. A Jew bought that building near the bank and will turn it into a Jew-only gym. That store where we buy our milk was bought by a German financier and will be converted into a warehouse. It'll be World War II around here! Her angriest comments, though, were about the Orientals. She'd drag Juan to the Bank of America, lean over the counter to tell her favorite teller, a young, sassy *gordita* with mushroom-cloud hair named Duchess, about the new mini-malls destined to take over Echo Park. More Oriental stores and restaurants, she whispered, exactly what we need around here, another Chinese restaurant. They paid no taxes, she said. Was Duchess aware of that? Of course she must be, because she worked in a bank. They got free money from the government because of the Vietnam War. Then she'd cast an eye at Juan and say, "Beautiful girl like you has to be on the lookout. They take *all* our young men away, *one way* or the *other.*"

On weekends, they argued next to my TV couch, more bickering couple than mother and son. By this time, Juan was in high school and I was a part of the gang in name only. Their fight over that Tran girl was the worst. When you talked to Ofelia, you were walking across a lake of frozen ice, and a misstep could plunge you into water cold enough to kill you in thirty seconds. That's where Juan learned his patience and diplomacy. God knows he didn't learn it from me.

"You love a *chinita*?" she asked. "What, again? They never like you."

"No, this one's different. She does like me. She doesn't like the fact I'm Mexican."

"How's that different from the others?"

Juan kept his cool. "Tran has a problem with me because I'm Mexican. Those other girls didn't like me because I was *me*."

"A Mexican *is* who you are! At least this girl's honest about it. *Ay,* why did I take you to so many Chinese restaurants growing up? That's why you fall in love with Chinese girls. They're all you saw!"

"Mom, don't be silly," he said. "Manny, can you explain?" he asked me.

"Leave me out of this, boy," I said from the couch.

"Who's silly?" she asked. "You're the one chasing someone who thinks you aren't good enough the way you are. What's the matter with a beautiful Mexican girl? You can have beautiful Mexican babies."

"Mom, I'm eighteen."

"I was eighteen when I had you. What Oriental girl's gonna want a Mexican baby? I've told you over and over, they want *gabachos*. Remember that Vietnamese woman at the hair salon who used to do my hair? Six months here in the country and then, *bam!*, driving a Mercedes and a husband with blond hair. Those *gringos* think those little *chinitas* are *so cute*. You think you're white? Don't you want a real woman instead of a little girl with no tits and no ass? Child molesters like Oriental girls. What about that nice Mexican girl at the bank?"

"The chunky one with the big poodle hair?" Juan asked.

"Don't be rude," Ofelia said. "She's a beautiful girl. What, are you afraid of tits and ass? You know how many boys lapped at these shores?" she said, cupping her breasts.

"Mom, could you please not fondle yourself in front of me?"

"*Ay,* so uptight!" she said. "These were good enough for you when you were a baby! And good enough for your father until he wanted a fresh pair to grow out of the television."

"Leave me out of this, woman," I shouted from the couch.

"That girl Duchess has a nice pair," she continued. "I'll take you both out for lunch so you can get a good look."

"Mom, I don't like Mexican girls," Juan sighed. "There's nothing you can do to change that."

"Her Chino parents will find a way," Ofelia said. "If her father's wallet goes missing, you'll be the one who took it. If their restaurant burns down, you lit the match. They will find a way to hate you."

The fighting got so bad I went to Tran's father's restaurant, Saigon Falls, across the street from a derelict gas station and next to Little Joy Jr.'s, a *jota* bar, to talk things over. Ofelia thought I was going down there to "take care" of him, but Tran was a good girl and her being Vietnamese didn't bother me one bit. I think I liked my son sticking it to Ms. *La Raza* by dating an Oriental. When I got there, Tran was packing Chinese food containers into paper and plastic double bags, dabbing her fingertips on lemon halves to keep them moist. Her mother came up behind her and hugged her around the waist, standing on her tiptoes to rest her face in Tran's shoulder-length hair.

"Mom, why are you acting so weird?" Tran said. Her father— a man named Phoc, who along with the restaurant owned a pallet-making factory in the City of Industry—invited me over to sit at a table he was setting. He sang along with an Oriental song on the stereo while he arranged white plates as thick as windowpanes, fat chipped teacups, and chopsticks sealed in Ziploc pouches.

"You like this song?" he asked, humming a seesaw melody that dangled in midair.

"It's nice," I said. "Sounds kind of Spanish."

"I sang this in Hainan, an island off the Chinese coast, growing up. It's about home, never seeing your home again."

"It doesn't sound sad to me," I said.

"I changed the melody," he said. "I can get used to not seeing home because I can have my home here, in America. My friends, my family, my employees, we the same, like in Hainan."

"You'd never have seen me in Hainan," I said.

"You right, you right, okay?" Phoc laughed. "But you have your own America, too. Inside, in here, it's Hainan. But out there, *your* home. Those people, Mexicans, like *your* home, Mexico. Right outside the door."

"My home's up the block on Portia Street," I said. "I've never been to Mexico."

"Who needs to, okay? Outside, Mexican on corners, Mexican at bus stop, Mexican at gas station, Mexican everywhere looking for job together. Why together? See, Mexican think of themselves. Too many on one corner means lower price for everyone. Chinese are not that way. They spread out so prices stay high and everyone can profit. We help each other because we want Chinese to succeed. Mexican want himself to succeed only."

"Phoc," I said, "my son works, so *he* can succeed. If he succeeds, that's good for him *and* your daughter. If what you say is true, how do you explain him?"

Phoc shook his head, clucking his tongue. "Maybe he Chinese!" He laughed. Behind a bamboo screen, Tran was filling teapots. "Her back's turn, but she strong enough to face her father, tell him how she feel. In here, she respect me. But out there, she can live how she want. She has to live with what people say, not me. Oh-kay?"

"It's their lives," I said. "Let 'em live them."

"Oh-kay," he said. "One day, maybe you go to the real Hainan.

You act too much like Chinese, okay?" He finished setting the tables and walked over to Tran, whispering something in her ear. Then he walked over to his wife and pointed at me. She shook her head as he talked, squealing in protest until he cut the air with his hands, silencing her. I laughed, imagining how much cutting I'd need to do to silence Ofelia. I'd probably need Paul Bunyan's ax.

Tran and Juan dated through college (Ofelia told him to major in Chicano studies; he chose European politics: "What's to study? Either way, the white man wins!"). It was difficult for both of them; the looks and leers they got on the street, in both Echo Park and Chinatown; *cholas* putting gum in Tran's hair in the movie theater; Orientals staring them down when they held hands on the street; Ofelia refusing to invite Tran for Thanksgiving dinner. Phoc invited me and Juan to Saigon Falls as a peace offering during the holidays.

I heard Juan's laughter in the kitchen. I crept there through a dining room decorated with Christmas lights, fish tanks, red Chinese New Year decorations, spiral foil mobiles, and out-of-date calendars with soft-focus photographs of Oriental women staring at koi ponds and flower beds. In between stacks of dented double-burner woks was an oak butcher's block the length of a dining room table. There, Tran had set out a large mixing bowl with a bowling-ball lump of moistened flour, a container with ground up crabmeat, scallions, onions, and paprika, and a small finger bowl of lemon water. Juan was standing next to her, at attention.

Rolling up her long white sleeves, Tran massaged a thin layer of flour onto her arms. The smell from her skin, bath soap and candied perfume, mixed in with the scent of the fresh dough she kneaded in the mixing bowl, overpowering the fatty smell of congealed grease.

"Here, let me show you how to make these," she was saying to Juan.

She yanked out a taffy-drop hunk of flour and, slapping it on the block, rolled it into a thin tent-flap-shaped pancake. Then came a morsel of crabmeat, followed by an index finger moistened in the lemon water, kissing the edges of the pancake to create a momentary seal. A quick swoop of her hand, and the pancake was folded over in half. Bunching her fingers together, she kneaded small, ridged impressions onto the dough's edges, plopping fat, raindrop dumplings onto the counter. He mimicked her motions, but his dumplings popped open, their deformed folds and ridges jutting out like baby fingers in clay.

"You're packing them too big!" Tran exclaimed with a laugh. "Give me your hands."

Her palms guided the backs of his hands across each ingredient, her fingertips dripping lemon water down his arms as their hands wrapped each dumpling together. Her breasts brushed his arm through her blouse, and the plastic buckles of her white bra straps, peeking through the top of her blouse, slid back and forth across her shoulder. The curve of her thighs leaned against the cutting block. Her black eye shadow brought out the delicate whalebone whites of her cheeks. And then, her face crinkled like wrapping paper when she stood on tiptoe to kiss him, with a look of either utter amazement at her recklessness or astonishment at the sincerity of her affection, right before she saw me looking at them and shoved him away.

They made plans to elope, but for a reason that escapes me, the plans fell through and what at the time was seen as a temporary setback became permanent separation, and the life I thought they'd be living now, the life I thought I'd see them have as a grandfather, haunted me—the hundreds of dinners they never cooked together, the photos I'd see from their family vacation trips to faraway places like Disney World or New York City left untaken, the children they never had tugging at my sleeves in a toy store asking me for a Barbie Dream House or a radio-controlled car, and me, hefting them up on my shoulders, planting a kiss on my daughter-in-law's cheek, then waking up from my dream and realizing nobody was there.

In time, the neighborhood changed, like Ofelia said it would. Phoc sold his restaurant to a gay white man named Brad, who turned it into Membo's Coffee Shop. I asked Brad if he had any way to reach Tran. He thought he remembered her visiting the restaurant once with her Chinese husband and newborn baby. He couldn't be sure, though; it may have been Tran's sister.

That's where I was, at Membo's, when the hospital called on the cell phone Ofelia gave me "for emergencies" and told me Ofelia had collapsed in a flower store picking up a bouquet of yellow roses for a baby shower. She'd had a stroke and was dead before I reached the hospital.

Each of us believes, when we are young, we know a way to cheat death. Then as we age, we tilt toward the end on a seesaw that never teeters back up. When that end arrives, we are surprised, gasping with shock, at last knowing the unknowable but not knowing how to tell anyone we know it.

Membo's became a new routine of sorts, to get me out of the house. One time, I held the front door of the coffee shop open for a two-year-old girl on unsteady legs, tethered to her parents, a mixed black and Oriental couple, part of the new wave of residents around here. A pair of elderly Oriental women in line with their daughters pushed the mother and father aside and cooed over the child, speaking to her in a mix of broken English and Chinese.

The girl, her skin a blend of her parents' but also a shade entirely her own, saw me and covered her smile with her hands. She could have been my grandchild, I thought, loved by those who didn't know how to love those who made her.

Juan finished his espresso. "I need to give you something," he said. In his back pants pocket was a thick, folded white sheet of butcher paper. A caricature of a beautiful woman in an elegant red dress was on one side. On its back was writing, in the form of a letter, and a signature.

"This is my 'last letter,'" Juan said. "This way I don't have to write each letter like it's my last."

"What's this it's written on?" I asked.

"This was that drawing I told you about. The one that . . . from that girl at the bank, Duchess, the one I dated for a while."

"Yeah, I remember her. Why are you giving this to me now?"

"I'm going to be with Angie at her place before I go. I didn't want her to see me give it to you. It's for her."

I unfolded the paper. "It's a drawing Duchess did of Angie," he said. "She gave it to me when I started dating Angie. I don't think Angie's ever seen it. Duchess said she'd want it." I tried to flip it over without Juan seeing me do it but I was never much of a confidence man and he caught me.

"You can read the letter if you want," Juan added.

"Hands aren't as quick as they used to be. You don't want someone else to hold on to this for you?"

"Who else could I ask?"

"I don't know," I said, unsure how to say I was petrified of fucking up this one simple task by losing the letter, ripping it up in anger, or worse, getting drunk enough one night and sending it to Angie in a fit of rage. That was a real possibility.

"It's for your woman," I said. "Someone else should hold on to it."

"You'll do fine," Juan said.

"I don't have a safe place to keep this in," I said.

"Since when were you the kind of guy who has 'safe places'?" Juan teased.

I wanted to say something more here, a promise that I would be faithful in honoring what could be my son's last request. Ofelia would have told me to go further. Say something to make him stay, she'd've said. Enough brown brothers have died for this country. *Por la raza, todo,* she'd've said. The best I'd done up to this point was concoct a series of plans and schemes to keep my son from leaving—a fake heart attack, threats of physical violence, and an appraisal of how much my house was worth, with a document giving three-fourths of the money to him and Angie as a no-strings-attached gift for their wedding. Yet each day when he came home from another round of preparations before basic training, I sat glued to my couch, watching a muted television and sharing wordless TV tray dinners before Juan sprinted out to Angie's.

This was a moment I might not have again with my son. It was a moment that required fearlessness, courage, the kind my father said he brought to take down those 18th Street punks. Why aren't you more like your old man, they'd say, even if he was a faggot who died of AIDS. He wasn't a *jota* (so he said), but they didn't know he was a baby killer. My old man told me tons of stories, but only one rang true. It came out one night while we were playing bones. I was on a hot streak and gloating.

"I'm killin' you, Pops, killin' you!" I said. "Time for you to go *deep* in the boneyard!"

"Don't disrespect your *jefe*."

"You're not my *jefe*." I laughed and slammed down a double six. "You ain't in the Locos no more."

He leaned over with a palmful of dominoes and slapped me across the face. "Talk back again," he said, "and I'll bury you myself."

"You never killed nobody!" I shouted, tasting blood on my lip. "They're stories, they're all just stories."

"I shot a baby girl," he said and carefully stacked up the dominoes into a wooden box shaped like a coffin. "Three years old. Dancing on a street corner. 'Baby Madonna.' In the wrong place at the wrong time. If that *puto* I was chasing hadn't cheated me out of a case of Bud, she'd be a young woman now. You might even be fucking her if you weren't a *maricón*." He chuckled. "If I could shoot a little girl, I could shoot my own son." He placed the domino box in the center of the table. "Put them away. We're done."

I tried to recapture his "courage" when I was in the gang, but I kept seeing that dead little girl lying out on the sidewalk—in my head, on that big-ass mural near the 101. I found out everyone in the Locos knew he'd done it but nobody turned him in. Why? We were supposed to have a code, rules to follow—don't hurt dogs, don't rape old women, don't kill kids. What kind of man shoots a girl, even if by accident, then doesn't turn himself in? And what kind of men protect that man? Whenever I went out on the streets, the image of a little girl bleeding to death froze me up, made me play things safer than my *carnals*, many of whom earned their Loco nicknames through fighting, stealing, dealing, or shooting. We were called *locos* for a reason; me, they called *El Pesado,* the "boring man."

When I "retired" a *veterano* at thirty-three, the Locos let me drift out of the life, nice and easy. It was like losing a factory job I'd had for years and not knowing what to do with the rest of my life because I didn't know how to do anything else. This moment with Juan, then, must have been the reason I outlived my gang, my wife, *mi barrio*—to keep my son from making a fatal mistake. The words would come now—they *had* to—in a way they never came for my dad.

"Are you done with that, sir?" The girl with pink hair motioned to my half-eaten sandwich.

In my mind, I was apologizing. That's all a grown son really wants from his old man. "I'm sorry"—and I *was* sorry, for being such a worthless father, for not loving Ofelia with the proper amount of respect, the drug scores, the anonymous dick-sucking tricks in men's rooms for money, the untold number of late nights I stumbled home drunk and punched Juan in bed at three in the morning to teach him to always be prepared to be attacked—here was my plea for forgiveness, for him not to leave me here alone in a neighborhood that was being stripped away one memory at a time and replaced with something foreign, cancerous, and final.

"Well, Dad?" Juan asked, rising to leave a tip on the table. He looked at me with a warm, peaceful gaze. "I think he's finished," he said.

6

The Hustler

The best sunrise you'll ever see is your first as a free man. That big gassy light that creaks out of God's cellar, wrestling the night away from a sky holding on to it with every star and streetlight, shining on a man who can rise when he wants, not when a 120-decibel buzzer tells him to—*that* is a sunrise. I should know. I've seen that sunrise over a dozen times, each one a promise that this will be the one that changes my life, this dawn will be witness to a new set of priorities, a new sense of hope. Of course I end up right back in the joint on a technicality (the technicality being that I get caught), and it's another stretch before I see that sunrise again.

You don't think about things like sunrises until you've gone without them, those unappreciated everyday moments you leave behind on the outside. You'd be amazed at the things people leave behind: being able to see your woman's hairy muff rise like dough when she comes out of the shower in the morning; your mother's *huevos rancheros;* the chance to give your son his first taste of beer on a summer's night. Hell, I know one guy who misses Kentucky Fried Chicken as much as some guys miss *pucha.* And then there are all the things out there changing, things you don't know about that you'd miss if you did. All you've got is faith that things change slow enough out there for you to catch up to them when you get out of here.

For me, this time out is different. I've changed. This sunrise here, the pale gray promise of one I can see hovering behind that line of palm trees on a faraway hill, is different. It's a sunrise that says: Welcome home.

I'm Freddy Blas, forty-two years old. Born in Mexico, raised in East L.A., and 100 percent American. I spent nineteen of those forty-two years locked up—juvie, youth camps, youth authority, Solano, Tracy, Soledad, Tehachapi, Chino—including my last stint up at Lancaster for aggravated battery (I had some trouble parking a car and got sent away for almost twelve years; can you believe that shit?).

I grew up over in Boyle Heights, where we caught the Night Stalker on East Hubbard Street, near Whittier Boulevard. I say "we" because I was *in* that mob that ran down and captured that *loco* serial killer during the summer of 1985. You wouldn't know this unless I told you, but *I* was the reason they caught that fucker, the first *chingón* (I need Spanish here because, for many of the best cusswords, there's no English equivalent) to start punching the shit out of him. Before I started throwing *chingasos,* people were flailing at him and missing, trying to catch a goldfish on hot sand. Everybody was afraid to touch him, intimidated by the indestructible bogeyman with supernatural powers they'd heard about on TV for months. They didn't see that thrashing underneath them was a skinny spic with a limp Jheri curl who tried to steal some *vato*'s broke-ass car in broad daylight. He'd have gotten away, too, if I hadn't thought, *Fuck, he'd stop squirming if he got punched in the kidneys a few times.*

I'm big for a Mexican and have these massive lobster-claw hands that made it easy for me to land the first punch. Once I hit him, my neighbors came to their senses and it was a kick-the-spic bonanza.

Too bad the cops got him when they did. We would have torn him limb from limb. Can you imagine, a *pinche* Mexican serial killer? Fucking *gabachos* in L.A. hated Mexicans enough as it was. First we took the whites' jobs; now we had taken the white man's claim on freaky serial killers, too. The city didn't seem to mind, though. People from across L.A. drove by the spot where he was caught, honking their horns in celebration and unity. That night was a real block party. Mayor Tom Bradley said it was "a spontaneous outpouring of good-will from the City of Angels," but he was always saying that kind of shit. The neighborhood thought this was the beginning of a renaissance. The potholes would get filled, the streetlights repaired, and the cops would keep the people safer. There were rumors of movie deals, keys to the city, seats behind the dugout at Dodger Stadium. But nothing happened. I sure never saw any reward money from catching that fucking Mexican—and wasn't it just like a Mexican to be caught, on foot, running. Fucking *maricón.*

Before I go on, I want to make it clear to you that I speak *inglés.* *Entiendes, mendes?* This is *America* and I speak *America's* language. No translation needed. See, I never had a problem speaking English. My old man told me that, to make it in America, all you need to do is keep talking. *Hablar hasta que las palabras no tienen sentido.* Don't ever shut up. The louder you are the better—that's the American way. Look at how much more respect Americans have for blacks instead of Mexicans. Rich black ballplayers, black movie stars, black comedians, a black president! That's because blacks tell you (they tell *everyone*) what they want to change. How can you do that if you can't speak the language? That's why I can't *stand* Mexicans who come to this country and keep their mouths shut because they never bothered to learn English. You say learning English is tough? I say sleeping on the floor of a room with fourteen people in it is tougher. Learn English and become your own boss. Stay speaking Spanish and you inherit a fucking crimp in your neck from nodding *"sí, sí"* all day long. I could make a killing selling neck braces to Mexicans who nod their heads instead of opening their mouths and saying "cut your own goddamn lawn." Can't let people push you around. You gotta be hard. Like Steve McQueen, or Kennedy. When that prick Khrushchev fucked with us over Cuba, Kennedy said, "If you don't remove those missiles on Wednesday, by Friday we'll turn this atmosphere to flames." That's what it means to be *ciento por ciento Americano, tú sabes?*

Capitalism is the best revenge against a *gringo.* And *gringos* love that "opportunity on every corner" bullshit. Mexicans don't understand that because they're too busy thinking about everything they don't have. Did you know the Mayans invented the number zero? Who else but Mexicans would know what it means to have nothing? Thing is, the *gringos* are *right.* You never know what you're gonna hear walking down the street. Did you know that one out of ten conversations you overhear walking on your block is about something illegal? Fuck, more than that if you live in Echo Park. Easy as sin to break into a conversation, too. Walk down the street with a twelve-pack, chat someone up, give 'em a few beers, smoke some weed, and *boom,* you got the score. You telling me that ain't easy? Easier than a day-to-day job bending your back or your knees twelve hours a day.

I've done those jobs, believe me. My first "straight" job was as a short-order cook at a twenty-four-hour taco stand. Graveyard shifters and rich, drunk club kids waited in the same line while I grilled ten pounds of shredded pork a night for eight months. It was here I saw how you could hustle to get something for free. Someone would place an order while a homeless person, some black guy, would amble back and forth in front of the counter where I laid out the tacos conveyor belt style. Black guy would pick up the tacos someone else paid for and score a free meal before anybody realized their order was gone. I didn't catch it the first few times because I was cooking the food and not working the register. Jimmy, the *pinche gringo* who owned the dump, saw what happened, took a spatula off the hot grill, and branded it on my forearm. The pain was like being in a dark room and someone turned on all the lights real high, blinding you. From then on, I never took my eyes off the counter. I gave people numbers and shouted them out when their orders were ready. If they didn't respond fast enough, I'd point my tongs at them saying, "Didn't you hear me call your number three times?"

One night, a guy forgot that he put a couple of loose dollars on the counter. I palmed the bills and told him they'd blown onto the ground. I tried it again and again that night, improving my technique. More like *inventing* my technique. Most of these kids were too drunk to register me as a person (they wouldn't have sober, either), didn't see how awkward I was when I snatched their money up with my lobster claws for hands. But I got better, got faster, and soon I could serve a basket of tacos and swipe a two-and-a-half-inch-thick wallet with the same hand in one single motion. Wasn't long before Jimmy wanted a cut. Lend me your van, I said, so I can get rid of the wallets. He gave me the keys, and I never drove back. No point in negotiating with a thief.

I never drove home, either. I didn't leave for any sinister reasons. My mom didn't beat me; my dad didn't try to suck my dick. I was crazy back then, never stopping to think things through past tomorrow. I ran away with the clothes on my back. Same reason I dropped out of high school. I was smart, never failed a class I showed up to, got suspended dozens of times for mouthing off at the teacher because I was bored (I'd throw shit up front to encourage them to pick up the pace), but the education I wanted came from hustling, an education that continues every day you're on the streets. You don't get it living the straight life. That's what I love about it. There is no direct line to becoming the perfect con man, no end of your apprenticeship, no place where you can look down from a comfortable perch and take a breather. Instead, there are a series of shortfalls, switchbacks, missteps, and flubbed cues, navigating a world of mazes. The one sure thing is that a straight line will take you right back to the beginning, and the beginning is not in the place where you remember but somewhere further away and harder to reach and darker to see into than you thought it was. Sometimes when living the life threatened to get too dark, I'd get this overwhelming desire to change, to do . . . right. Get a wife, couple of kids calling me Dad, and for fuck's sake, a minivan. It was a terrifying vision, worse than any jail cell, and I've been in a *lot* of jail cells. I've never been able to channel those fleeting, euphoric intentions into *doing* good. Good is too much work.

I'm not trying to make this life sound like a woman, all depressing and deceptive. Like a woman, this life has its perks—you get the best out of both if you treat each as a job and not a hobby. People don't know when they see me in a bar or a back room and I trick them up for some pool or a card game that I'm a professional gambler. *Hustler* sells short what I can do. Could a "hustler" run any pool table in the city like I can? I made eight thousand dollars in *one night* when some movie execs went slumming in the Eastside and made the mistake of challenging me in my local. I've stolen cars in front of post offices and video stores when someone dashes out with the keys in the ignition, TVs by picking up display models at electronics stores and walking right out the front door with them, money from bank drawers and kids' piggy banks. I've run drugs for the Mexican mafia, who wanted to recruit me, except I had to take a blood oath and put a bunch of damn tattoos and shit on my body.

I didn't need to be part of a gang to have respect. I've got contacts from here to Laredo, Texas, have my pick of any town to set up shop, but I chose Echo Park because *mi barrio* never sold me out, even when half the LAPD was looking for me. The shit I pulled here, man. People still talk about it, still write me letters in the joint about it. I got papers by the boxful from all the homeboys here asking, When are you coming back to the 'hood, Freddy? That's respect, see? None of us knew it'd be twelve years, but experience tells me time doesn't change shit. Every con knows that. My woman Cristina knows that.

We met at Pilgrim's Supermarket, where she was a checker. She was a dyed blonde who'd spilled an ink bottle in her roots, and had long fake eyelashes, luminous green eyes, and these perky, upstanding titties that made me howl like *un lobo*. I was trying to sneak out four bottles of Tanqueray under my shirt, but she caught me. Keep the bottles, she said, but come back when I'm off shift. I thought it was some kind of setup with the cops, but she shook her head. As long as you come back, she said, you can have me. I'd finished the second bottle by the time her shift was over. At her house, her teenage daughter, Angie, plugged into her Walkman without being asked while Cristina led me to her bedroom and showed me that pert, dimpled curve of a woman's ass that gets me excited. I moved in her like the rhythm in a seventies rock song—all bang, no shuffle, baby—and then I moved into her house. We were married in an "alternative" religious ceremony by a group that's considered a "cult" in the state of California, and I stayed with her and Angie off and on (I always came back) for almost five years.

Funny enough, my one attempt at a straight job while I was married was what got me sent to Lancaster. This is the parking problem I was talking about. I was working as a valet at a new club in West Hollywood called Reflection. It was a short application process. Could I speak English? Could I drive a stick shift? Could I run (running, it was understood, was always preferred) for short periods of time? And could I work any day, any shift, day or night?

They paired me up with this guy, Javier, from Highland Park. We weren't friends, but we had enough to bitch about in common—the low pay, erratic hours, cheap tippers—that always gave us something to discuss. We swapped shirts, several changes of which we needed to keep in a nearby chest, along with fresh vests, white towels, and lots of deodorant (all this came out of our paycheck). Running in the warm, muggy Los Angeles summer nights drenched us in minutes, and customers would complain if any of our sweat was on their leather seats or steering wheels.

Javier didn't talk much, which was fine with me, because parking these rich assholes' cars gave me a new perspective on things. I ran these opinions by Javier whenever we had a free moment. Seeing the way these restaurant types fell all over themselves whenever a black Laker or a black Dodger came by, I realized Mexicans' status would change overnight if soccer became a popular sport in America. And the white girls these black guys ran with! *Ay, Dios mío.* These black guys had it all figured out. The first time I saw a black guy kiss a fine white girl, I thought, *Holy shit, can we do that?* This was the *real* path to being American—find a white girl and fuck her real good.

Javier didn't have many thoughts on these subjects. He was always angry. His anger rose off him like a fever I didn't want to catch, one that swelled with the length of our shifts and the size of the crowds. That's what happened that night. There was a movie premiere party, the two of us trying to park a line of cars a mile deep. Javier was parking one of those black basketball player's cars while I was in the car behind them, a Mercedes with an open wallet with several one-hundred-dollar bills sticking out of a compartment next to the gearshift. I'd been working on the level for three weeks and gotten screwed in my wallet and blisters on my feet. Wasn't it time for a little bonus? And who better to give it to me than someone who wouldn't miss it anyway?

I tried to pluck one of the bills out of the wallet with my fingertips but missed, knocking the wallet to the floor. I was rusty. In front of me, Javier and the black guy were talking. Something was up because, nine times out of ten, these people don't want to know you're alive, let alone have a conversation with you. Fingers were pointed, voices raced. And there on the floor by my feet, an open wallet with a crisp one-hundred-dollar bill I'd grabbed at, ripe for the plucking.

Peeking up over the steering wheel, I could see the black guy towering over Javier, pointing these massive fingers down at him like he was talking to a small child. I gotta hand it to Javi, though. He didn't back off. He stood there, shoulders forward, looking real dignified, I thought. There was a dignity in the way he stood up to a guy two feet taller than he was. Where does strength like that come from?

I saw the owner of the Mercedes walking over, his one-hundred-dollar bill stuffed in my hand. I ducked back down to pick up the wallet, and in my panic my big, heavy foot punched the accelerator. The Mercedes plowed into Javier, slamming his head into the support bar of the windshield, sped onto a side street with a forty-five-degree-angle incline, then flipped through the air at a center divider, ramming into an island of streetlights.

I remember the EMTs' feet crunching on the glass and pebbled shards of metal. The photos they showed me in the hospital of Javier's contorted body, the impact throwing him fifty feet, unrecognizable except for his uniform, told me the rest of the story.

When I got sent to Lancaster, Cristina told me she'd never stop loving me, unlike the asshole that knocked her up, some *cabrón* named Hector. Of course she'd fuck other men, move 'em in when she got bored, kick 'em out when they bored her, but there was no doubt that she'd leave a spot on her bed for me when I was ready to claim it. Some women you can count on waiting forever. I dreamt about that spot on her bed, and that sweet pert spot on her ass every night I was inside, my body fitting into the curves of her body like the outlines of shadows in an eclipse, one moving across the other, then together as one, blinding everyone who dared steal a glance at us, then pulling apart onto our separate orbits, night turning back into day.

Beautiful, ain't it? I wrote Cristina that in a letter. Cons make the best letter writers because inside every man is a poet. You just have to throw him in jail to find it.

It's the dark half of morning before dawn when I get off the bus at the Greyhound station on Skid Row. You can hear the hum of traffic from the 101 a couple miles away, gentle and constant like a steady rain. The sky lightens to a cobalt gray, and I imagined I'm one of those great ancient Greek conquering heroes returning to his kingdom to reclaim his throne.

On the starting tip of Sunset Boulevard (which is now called César Chávez Avenue—when did that happen?) I survey my territory—the new apartment buildings and stores, the fresh coats of paint on the doors and window frames on abandoned shops, new storefront signs in English covering the old sun-bleached Spanish ones (which themselves were molded over the old English signs from the forties and fifties), the odd presence of young bearded white men with coffee, not six-packs, on the street corners. Where are the *Chicanos*? Or the *Chinos*? To keep me going, I picture Cristina's robin's-egg-blue kitchen and my face buried deep in a big home-cooked breakfast of *chorizo con huevos,* and a warm pair of loving thighs. Then I call my *carnals,* who must love all the fresh money walking around here, and by this time tomorrow I'll be up a hundred? Five hundred? Hell, maybe a thousand dollars, enough to relax on for a couple months.

Cristina's house is a flat bungalow atop a hill with a straight staircase pointed down at the street like a gun barrel. My stomach and dick throb in unison at the homecoming I'm expecting, one that'll be more exciting for Cristina because I didn't write ahead and tell her when my parole date was. It's been about four years since we last exchanged letters. (Through a prison "pen pal" newsletter, I'd started dating a forty-seven-year-old woman in Canada who sent me cigarettes, money, and pictures of her standing next to a nickel-plated lake, but why would I freeze my fucking ass off in Alberta?)

When Cristina and I were living together, I'd go out for days at a time, wouldn't call or send word where I was, then when I'd drunk and scored and fucked as much as I could handle, I'd creep up the stairs at three or four in the morning, tap on the security gate, and shout out *"Hellooooo!"* drawing out the *o*'s into *aww*s, like a drunken crow. Her daughter, Angie, would open the door, tell me to "die in the gutter," then slam the gate in my face. Man . . . what a bright kid she was.

Then Cristina would storm out onto the porch in one of those skimpy white nightgowns with a slit up the front that didn't—hell, couldn't—cover her breasts, yank me into the house, and unleash a shouting tirade that'd go for thirty minutes. She'd tire herself out, which is when I'd moisten her up with a few promises and a neck massage. By morning I was between her legs and good in her eyes for another two weeks. She liked it better when I didn't make excuses about where I was or who I was with anyway. Stay here or stay away, she'd say. God, what a woman. I hope she hasn't gained too much weight.

It's an easier climb up the stairs than I remember. The gaping cracks in the hillside foundation that ran up and down the uneven staircase like varicose veins have been filled in, the threads from my old patch-up caulking jobs paved over with a smooth frosting of flat, even concrete. Potted plants arranged in neat rows line either side of the staircase, and there's a wicker sitting bench on the porch, both new additions. The security gate's been removed and replaced with a separate front door with a stained-glass inlay. On the brass mailbox next to the door is a different last name than Cristina's, which I assume is her new husband, a man I've never met and almost feel sorry for. Whoever he is, he'll never be in my league. He'll have to accept his demotion; I was here first.

I knock and see a rustling of blinds before the door opens. A white woman with short black hair and a tight T-shirt that somehow makes her look like a man answers. I speak first, because when you're on the locked side of a door you're trying to open, you always speak first.

"Morning. I'm looking for my wife, Cristina. Are you a friend of hers?"

"There's no Cristina here," the woman says.

"Is she out?" I say. It's time to apply a little grease to the situation. "If she's shopping, I'd love to come inside and cook up a warm meal that's waiting for her when she gets back."

"Nobody named Cristina lives here," she says.

"Did Cristina tell you not to let me in? Cristina's a forgiving woman, and if she told you otherwise, she was saying what comes natural to a woman that hasn't seen her man in a while. What's your name?"

"There's no Cristina here," the woman says and, through the crack in the door, looks me over. "I need you to leave."

"Miss, there's no cause for that. I'm scruffy because I've been on a bus all night. Been visiting my sick brother in Bakersfield. He and Cristina are real close. She'll want to know how he's doing."

"Please leave," the woman says. She closes and double-bolts the door. I knock again, harder this time. She's not gonna get rid of me this easy.

The door flies open, like in the old days. Cristina's going to let me have it. That old fire's still burning in her!

The woman reappears with a phone in her hand. "If you don't leave," she says, "I'm calling the police."

"Miss, let Cristina speak to me for five minutes."

"I'm dialing," she says.

"Lady, you're making a big mistake." I laugh, backing away and staring over my shoulder, wondering how far this will go. I could force my way in, but trouble with the cops on my first day out of the joint is the last thing I need. And I'm a gentleman about certain things; I don't like getting rough with a woman I've just met.

I'm down the stairs and on the sidewalk before she closes the door. Cristina must be angrier than I thought. Looking up and down the block for another staircase I can sit down and think on, I see Julianne's old bungalow, tucked at the rear of a driveway adjoining a house that's being renovated by some Mexican day laborers. Julianne was one of the last white women who lived here, a holdover from when her mother bought a place here in the 1950s. We used to smoke out, get drunk, and fuck at her place when our spouses were working. She had two kids back then and was proud—get a load of *this*—of never having lived more than five hundred feet away from her mother. That kind of shit almost sounds like it makes sense when you're high every day.

That thick, caked-on skunk stench hits me through a punctured screen door. She comes out in a sweatshirt and ripped, pissed-on cutoff shorts. Her stringy hair's a ball of earthworms, and there's thirty pounds more of her; she leans out of the doorframe heavy, like a tottering pole that's been bent in a hurricane.

"Helloooo!" I bellow. "Julianne, it's me. I'm back."

"Oh, hello, hello. Come on in and sit down," she says and offers her sofa, its plastic slipcovers dotted with cigarette burns.

"So which one of Pete's friends are you?" she says.

"Julianne, it's me. Freddy. I lived across the street a few years ago."

"You did?" she asks. It's no wonder her memories of this period of her life are vague; the bitch got high so many times you can't find Acapulco gold anymore because she smoked most of it herself. Then her creased face unravels into something soft, feminine, and it hits her, who I am, the moments we shared lost for these many years. Those times come flooding back, and she's not happy that the dam couldn't hold back that much water.

"Freddy. Yeah, you lived with Cristina. Why are you here?" she asks.

"I'm back. I was away and now I'm back."

"Oh. How long's it been?" she asks.

"A few years. Not long, really. I've got catching up to do, though. How're your kids?"

"Got kids of their own," she says. "A lot's changed. Most of the old neighbors sold their homes and cashed out. Made a lot of money."

"Cristina hit it rich!" I say, slapping my thigh. "She's gonna be in so much trouble when I see her. Where'd she move to?"

Julianne sits down on the opposite end of the sofa, arms and legs crossed. "Cristina's dead," she says.

I'm used to death sneaking up on me, disappearing homeboys in puffs of smoke or for life sentences behind bars. I never knew how it felt to lose a woman, forever, until today. Women were doors left a little bit ajar at the ends of darkened hallways—always open, but you had to find your way to them first. Dead women were grandmothers in their seventies and eighties, not women I'd made love to, held close, slept beside.

"I saw them taking her body down those stairs," Julianne says and lights a cigarette. She offers me one, and I take it. "Worked every day of her life. Crazy."

"But she was so . . . young."

"Cristina gained a lot of weight, stopped leaving the house. Then one day they're taking her down the stairs on a covered gurney. A For Sale sign goes up on the front lawn 'cause her daughter, Angie, didn't want to live there anymore. Then some dykes buy the place. It's been that way up and down this street."

"You know where Angie is?" I ask.

"Such a nice girl," Julianne says.

"I was her dad for a while."

"Were you as good a dad as you were a husband?" Julianne cackles, puffing out a cloud of smoke in front of her like a veil. "You ever tell Cristina that you cheated on her with me? Or the five other women on this block?"

"That was years ago," I say. "You were cheating, too."

"I was being cheated on. I had to cheat back. How else do you get anything around here? And I came clean. Did you ever come clean with—"

"No, god no. I'm glad I didn't. That kind of thing would've killed her."

"Someone beat you to it."

Why do men cheat? Hell, why do women own more than one pair of shoes? It doesn't matter that I cheated on Cristina with another cheater. It doesn't matter that I came home to her most nights, paid the bills when I had money I didn't piss away, and when I told her I loved her more than anyone it was usually true. It doesn't even matter that it wasn't Julianne I cheated on, it was Cristina I was cheating on . . . *with her.* Well, that may have mattered a little bit. Point is, there's no expiration date on cheating. Women treat cheating men the way society treats child molesters. Never forgiven, never forgotten, and no amount of rehabilitation is enough for you to earn back your status as a human being.

But that doesn't mean you can't get lucky.

"Where are you gonna go?" she asks.

"I got lots of friends here," I say. "Bound to be something I can cook up."

Julianne moves next to me on the sofa. "You can't stay," she says. "Pete will be back at three."

"What happened to the guy you was married to? What was his name?"

"I told you a lot of things changed," she says and leans in, sticking her tongue in my mouth. She rubs her hands on my thighs, and I wait for the bulge in my pants to rise, that bulge that's been waiting twelve years to be inside a woman. She's not any of the women I'd dreamed of and fantasized about and jerked off to, but she's a warm body, jagged around the edges but soft in the middle. Fresh-out-of-jail pussy's much better than fresh-out-of-jail sunshine, but I still have to concentrate to get hard, grunting and wincing in pain as Julianne's mouth slides up and down on a semiflaccid piece of flesh. There's a hissing, farty sound when I enter her pussy, a hiccup of cum, a few dribbles, like what spits out of the bottom of a shampoo bottle, then I'm crumpled over in a quiet U shape for a minute or two.

I sit back up, buckle my pants. "I've gotta go," I say. "Can you lend me fifty bucks?"

Julianne slides back on her sweatshirt. "Don't got any money until the first."

"I need to piss," I say. She motions to her bedroom. Next to her bed is a purse. I steal nine dollars and a pack of Kools; in the bathroom, I take two bars of Ivory soap, then hop out an open window, back to Sunset Boulevard.

* * *

Not counting Cristina and Angie, I learn throughout the day there's eight families I know who sold their houses and moved away, five guys who "disappeared," two guys in jail, and a handful of nobodies who'd never heard of me. "Shit, granddad," one asshole said, "you ain't even got a cell phone!" Where did all these people on telephones come from anyway? Big phones, small phones, video phones, phones that stick out of their ears like mechanical worms trying to burrow out of their heads because they can't stand all the noise inside those skulls. And the things these *cabrónes* talk about! *Putos* screaming into their phones like they're fucking them, walking down the street like square-dancing zombies—punch some buttons and stagger to the left! Punch more buttons and shuffle to the right!—trying to conduct business shit from a phone on the street. Send this memo, write that letter, and of course, call somebody to tell them what you told somebody else thirty seconds ago. Listen, if you ain't a hustler, the street *ain't your motherfuckin' office.*

The liquor store where I used to pick up scores and run lottery ticket hustles is now owned by a pair of "you buy, you fly" Arab pricks who chased me away when I'd hung around the lotto results posters (always a prime location for meeting other hustlers) too long. And shit got *expensive* while I was in the joint! How can shit cost so much when a black man's running the country? Farther up Sunset, the hardware parking lot has men looking for honest, pathetic, back-breaking work, and since that sure as hell ain't me, I walk over to a sunny coffee shop, where I order a "latte" and a bran muffin and get caught not paying for them by a skinny, tattooed white bitch with pink hair and a cluster of spike piercings around her neck.

Down to my last three dollars, I walk into the Little Joy Jr. bar, determined to hustle up enough money for a motel room downtown on Skid Row and a chance to find Angie tomorrow. There's a weird ammonia smell in the bar I can't place and graffiti in English—who writes fucking graffiti in English in *Echo Park?*—covers the walls of what was once a low-key *jota* bar. The bathroom used to be as reliable as an ATM—always money there if you didn't mind sucking dick ("straight" Mexican guys do it, and get it done to them, all the time). A stereo blasts something loud that isn't oldies or Motown. I order the cheapest beer they have, a PBR, and search for my mark. Over by the pool table with a young white girl who'd be gorgeous if not for her tattoos and shaved head is a white guy in his thirties with thick Buddy Holly–style glasses, a short-sleeve shirt that changes color depending on what angle I look at it from, baggy black pants with a chain dangling from his right pocket, and spotless black "work" shoes.

"You up for a game?" I ask.

"Sure," he says. I offer to shake hands, which for me isn't a pleasantry but a calculated business move. I have an almost supernatural ability to gauge a person's character by his handshake. I've figured this guy out in seconds. If this man were currency, he'd be the loose change you find in your couch. I'm gonna make it rain money in here.

"Ten bucks a rack?" I ask, starting out small. My game here is to appear that I have no game, and after an hour, I'm up eighty bucks. The guy plays along, aware he's being hustled by the third game, but too drunk or too proud to pull himself out of it. By midnight, he's made three trips to the ATM and I'm up to two fifty. That's when I offer him double or nothing that I can't make cigarette ashes go right through the palm of his hand. He's drunk now, loud and defiant, but agrees to the bet.

I light one of Julianne's Kools and search for an ashtray. What I do is lick both my thumb and index finger and rub them together. Then I swab both fingers in the ashtray and place my thumb on top of his hand and my index finger in his palm. Boom, ashes through your hands. That's five hundred dollars, *pendejo*.

Except there's a problem. I can't find an ashtray.

"Outside," the guy says. "We gotta do this outside."

"What are you talking about?"

"Can't smoke in here."

"Since when?" And that's when I realize what the weird smell in the bar is. It's "no smoke," the smell of no one smoking in the bar. I can smell the moistness of spilled alcohol and fresh piss from the bathrooms. Turns my stomach.

"Since years ago. Man, where have *you* been?"

Out on the street, I have to take a long drag and almost burn my fingertips to get enough ashes for the bet. I grab his hand like a pincer, and he snatches it away, brushing ashes from his palm.

"There it is," I say. "They went right through your hand."

"That was a trick," he says.

"A bet's a bet. That's five hundred dollars."

"I'm not paying you shit," he says louder. "That's a stupid fucking magic trick."

"Don't get mad because you didn't see it coming," I say. "Stick around, you'll get a chance to win some of it back."

"Fuck you," he says and shoves me against a wall.

I don't want to fight. I want the money. You gotta talk angry guys down to get their cash, then string them along until their money's gone. It's time to start talking.

The hustle is on the tip of my tongue. The old pat routine I used to run, the words that poured a soothing balm over any man who was pissed because he had a shitty job, was stuck with a whale or a tramp for a wife, or was down to his last couple bucks of drinking money, the pitch I gave to befriend and defraud—those magic words are there for the taking, if I can summon the barroom gods to help me this one time until I have my sea legs back. But where are they? Where are the gods and the words they brought with them, those precious words that had gotten me into a thousand wallets and out of a thousand brawls?

"Fuck you," he says and shoves me again.

"I don't want to hurt you," I warn. "I just got out of the baddest joint in the state."

He sucker punches me in the gut. I fold shut around his fist. He kicks me in the balls and smacks my head against the curb. I cover my head with my arms, crawling away on my hands and knees. He kicks me in the gut again, and I land facedown out in the street.

"Don't come back," he says.

"Are you kidding?" I laugh, coughing up what I hope is spit. "It's yours!" I say and point down the block. "This street, this shitty neighborhood! It's all yours!" Scuffing my elbows and knees on the pavement, I crawl to a parking lot and collapse on a stack of pallets, dreaming of Cristina wrapped in a sweat-drenched bedsheet walking to a window and letting in the cool air, the breeze dancing around her body and a warm sun turning her dark silhouette into light.

I hear the street noise first. The ear-bludgeoning din of a garbage truck picking up what must be a large metal box of boulders. Then the metronomic clicking of traffic lights. A bus's hydraulics exhales in front of a gas station on Sunset Boulevard I slept behind last night. My back's in such pain it's radiating a high-pitched sound on a frequency only I can hear. It's the cold gray of morning again, not yet light but past being dark. There's a sun coming up in the sky, the second sunrise I've seen in a row as a free man.

Using their air and water dispenser, I wash the blood and vomit from my chest, then take out of a Dumpster pieces of a cracked pallet and washboard my shirt on it with the soap from Julianne's house.

My eyes adjust to the grayness. Parked on the curb is a city bus. If the driver's gone for a coffee, I can sneak in and crash in the back for a couple hours. Or I could ride the bus to wherever it's going and get the hell out of here. Forget about finding Angie. The beating I took last night hasn't given me a chance to think too far ahead.

The bus's back doors won't pry open. Up front, I can see through the doors the driver asleep behind the steering wheel. I fish through my pockets and come up with forty-seven cents, not enough for a fare, but maybe all the coins will fool him. I kick on the doors, but the heels of my shoes keep slipping on something greasy and slick that's smeared on the glass. When the doors open, I drop my change in the fare box, knowing he won't throw me off as long as I keep talking. To my surprise, he talks first.

"I'm out of service," he says. I've spent enough nights out on the street—including last night—to know he'd slept in this bus. If he'd stolen it, he didn't seem too worried.

"I am too," I say. "But here we are."

"No, this bus is out of service," he says, cutting me off.

"Okay," I say. "When you going to be ready to roll?"

"No, mister, the bus, totally out of service. *¿Comprendes? Tienes que coger otro autobús.*"

"I understood you the first time," I say. Can't he tell I'm not some *pinche mojado* fresh from the desert?

"Then why are you still here?" he asks.

"I have somewhere to go and no other way to get there," I say. Isn't this obvious? I've never had to encourage a bus driver to *drive* before.

"Why is that my problem?"

"Because that's your job, right?" What's wrong with this guy? Either kick me off or get going. There's a lot I can do today and I don't want to waste my time here in Echo Park.

"You're right," he says and looks at the fare box. "You put in too much."

He's wrong, but I don't call him on it. "That's okay, man," I say. "It's a first for me."

"How do we get to where you're going?" he asks.

The nearest shelter is Downtown, about a mile or two away. I'm not sure what direction I want to go in, though.

"I don't know."

"How far away is it?"

"I'm not sure."

"How will you know when we've arrived?"

If we go a few stops and park somewhere, I can crash in the back and rest up. I can talk to this guy, get him on my side. We're both on the same bus, right? If he drives me to Venice, I can beg enough on the boardwalk for a big lunch. I have a lot of options. Why choose one?

"I'll know," I say.

"Okay. I will get you there."

The bus shifts gears as we drive through pools of rusty streetlight blending with a rising sun fighting its way out of a gray, overcast sky. On the floor next to a long bench seat in the back are about a dozen unopened Skittles packets—enough sugar to keep me going at least another day. I can't believe my luck. Isn't it amazing, the things people throw away? Isn't it amazing, the things people leave behind?

7

Cool Kids

I wish I could be Gwen Stefani. I'm not *cool* enough to have ever become her, or someone like her. I wish I was thirteen again, though, so I wouldn't have to hide my girl-crush on her. If I was young, I'd answer my Hello Kitty cell phone with the "Spiderwebs" ring tone *("I screeeeeeeen my phone calls!")* everywhere and not just in my apartment, dance up and down the supermarket aisles with my limited-edition No Doubt iPod because only kids can dance in public without embarrassment, and wear things from her clothing line L.A.M.B. (Love. Angel. Music. Baby.) to school every day. Have you seen the cool things Gwen designs? I have every Gwen top and hoodie she's created—the ones with that classic *chola*-style writing on them are my faves. Then there's the limited-edition handbags in leopard print or glossy, pimped out lowrider colors; rows of sneakers, slip-on scuffies, the supercute high-heel sandals and peep-toe oxfords, penny-loafer wedges and those "Chiquita banana" pumps with the blue labels on the heels, and the limited-edition "Rock Steady" wool Rasta hats, which is silly because it never gets cold enough in Los Angeles to wear a wool hat. Juan told me I was a "completist," one of those people who, when they like someone, have to own everything they do.

If Gwen Stefani was born in my zip code, she could have been my best friend Duchess. Sounds like a *chola* nickname, doesn't it? That's what I thought when I met her. She was part of White Fence for a while, whose roots go back to the Zooters in the forties, but didn't do much more with the gang than hang out to get away from her mom and stepdad. Thugging was boring, and their colors—black Raiders Starter jackets, baggy khakis, or ass-riding jeans, and crisp as the morning wife-beaters—why would *any* girl wear that kind of shit? They were supposed to be badasses, so why did they dress like middle-aged sports fans? Duchess was too stylish for that, and could've designed new *chola* outfits if they'd let her. She could look at a department store dress, find the exact same fabric the next day in the Garment District downtown, measure out a pattern, cut, sew, hem it, and have a dress impossible to tell from the one that cost eight hundred dollars. Her own designs were inspired by her Mexican grandmother's zoot-suiter clothes: tight around the bust ruffled blouses, drape skirts with vertical black and white stripes, and bow-box ribbons for her long, curly hair that ran down her back like melting licorice. She sketched on big white pads and carried a constellation of colored pencils with her. Bright reds, icy blues, fiery greens, and milky blacks fleshed out her neat and perfect lines, freehand compositions that could pass for patterns traced out of a book.

Duchess had looks, too; five ten, busty, with a simmering butterscotch complexion and a foundation-free face that wasn't torn up by acne or chicken pox. (I had pasty skin, and my face was cratered like the Moon's Sea of Tranquillity.) Her forearms and upper lip weren't hairy. That lilt in a Mexican girl's accent, the way it rises and falls, like a surfer riding a choppy wave, sailed out of her mouth at an even monotone, her voice sounding clean and plain as a cup of yogurt. She always did her own hairstyles and makeup, and not even her mother sending her to the Las Bonitas hair salon on Sunset for what she thought would be a thoughtful gift—a first day of spring makeover—could change that. Duchess was so appalled by the breast-popping blouses and short denim *Guess?* skirts the girls wore there to attract men for haircuts, she ran home and came back with a homemade picket sign. Luring the girls outside, she lectured them on how they could dress and put on makeup without looking slutty. For the rest of the afternoon, Duchess gave *them* makeovers.

Duchess had this effect everywhere, on everyone she met. If she came to school on Monday a platinum blonde, by Friday a dozen shimmering blond heads (a rare sight in Echo Park) charged through the halls like a marching band. To the boys she was sexy, irresistible, and sweet natured; her maturity didn't intimidate them but encouraged them to defer to her out of a mix of respect and desire. She carried herself with a grace and elegance you'd never see in a high school, where we stole what we passed off as sophistication and coolness from what we saw on TV. I've seen Gwen carry herself the same way in her videos, interviews, and at that award show where Snoop Dogg grabbed her butt and in one swift, firm move placed his hand above the equator. Total Duchess move.

Yeah, she could've been a Mexican Gwen. It's not so far-fetched to believe, except there's always a seed of a fatal flaw in someone who you think could be a famous person but isn't. Some hairpin curve in their personality that keeps them right where they are, instead of where you think they could be. Thing is, Gwen acts like a badass *chola,* but you can tell she's a straight-up rule girl at heart; she wants to hang with the bad boys but doesn't want to *do* anything bad. I think that's why I like her. I didn't think you could make that kind of choice. I never believed you could live in two worlds at once.

Not to change subjects, but did you ever notice how friendships are a lot like pop songs? They are for girls, anyway. First there's the newness of it, the melody that streams into your head and makes you wonder—will I like this song? Then come the vocals, what the song's heart *truly* sounds like, and with it the song's purpose, its lyrics—will they say something meaningful about my life? Will these words help me through a difficult time, or create a memory that will make me smile whenever I hear this song again? And then you keep hearing that song—in a department store, on the radio on your morning drive, from a rooftop window walking down the street—and you know that you are in love with this song, and *only* this song. You can't live without it, and have to play it twenty times a day for the rest of your life. But the rest of your life *doesn't* last the rest of your life, because once you've memorized the song and can't imagine a world where this song doesn't exist, you discover you've grown tired of it, are bored with its melody, and wonder how and why did that happen? Will I fall in love with another song the same way? And, after falling in love with a thousand other songs in the exact same way, will I fall in love with this one song I cherished so much again?

I think about weird things like this when it's late and I can't sleep, stuck in that place between the night and the dawn. When I close my eyes, I dream I'm back in my high school bedroom, the one Duchess and I had a hundred sleepovers in, staring at the water-damaged ceiling, its skin bubbling like hot milk froth.

On the nightstand, underneath my cell phone, is a sheet of drawing paper. Sketched on it is a young girl, on the cusp of becoming a woman, in a red dress. I'm listening to a bootleg recording of a Gwen Stefani concert (like Juan said, I gotta collect everything) to help me go to sleep, and as my eyes get heavy, Gwen starts singing a cover version of a song that was popular in high school:

> *Cool kids,*
> *will you come out to play?*
> *Cool kids,*
> *will you come out to play with me?*

My cell phone whirs like a windup toy, stops, then, a minute later, whirs again. There are eleven new messages in my voice mail.

*　*　*

We met the winter of senior year of high school, 1991, at the windows of Father Alemencio's *casita,* where he was conducting a practice *quinceañera* ceremony for my then–best friend Rosa's younger cousin. These things can drag on and on, so I waited behind the house in an alley for an hour. I arranged a stack of greasy box crates beneath a window to see if they were finished. While I was inching up on my toes to peek inside, a girl walked by the alley. I tried to duck back down but slipped and fell. The girl slowed, and I could see her head turn as she checked me out, flat on my ass atop broken box crates and split-open trash bags. If her boyfriend, walking behind her, hadn't laughed at me, she might have turned her head and disappeared. He stepped ahead at a determined pace, hadn't noticed she'd walked away from him until she was standing over me.

"It's bad luck to peek in a father's house," she said.

"He didn't see me," I said. "I don't know what happened."

"God knocked you on your ass so you could get a better look at the ground you're standing on," she said, helping me up.

"That's funny. Did you make that up yourself?"

"Nah, my mom says that. My name's Duchess."

"Duchess?" I asked. "Is that your real name?"

"Yeah. Because my mother's a princess. That makes me a Duchess. What were you doing looking into his windows?"

"My friend's *prima* is practicing for her *quinceañera.*"

"Oh, I *love* those!" Duchess ran to the window and jumped up to see. Her boyfriend shambled over, grinding the soles of his bright, new Air Jordans. "*Prima's* strutting around in there like this," Duchess said and, cocking her hips back, waddled around on the balls of her feet. "Bossing her *damas* around. Looks like a real bitch. Let's make faces at her," Duchess said.

"I thought you said it was bad luck to look in there."

"We're not looking. We're trying to scare away a demon."

"We gonna stand around here?" her boyfriend said. "This is boring."

"You can go," Duchess said.

"I ain't comin' back," he said.

"Okay. We won't be here when you do." Duchess waved me over to the window. Her boyfriend stormed out of the alley, kicking trash cans and cursing.

"Boys are so noisy when they lose," she said.

"Who is he?" I asked.

"My ex-boyfriend. Come stand next to me by the window."

"Ex-boyfriend? When did you break up?"

"Just now."

"Shouldn't you go after him?"

"Why chase a bus when another one's right around the corner? My mom says that, too."

I was in awe. It was love at first sight, and by *love* I mean "I want to copy everything this girl does and maybe a tenth of her coolness will rub off on me."

Duchess hopped up to the window again. "She's looking this way. Get ready."

"I shouldn't. My friend might get upset."

"Oh, we're not making fun of your friend, we're making fun of her bitchy cousin. C'mon."

She grabbed my hand and jumped up, rapping her manicured hot pink and emerald sparkle nails on the window. It took us a couple tries to synchronize our moves, but we got an up-and-down trampoline rhythm going. Duchess twisted and scrunched her face, stuck out her tongue, then gave Rosa's cousin the finger.

Rosa pointed at the window. "She's seen us!" Duchess screamed. A door slammed open, and a pair of shoes clicked over to the side of the house.

"What the hell are you doing?" Rosa screamed. Her arms flapped over a fountain of ruffles cascading down her dress.

"The bitch is loose!" Duchess laughed. "Run for it!" We held hands as we raced down the alleyway.

"You cursed outside Father Alemencio's house!" Duchess screamed. "Now you'll never get married!"

When we stopped to catch our breaths, Duchess said, "I had to do that. *Quinceañeras* are so stupid."

"I didn't have one," I said.

"That's so cool!" Duchess said. "How'd you get away with that?"

Truth is, I didn't want one, but skipping your *quinceañera* was an indictment of your friends, neighbors, and relations who went through the trouble of having *quinceañeras* for *their* girls, and it could make you and your family real unpopular. And not having enough money, or one parent working, wasn't an excuse. Families on our block didn't have enough money, but that didn't stop them from taking out loans with 50 percent interest rates, second-mortgaging their houses, and maxing out credit cards for stretch limos, banquet halls, photographers, and tailored dresses you wore once. It seemed so embarrassingly . . . *Mexican*. That's a shitty thing to say, but with my mother supporting the both of us with the same job she'd had for years at Pilgrim's Supermarket, a vanished father who never supported me, and a deadbeat stepfather in and out of jail, why spend money we didn't have to brag about the fact I was "a woman" in a neighborhood full of women-abusing men? To get out of a *quinceañera* though, you'd need an excuse note from Jesus. Or you could do what I did.

"I told my mom I was a lesbian," I said. "And that seeing my *damas* in those fancy satin dresses would get me hot and excited. '*Dios mío*, we can't have that in a church!' she screamed. I went to the movies instead."

"I should have thought of that!" Duchess said.

"I wonder if Rosa's going to forgive me," I said.

"Why do you need her?" Duchess laughed. "You know how you

made a bunch of new friends when you went from grade school to junior high? I had this one friend in elementary school, Aurora. We did everything together. Best friends. Then we got to junior high and we'd both changed. We didn't notice it until then. She started getting into that white music, MTV shit from England, made a bunch of white girlfriends. That wasn't me, so we stopped hanging out. It's okay, though, because you need to change your friends once in a while. That's how you become the person you're meant to be."

There was such a thrill of being drawn into a new friendship that I didn't realize that I'd just had a "friendship ending" moment with Rosa. One day she was there, my best friend, laughing next to me at birthday parties, sharing *paletas de limón* under shady trees, going to each other's houses for backyard plastic wading pool parties, then she was gone, passed through my life to become someone else's best friend.

The alleyway emptied into a barricade of Dumpsters. We turned onto a one-way side street, stopping next to a palm tree that'd been tagged by three different gangs. "I live up this way," Duchess said. "What are you doing tomorrow?"

"I have to clean the house. Why?"

"'Cause I'm asking you out, lesbian! I need someone for the party."

"What party?"

"Party of two, me and you. C'mon. Swear on it." She held my pinkie's chipped peach polish against her manicure.

"We gotta do something about these nails," she said.

I could tell you about the things we did the next three months that "bonded" us—drinking forties on my backyard brick wall in our bathing suits and dangling our flip-flips off our toes over a neighbor's tomato patch; smoking joints at the back of a movie theater during the night-vision scenes in *The Silence of the Lambs,* then giggling our heads off as we told everyone we met on the street we were FBI agents and would they mind "answering a few questions"; and so many beach trips and park picnics they blur into one long, endless memory of riding in a car with the windows down, the radio blaring, and a cool breeze running through my hair—but the moment that pushes your friendship into something deeper, from friend to best friend, can't be seen when it's happening.

Our moment came under a wrinkled jacaranda tree on Portia Street on a balmy June afternoon. This fresh sea-air breeze had somehow fought its way from the beach miles away to caress our bare arms and legs.

"What are we gonna do after summer?" I asked.

"Whatever we want," she said, distracted. She was sketching an outfit. "We could be Thelma and Louise, steal a car and shoot all the assholes we know around here. But we'd run out of bullets before we left the neighborhood."

"You want to, right?"

"Want to what?"

"Leave the neighborhood?"

"Sure, maybe," she said, digging through her pencil case. "There's a blood red in here."

"I love your drawings. You could go to art school."

"For what?" Duchess laughed. "To pay someone to teach me what I know? I'll find something to do around here. Aren't you doing the same? Doesn't your mom like your company?"

"She *has* a lot of company," I said, hoping she'd get the hint.

She did. "He's not your dad, you know. He's some dick that comes and goes when it pleases, like every dick that has a man attached to it. That ain't no life for your mom."

"That's the life she's choosing. You have to choose your own, too."

"Thank you, Daddy," she said. Duchess's sharp pencil cut across the paper in gentle but deliberate swaths.

"Don't be in such a hurry to leave," she said. "You're not a man. Or my father."

"At least you know who your father is," I said.

"I'm sorry," she said, and we sat in silence for a while, listening to the jacaranda tree sigh in the wind. The breeze rattled plump flowers, tiny lavender petticoat slip dresses, off the tree and plopped them on our heads.

"I could stick around," I lied. "And you?"

A jacaranda blossom landed in her hair, its pulpy white tip sticking out from a wavy curl. She put down her pencil. "I'm your shadow. And you're my sun."

"Your mom said that, didn't she?"

"Yeah." Duchess blushed. "But I never said it to anyone else." She leaned back down to finish her sketch. It was an intricate drawing of a young woman in a dazzling off-the-shoulder red dress.

"It's beautiful. Is it you?"

"Yeah," she said. "I think it is. I don't know. It's not finished yet."

"You going to make the dress?" I asked.

"When I can afford the fabric. This dress needs a special material."

"You have something in your hair," I said. My fingers brushed against her scalp, popping the blossom's milky tip in her curls. Duchess crooked her head so that it followed my hand, the way a cat arches up to someone stroking its spine. Our breathing slowed until our rhythms were the same. Tracing a circle on her head, my fingers grew warm enough for me to slide the blossom out without yanking strands of hair with it.

"Did you get it?" Duchess whispered.

There were bits of ripped jacaranda stuck to my fingers. "No. It's tangled in your hair."

She pulled out her mirror. "They're a part of me now," she said, looking at my fingertips. "So are you." With a purple pencil she shaded in a blossom barrette in the girl's hair in the sketch. Then she led my hand over her lap, up to the top of her sketch pad, and using both our hands, ripped the page out and tucked it away in her purse.

*   *   *

It takes a lot more time to realize that a best friend has become a member of your "new" family—"water dripping in a bucket" time, or "learning to play an instrument" time. It's a surprise because, when you're a teenager, you don't realize you have the right or the ability to make a new family. You do it by accident. When you pull away from your parents—easy for me, harder for Duchess—you're creating a hole in your life for someone else to fill, a hole that did not exist before you knew them. It's like a crack that expands each time you see it, yet you never see the crack getting bigger. The more time you spend with someone, the bigger the hole gets. I learned to see things through her eyes, enjoyed her music, her movies, and hanging with gay boys with her tastes, copied her dress and mannerisms, and used her catchphrases. I was saying, "Why chase a bus when another one's right around the corner?" in situations where it made no sense—my English teacher warned me not to raise my hand anymore if I offered this as an answer to why all the major characters in Shakespeare were screwed up. You do this so people can see you the same way they see your friend. Of course they don't—can't—see you in the same way; what they can see is the copy you've turned yourself into, and you ignore that pinprick sensation in your head each time you surrender a piece of who you are to become someone else. You do this because, when you act like your friend, you no longer feel alone.

You also do this to ignore the scary parts of your friend's personality that creep up to the surface when you aren't looking. Remember that fatal flaw I told you about? That keeps people where they are instead of where they could be? A week before graduation, we went to the Glendale Galleria. I was returning something my mother bought a month before from a catalog and couldn't fit into, which was happening to her a lot. Duchess hated shopping malls but agreed to keep me company. What I didn't tell her about was my plan to scout out a summer job. In Glendale, the streets were clean, there were tons of movie theaters and real air-conditioned restaurants (not the ones with crappy plastic oscillating fans that trap flies), and you could walk around wearing whatever you wanted without getting hassled by every *cholo* on the block. And I was too shy to say it to Duchess, but I'll say it here—the *gabachos,* the white boys, were cute.

Duchess wouldn't sympathize with any of that; she was working at a Bank of America three blocks from my house that had been held up four times in the past two years. She offered to get me a job there, but I kept stalling about when I would come in for the interview.

At the galleria, I made mental notes of the department stores and shoe stores that had the things I liked best, and the food stands that attracted the cutest boys. The plan was to come back another day and pick up the applications; there was no way I was doing it in front of Duchess.

Upstairs on the second level, we wandered into Contempo Casuals. The place was like a fun house; checkerboard tile floor, mirrored ceilings, tilted mirrors, and rows of television sets on the walls. The back of the store seemed to stretch out forever. On the screens, a computerized man in a red chrome suit with a blond skyscraper hairdo was singing in a robotic voice:

> *Cool kids,*
> *will you come out to play?*
> *Cool kids,*
> *will you come out to play with me?*

"Clothes for hos," Duchess said. "Can we go?"

"I'm going to take a look around," I said.

Near the five-dollar scrunchie rack by the cash registers, a salesgirl with short strawberry blond hair started following me around. She wore a zip-up, powder blue hoodie with a drawstring tie, white Vans slip-ons, and ass-tight jean shorts with knee cuffs. Her name was Debbie; she was a wannabe surfer girl with propane eyes whose vacuous stare one could mistake for intensity or Zen. Duchess was nowhere in the store, so I asked Debbie for an application.

"You'll be sick to death of floor sets when you're through," she said. "Where you going to school in the fall?"

"L.A.C.C."

"There's an *L.A.* college? Why aren't you going to Glendale CC? It's a short drive from here."

"Really?" I asked, not letting on I didn't live near the mall, nor did I have a car. "Lots of cute guys?"

She cocked her head, a crooked grin on her face. "Um, yeah, they have some total babes there. Lots of blonds, you know?" There was an awkward pause. "Let me get you a pen."

Duchess was waiting for me by the clock tower elevator. She jabbed the Down button.

"What were you doing in there?"

"Filling out a job application," I said.

"You going to work in that *puta* store?"

"I don't know," I said. "Maybe. I need a summer job."

"Look at their trampy clothes!" she shouted. "Rayon leggings with fake lace around the ankles. Flimsy baby doll dresses that come apart in the wash. Denim scrunchies you could make for a nickel. Petticoat slip dresses. And size zero jeans? White girl jeans for white girl asses!" she shouted.

"They seemed really nice in there," I said.

"Who? That *puta blanca* following you around the store like you were a *ladrona*?"

"Following me arou—— How long have you been standing out here?"

"You too good to work at the bank?"

"It's not for me, okay? There's nothing wrong with this place."

"You think you're better than everyone, huh?" she said. "Because you're lighter than me? Because you want to live someplace nice and clean? No graffiti, no trash everywhere, no thugs hassling you just for walking down the fucking street!" People stared at us. It didn't feel right to act this way in a white neighborhood. I was worried that we'd be thrown out of the mall, maybe even arrested.

"I'm going home," I said.

We stormed off together, in silence, sulking from the bus stop bench to our hour-long bus ride back (sitting at opposite ends of the bus) to the gas station on the corner of Glendale Boulevard and Montana Street. She stormed ahead of me, but not before she said, "I'm surprised you still remembered your way home."

The time between your first major fight with your best friend until you make up is, for a teenage girl, about as long as it took for God to create the universe. First, you make your declarations: *She's being the world's biggest bitch! I'm never speaking to her again!* Next, you console yourself with how unreasonable her actions were: *Why is she being such a bitch? Can't she see I'm totally right and she's totally wrong?* You console yourself with how much you'll make her do when she comes crawling back to you: *I'll speak to that bitch again* only *if she calls me first, admits she was wrong about everything, and begs me to be her friend again.* As the days pass without a word, your mind races with scenarios of how she's spending her time and who she's spending it with: *How could that bitch be living her life without talking to me?* Then you realize there will not be a scene where she crawls on her knees for your forgiveness and you accept that having her back in your life again, no matter who's right or wrong, is enough. It's excellent training for having a boyfriend.

We didn't speak to each other until graduation, held on a muggy June afternoon at an outdoor amphitheater in Hollywood, where several high schools had their graduation ceremonies at consecutive times throughout the day. It had been three weeks since our fight.

She wore a tight orange and purple dress that flared up like a pilot light flickering out of a fissure on the street. It was a homemade dress, not the one from the drawing, and it was stunning. Girls in street hoochie outfits came to Duchess and ran her material through their fingers as if they were dipping their hands in the springs of Lourdes, hoping by some small miracle their dresses would magically turn into something beautiful. In that outfit, Duchess had the gait and poise of someone who hadn't made a single decision in her life she regretted. I was angry that she was so confident, but there would be no moment of surrender, no gloating or begging forgiveness on either side.

"That's a pretty dress. I'm so happy to see you in something you made," I lied.

"Thanks," she said. I'd worn a sheer, royal blue and scarlet red Hawaiian floral print dress Debbie helped me pick from Contempo. It was stylish and sexy in the store, with those slanted mirrors, checkerboard floors, and loud music disorienting me, but here, out in the bright sun, around actual people, it was hideous, part grandma muumuu and part exterminators' tent. The material was cheap, flimsy; the spaghetti straps were fettuccini size. You know those outfits you see people wear from twenty or thirty years ago in those faded photos and you say, "Damn, that was *ugly!*" *This* was that outfit. It was the kind of dress you pray strikes everyone around you with blindness *and* amnesia.

"Yours is nice, too," she lied back.

"What're you doing now?" I asked.

"Family's going to Sizzler. You?"

"Mother couldn't get the day off at the supermarket. I have to go to work, too. Big sale this weekend, and we have to do a ton of floor sets."

"Floor sets?" Duchess asked. "Sounds . . . important."

"No, they're what we call the displays in the store."

"Why don't you call them displays, then?" Duchess asked.

"I . . . I don't know." I shrugged. "That's what they're called." It was tough pretending our fight hadn't affected me, hadn't sent me to sleep crying every night. She was acting so cold, so . . . hard. Why wouldn't she meet me halfway?

"We're gonna get going. My boyfriend's here," Duchess said. She'd never even mentioned a boy she was crushing on. Now she had a boyfriend?

A tall, light-skinned Mexican walked over, standing next to her at an awkward angle. Duchess slung an arm around his waist, which made him blush.

"Hi, I'm Juan," he said, holding out his hand. I shook it, and as I stood staring into his eyes, a sudden rush ran up and down my body. I could feel the heat rising to my face, embarrassed that I was smiling. Duchess wrapped her arm around his waist tighter. He broke free and leaned in closer.

"Congratulations," he said. "Both of you going to celebrate the big day together?"

"Angie has work," Duchess said. "And we were going to leave."

"Is that true, Angie?" Juan asked with those deep eyes of his, as chocolaty brown as a teddy bear's. "You have to work on your graduation day?"

"Um, yeah, I do," I said, looking at Duchess. "I have a crazy schedule."

"Where do you work?" he asked.

"Out in the Valley," Duchess chipped in.

"At the galleria?" Juan asked.

"She likes it out there," Duchess said. "It's clean."

"I have to get going," I said. "I have a friend from work picking me up. It was nice meeting you." I ran down a dirt hill in my best shoes to wait for Debbie at the driveway into the parking lot. Then I heard his voice.

"You sure you don't need a lift?" Juan asked.

"Duchess is going to be furious you're here," I said.

"Why, because I'm talking to you?"

"Aren't you her boyfriend?"

"Did Maria tell you that?"

"That's her real name?" I asked.

"Yeah, Duchess was her mother's old gang nickname. She told me on our first date. Said she doesn't like to keep secrets. So can I see you sometime?"

"Are you joking? You're going out with my best friend."

"You two didn't seem too friendly back there."

"Juan, you should go. Please," I said. "She's my—"

"Look, we're not serious. I'm seeing Duchess to make my mom happy," he said. "You and I don't have to date. We can just hang out. No pressure."

Debbie's shiny Nissan sports coupe idled its way up the hill amid a caravan of school buses and cars from the next school to graduate.

"I can't decide this now. I'll think about it. Okay?" He nodded, then leaned down to kiss me on my ear. I felt my arms melt into his shoulders, felt my legs grow weak, felt my flesh jump. Then he was gone.

Debbie pulled up to the curb, and I climbed in. She pointed at one of the buses.

"Are those guys from your school?" she asked.

"No, the one graduating after us."

"Check out those babes," she said and pointed to a blond Adonis in a basketball jersey shaking hands with a black guy in a cap and gown.

"God, I love jocks," Debbie said. "I'd *so* fuck-and-run him. You can go for the black guy."

"I like the blond."

"But he's . . . not black."

"Neither am I."

Debbie rested her head on the steering wheel. "Don't hate me because I'm stupid," she said. "You're going to teach me about this, right, Angie?"

"Party of two," I said. "You teach me, I'll teach you."

*   *   *

You never realize the final moment when a friendship ends. One friendship fades out, and another one fades in to take its place. Duchess's stock question "Why chase a bus when another one's right around the corner?" was replaced with Debbie's "I'd *so* fuck-and-run him," which is what she said meeting Juan for the first time. It took three months of dates, and a night of margaritas at a restaurant that didn't card, for that to happen. Juan's after-sex sweat glistened on his skin like the glossy sheen on a street following a sudden rain. He said romantic things—things he liked about my personality, little traits and mannerisms of mine I never noticed—but when he tried to tell me about the moment he knew he'd fallen in love with me, I cut him off. "Juan, this is too soon." He stopped talking, went to sleep.

I snuck out before sunrise, into that cold raw darkness where you don't hear a sound or see another soul. I didn't return his calls, his gifts and flower bouquets, or respond to his letters asking for some sort of explanation that would make sense. Nothing I could say would make sense to him because it made no sense to me. In my mind, I had a specific plan for how I would fall in love, and getting drunk on margaritas (like two stereotypical Mexicans) wasn't it. It was easier to pretend nothing had happened between us, a gift I am thankful women excel at with men.

Debbie counseled me on what happened. You had your first "fuck date," she said. Fuck dates were like Chinese food—you're satisfied at the end of the meal but hungry for something substantial four hours later, and I'd better get used to that if I was going to survive in college. I took her advice, and I'd like to think she took some of mine in return. We'd go out for margaritas at Chevys (a chain restaurant that served watered down Mexican food—some education I offered!) and attempt to seduce Valley boys and police officers by flirting in Spanish. Debbie followed my lead, grabbing those thick, sexy Spanish words by the scruffs of their necks and rolling them around in our mouths, gyrating our hips in time with our rolled *r*s and trilled *t*s. She in turn educated me—with frequent visits to her mother's flat, one-story, cul-de-sac house—about how life in suburbia was clean, safe, . . . and super-boring.

While I was enrolled in Glendale Community College, my mother's house had become a shrine to dead movie stars. Since being fired from her checker job at Pilgrim's Supermarket for gaining too much weight, she'd stopped going outside. Mother was now capable of savage blowups followed by startling moments of tenderness, suffering from a kind of selective emotional amnesia, the result of cocktailing speed and Fen Phen to lose weight. Her new routine consisted of scouring magazines in the morning for photos, clipping them out and mounting them in cheap seashell-ridged frames, then spending the rest of the day cleaning the over two hundred framed photos around the house. Movie stars both white and Mexican, from Pedro Infante to Bette Davis, mingled with photos of distant, nameless relatives, sad immigrants with rangy saddlebag faces standing next to each other in corpse suits and neck-to-ankle dresses. You'd think these famous strangers were actual parts of my mother's life; there were more photos of them than there were of me.

One afternoon my mother lost her train of thought and stopped cleaning altogether, something I'd never seen her do before. In her hands was a photo of herself standing outside The Option restaurant in Hollywood. My mother had been set on me seeing the place, though I didn't get what the big deal was. Maybe she dreamt of eating there on many a glamorous Saturday night years ago in a sheer cocktail dress with Jorge Negrete or Cary Grant. When she was able to make a lunch reservation for the both of us, the once exclusive restaurant was a bare carcass of its former self. Its famed wall of caricatures had been removed, and the building was weeks away from being closed and demolished. The service was distracted (our busboy, someone she kept calling for by name, totally ignored us), the interior murky, as if sunlight was being filtered in through fish tanks in the windows, and the "famous" Cobb salads were blistered with mold. My mother said nothing through our lunch, making a few bratty stabs at her meal. She'd brought a camera to photograph the restaurant's caricature of Rita Hayworth, but the asshole maître d' asked us to leave. I took her picture by the bus stop instead, snapping the photo midconversation.

Placing my hands over the photograph, I asked my mother, "What were you saying?"

"Rita Hayworth," she said. "She was a Mexican movie star who was discovered at a bus stop. Her skin was so light she could pass for white. How lucky she was."

"You're lucky too, Momma," I said and caressed her scoured hands.

She hung the picture back on the wall, undusted. I reached out to clean it and she slapped me. I threw down my towel and didn't come back home until the police called me to identify my mother's swollen body, crumpled atop a stack of movie magazines and The Option's famed caricature of Rita Hayworth. I never found out how she got it. Some things in life you're just not meant to know, I guess.

Juan saw the For Sale sign I'd put on the front lawn and left a note in my mailbox inviting me out for coffee. Transferring to UCLA for an English degree had left me $60,000 in debt. Selling the house would be an easy way to pay off my loans. What I needed in the meantime was a temp job nearby.

It had been six years since Duchess said she was working at the Bank of America on Sunset and Echo Park. I thought there was no chance she'd stay in the same job that long—that kind of commitment seems an eternity when you're in your twenties—but I spotted her right away. She was wearing a pin-striped jumper dress with sparkler streaks in her hair, sheer stockings, a faux pearl necklace, and espadrilles. Her name tag had glitter and stick-on stars around the word DUCHESS. She was carrying a stack of papers, had gained a lot of weight, and was heavy around the belly the way a new mother is. Her eyes, though, were as fresh as a sunrise, betraying none of the weary sleep lines you'd find in a new mother's face. "Late-term miscarriages," or second-trimester abortions, were common around here.

"Can you help an unemployed college grad out with a job?" I asked, my voice breaking.

"We're only hiring summer temps," she said, acting like we had just spoken earlier in the day. Her eyes watered, but she was not going to give me that satisfaction of her tears, and I was glad for that. "Is that okay?"

We hugged as if we were made of eggshells, holding with the delicate fierceness of frail *abuelitas*—pure intent to connect, but not enough strength in our muscles to show it.

"Let me get my purse," she said. When she returned, her mascara had been reapplied.

Over burritos at her "regular" lunch spot (the thought of eating at the same place every day sounded like death to me), she covered a long expanse of post–high school time with an incredible economy of words: bank job, community college dropout, abortion, unemployment, bank job. My update was as brief as hers. How was it that we could cover years of day-to-day, second-to-second life—so precious, so fleeting while we were living it, so filled to the brim with the annoyance of everyday occurrences that took up so much space in our heads—in minutes? Perhaps we were both eager to talk about Juan; seeing Duchess stirred up old feelings for both of them. She brought him up first.

"He misses you," she said. "You should call him."

"He sent me a condolence note. But I couldn't call. I humiliated him."

"Sex helps guys get over humiliation pretty fast."

"Do you think you can get me a job at the bank? For a few months?"

"Maybe. Let me speak to my supervisor. You can apply for her job."

"You want me to be your boss?"

"Sure, why not?" she said. "She's leaving soon. I'll be glad to see her go. She's a real fascist, makes a big deal out of everything. You'd be perfect for her job."

"Um . . . thanks?"

"That's not what I meant." She laughed. "Need one of these," she said, brushing her bangs like a tassel from right to left across a non-existent mortarboard.

This was the time, I thought. This was the natural pause in our conversation. We'd caught up on each other's lives and settled our past loves. Now we could talk through our hurt feelings, make amends, maybe set off on the long road back to a different kind of friendship, stronger than before.

"That's a cute dress," I said, and meant it. "I think it's great."

"Thanks, I got it on sale."

"You didn't make it?"

"Nah, I don't do that anymore." Her plastic knife cut through her burrito and sawed into her Styrofoam lunch tray.

"Why not?"

"No reason."

"You could start up again. Maybe in your free time."

She set her knife down and covered it with a napkin. "I just don't feel that way anymore," she said.

We both kind of nodded, cleared our table, and walked back to the bank without saying a word.

"We should do something," I said.

"Yeah, we should," she said. "And we'll see each other at work. There's no rush."

"Right," I said. "Because 'why chase a bus when another one's right around the corner?' You know, what you used to say? Back in high school?"

"I don't know what you're talking about."

We hugged good-bye. I'd taken about ten steps when I heard her voice. She was pointing to a Glendale bus on Sunset Boulevard pulling away from the curb.

"You missed your bus!" she shouted.

Of course I never went back to the bank. I didn't have the courage to see Duchess every day, let alone be her boss. I'd rather have worked at McDonald's, which I did instead for six months, until the house sale closed. The next time I saw Duchess on the street she didn't mention it. We scheduled another lunch, then canceled. Several more months passed before we saw each other again, friendly waves this time, no conversation. Our days together would keep coming, albeit with greater distances between them, until we reached the point where we both knew how to get in touch with each other but didn't.

Selling the house meant I was out of debt, free to go wherever I wanted. I discovered I didn't want to go anywhere after all, especially once the neighborhood started changing. House prices went up, neighbors cashed out, and there were new bars, new restaurants, fewer *cholos*. I welcomed these fellow white, affluent (and sometimes openly gay—a shocker for the old-timers) strangers into a land that I'd inhabited for most of my life and that was now a foreign tourist destination. These new shops had so much beautiful, useless . . . *stuff*—handmade designer handbags; overpriced "folk" art paintings; hand-me-down T-shirts with iron-on decals of cereal boxes, cartoon raccoons smoking joints, and eighties icons like Michael Jackson and Madonna, shirts that my friends growing up had handed down enough times they were being handed back to us at a thousand percent markup. And I loved these stores for this, for their nice . . . *things*. They made this place feel more like my home.

I rented an apartment around the corner from Membo's, where I shared chaste cups of espresso with Juan. He never pushed us into dating (we dated other people), but we remained friends, and it would have stayed that way had not a young *chola* walked into the Bank of America and gotten into a screaming argument with one of the tellers over an iPod. She was told by the bank manager that if she didn't leave, the police would be called and she'd be arrested for creating a disturbance. Duchess thought the manager was overreacting and came out from behind the safety partition to mediate the dispute. The *chola* grabbed a letter opener from the manager's desk and tried to slice his cheek open. The blade missed and gouged Duchess's jugular vein. She was killed "instantly," I was told.

An event so common before was now a call to immediate action. Police patrols were stepped up, Guardian Angels walked the streets, neighborhood watches popped up overnight. None of that changed how much I hated that word *instantly,* implying Duchess didn't suffer any pain. What kind of consolation was that for me? I couldn't cry my tears instantly, couldn't heal my heart instantly, couldn't move on with my life instantly.

Juan picked me up outside the funeral home where she was cremated. We spread her ashes underneath the jacaranda tree she and I sat under when we were young girls and lived our lives as sisters.

The next morning, Juan asked me to marry him. I said yes, because I realized some things make more sense after a tragedy. There was enough left from the house sale to buy a small bungalow a few short blocks from the house I was raised in. We married in a simple ceremony at City Hall to the soundtrack of my favorite Gwen Stefani song, "Underneath It All," two weeks before Juan reported for basic training.

The phone stops ringing. My Gwen CD finishes then repeats itself back to the first track. Around me on my walls are layers upon layers of Duchess's drawings that her mother gave to me. I slide the phone off the drawing on the nightstand. A young woman is standing proud in a timelessly stylish red dress with violet blossoms in her hair. This is the drawing Duchess made that day we sat under the jacaranda tree. She wouldn't let me have it then; here it is now wrinkled and folded over, yet it's not as I remember it. The face is different. The strong cheekbones, the squat pug nose, the acne scars flecked on the face like buckshot. The face is mine. It wasn't a drawing of her, like she said. It was a drawing of me.

Somebody left this drawing for me in a manila envelope outside my front door. On the other side is a letter from my husband, Juan. He is telling me the story of how he knew he'd fallen in love with me, the story I'd never let him finish. It was the moment he first saw me in that hideous Contempo Casual dress. The memory's as bright as a chemical fire. Any woman who could wear a dress that bad, he said, and look good, was a woman he needed to make his own.

He is telling me he had that picture of me in his mind—a goofy young girl in a shitty dress—when he fell. He is telling me this is his "last letter"; he has been killed in action.

Cool kids,
will you come out to play?
Cool kids,
will you come out to play with me?

It's almost daylight. The phone's ringing again. I open my bedroom window to breathe in the warm Los Angeles dawn, and the murderous heat I can tell is coming with it. There's the sound of the street, the garbage trucks grinding the quiet air, the police helicopters searching for *cholos* running from their pasts, and if I listen close, above the noise, the heartbeat of a little girl, kicking in my belly, as I dance around the room to a silly Gwen Stefani song. Her name will be Maria, and she will hate this song when she's old enough. She will dance to the songs in her own head.

8

La Luz y la Tierra

My first name comes from the last woman evicted from the ground that would become Dodger Stadium. In an effort to lure the Brooklyn Dodgers to Los Angeles, the city agreed to construct a new stadium on a large tract of land north of Downtown called Chavez Ravine. Mexicans racially steered from buying houses anywhere else in the city lived here for years in the long shadow cast by the City Hall building, unnoticed and unmolested. Chavez Ravine was immune to time. Dirt trails, along with a paved road or two tossed in like bleached bones, connected backyards where goats and stray dogs roamed free amid houses and shacks with crooked walls, wooden outhouses, and pie-tin roofs that baked your arms and legs throughout the year. Men pushed trolleys and wheelbarrows laden with fresh fruit, ice blocks, and jugs of water from house to house as if Chavez Ravine were still part of old Mexico and not "modern"-era Los Angeles. The land's serrated mesas and loping glens nestled its residents in a sense of forgottenness, which was fine with them.

The notorious *Herald Examiner* (founded by the anti-Mexican racist William Randolph Hearst) branded Chavez Ravine "a shantytown" where "descendants of blood-lusting Aztecs squatted in piece-meal huts, drawn to these undeveloped dirt mounds the way flies are to horse dung." Despite the hard, brown earth that stretched for miles up and out of the valley, this was fertile ground. Mexicans were born here, among the smoky bouquets of the toyon shrub, made love on hills of elderberry, honeysuckle, and fistfuls of lilac fiesta flowers, married each other by a ring of deodar cedars, grew old walking the long, open fields of sage scrub and giant wild rye, and died in ancient forests of pine and eucalyptus. Trees older than the Chandlers and the Spaniards, whose last names christened streets and parks throughout Los Angeles, dotted this land, which if you believed the old folk (and who ever believes the old folk?), was a crater made by God's hands, a special piece of land scooped out for the Mexicans to stay Mexican, to remember who they were before they became Americans, when Mexico ceded California at the end of the Mexican-American War.

But God's hands couldn't stop the bulldozers. Families were first told their homes were being torn down to build them brand-new public housing—townhomes with running water, washing machines, lush green lawns and playgrounds, shopping centers, and a "super" market where you could buy Swanson TV dinners and bring them home to cook them in state-of-the-art "Dyna-Warm" ovens, one in every new apartment. Then men in large machines came flying crisp white banners, conquistadors in hard hats bearing royal standards emblazoned with baseballs soaring over a large red treasure map X. The speed with which dozens of houses and trees with deep, ancient roots were pulped into smooth asphalt was extraordinary, something you'd see a child do in a sandbox, wiping a self-contained world clean with the brisk sweep of his hands (not God's this time).

It took more than God's hands to move Aurora Salazar. Four pairs of hands, to be exact, carried Aurora by her wrists and ankles out of her house in front of news reporters and photographers, down a flight of stairs, and onto a swatch of cracked desert floor. Four Mexi-can officers from the Los Angeles Sheriff's Department with badges and guns to restrain an unarmed, barefoot woman, clad in a sleeve-less white blouse and pants with large appliqué butterflies fluttering up and down her legs, from ever entering her own home again. Four men to contain one woman's fury.

Here my mother, Felicia, smiles (she is telling me this story, *again*—thank God she's not showing me the newspaper clippings) and looks somewhere across a field of flaking lime green sunflowers painted on her kitchen walls, whistling low as if to say, *"Ay, that* was a woman." She holds out her hands as she speaks and sculpts the land Aurora walked—and was dragged across—with fierce, swift strokes. Mother believes it was the land, those hills, that made Aurora so pas-sionate, those rich, brown, curvaceous mounds and valleys that she'd tell me, stroking her hips, resembled her own body in her youth.

I didn't know those hills; I didn't know that woman. What I knew were tunneled-out highways that unfurled like streamers tossed off a balcony from atop Dodger Stadium and endless days of riding my bicycle through its saucer-tiered parking lots, flat and featureless, my mother said, like that light-skinned, hair-dyed *telenovela güerita* my father left us for. That was when my mother took back her last name, Esperanza, which means "hope."

Put these two names together. You get me.

My mother owns a house in Echo Park, a neighborhood beneath Dodger Stadium whose boundaries sit on a map of Los Angeles like a busty teenage girl with scoliosis and a hooked nose. Echo Park was once a secluded enclave for Hollywood's silent-film-era movie stars. (Charlie Chaplin lived in a large Victorian mansion that over-looked Echo Park Lake; Tom Mix built the first movie studio in Los Angeles where a public storage facility and a Jack in the Box now sit.) The whites moved away after one war; Cambodian and Viet-namese refugees from another war took their place. Then an influx of young white Westsiders who knew nothing of war trickled in looking for cheap property. By the time I turned thirty and returned to Los Angeles after a failed engagement to a white college grad named Gerald, and a series of uninspiring rent- and food-paying jobs, they'd realigned Echo Park's nose and straightened her posture with coffee shops, "funky" boutiques that sold *just* purses or *just* cell phone holsters, cafés with outdoor seating and Internet access, and bars that were written up in lifestyle magazines and served imported beer on tap. I was thrilled at first when they ushered those dilapidated *tiendas, lavanderías,* and *taquerías* out of the neighborhood. Without my mother to barter for things we needed with her currency of shared history, overzealous laughter, and hot *chisme,* I was shortchanged and ignored. Now that these *gringo* hipster stores are everywhere, I'm not sure this *is* my old neighborhood anymore. I drive in, visit my mother, then drive out. I haven't explored around here for years for a reason; Echo Park has a hard time letting you go.

My mother watched with guarded cynicism the real estate boom that brought the whites to our front door. For over thirty years she's worked as a cleaning lady, many of those years for white B-list movie stars and studio executives in the Hollywood Hills. When I was younger, I'd beg to go on her cleaning trips, but she'd never let me. You're cleaning their filth while they devour your health, she'd say, and send me back to my schoolbooks.

When I got older and discovered tabloids and *Entertainment Tonight* on television, I'd ask her for secrets, little black books with addresses and phone numbers of other movie stars (with the way these stars dated, I thought they enjoyed *only* each other's company—one big, happy, rich, and famous family), descriptions of drug caches, sex tapes, something we could profit from. She thought this way of thinking was crass, something that was endemic among people my age. When she arrived to clean in the mornings, she said, anything exciting that had been happening had happened and moved on. And if anything *did* happen, she's liable to tell a complete stranger more about it than her own daughter.

My mother's house is halfway up a block of prewar residences, most of which have changed owners in the past few years. Perched atop a tilting hill like an old cat that can do nothing but sleep all day in a sunny window ledge, it was built in the 1920s and has survived five major earthquakes. Out front, a large jacaranda tree with cracked bark spreads its heavy blossoms across the jagged, pitched staircase that leads to the security gates that protect the doorway and the front windows, relics from when the neighborhood used to be rough. For years I tried to convince my mother to move away because it was dangerous. Now I try to convince her to move away to cash in on the gentrification march. Either way, she won't budge.

I come here each month to help my mother, who lives alone, clean her house. I knock on the security gate because I don't have my own set of keys. Through the open front door I hear a transistor radio playing loud *ranchera* music in the kitchen over the sound of church bells up in the hills tolling the start of Sunday service.

"You're just in time to help," my mother says from the kitchen, something she tells me no matter what time I show up. "The gate's open. Lock it behind you so I can let Blackjack out. The towels are next to the storage room."

The storage room used to be my old bedroom, though my mother hasn't called it my bedroom since the day I left for college. I set my purse—a large, unfashionable taupe sack with worn straps—down in the living room on a ratty couch with reversible pleather/corduroy cushions that one of her bosses handed down to her years ago and start to clean.

The sticky-sweet smell of fresh varnish and lemon ammonia is overpowering. I unlatch a series of French-door-style windows that open onto the front porch to breathe in the smoggy air outdoors. It's early, and the sky's coated with a wispy molasses glaze. Strong puffs of wind swirl dust devils around my feet. Cleaning the mantel above the fake fireplace, I find a row of family pictures of me, my mother, and bits and pieces of my father, Hector. She cut and excised most of him away in these photos, leaving behind a stray hand on my cradle or a phantom arm caught midwave. In Hector's place are portraits and magazine clippings of Morrissey, an English rock star from the eighties.

That jagged space where my father used to be never looked right. When I was in high school, I overlaid Morrissey's image from glossy magazines into shots where my mother was holding on to a headless neck or kissing a crisp rip in front of a tree that had been sliced in half. I pasted in Morrissey's picture because he was the kind of man who would never leave my mother, or abandon a child. His songs contain stories of endless devotion and his incapability of being loved by anyone. Why not give him, then, to someone who no longer had anyone to give her love to? Judging from these photos, Morrissey was a better father than my own was.

If second-generation Mexicans could canonize a living saint in Los Angeles, it'd be Morrissey. Like most of the Mexican girls and gay boys I knew, I went through a vicious, life-consuming Morrissey phase in high school, one that for a period of time made me hate the queen of England and Margaret Thatcher more than I hated the Los Angeles Police Department. White girls who could tell what kind of music I listened to by the way I dressed would come up to me and say, "You like Morrissey, too? Why? He's not Mexican." I'd say, Then why do you love Prince? Or hip-hop? I never understood why when a white person likes a musician who's not white, they're cool, but if a person who isn't white likes a musician who is, they're a freak or, worse, a sellout.

I couldn't explain to you why Morrissey meant so much to me, or still means so much to me that one of my life's ambitions remains seeing him in person. Not at a concert but in an actual Los Angeles *place*—eating dinner at Astro's Coffee Shop or shopping for organic tofu at Trader Joe's. While it sounds far-fetched, he does live in L.A., somewhere in Beverly Hills I've read, driving himself around in a silver mist Porsche that has on occasion been spotted on my side of town. It's a fanciful yet unrealistic possibility; I've calculated the odds and thought about ways to improve my chances of an "accidental" encounter, but I place no faith in an actual meeting. Faith is a luxury for those who are able to ignore what the rest of us must see every day. Pessimism, distrust, and irony are the holy trinity of my religion, irony in particular, and I will be the first to point out the irony of a woman whose last name means "hope" placing no stock in faith. Hope is my mother's name, and faith my mother's cause, not mine.

Not that she's given up on converting me. Her idea of faith has nothing to do with God, at least not anymore. She was a religious young woman who could quote Bible passages, but with the passing of her years and the aging of her muscles, she's come to equate faith with hard work and hard work with having a successful, happy life. Forget faith is a word, she'd say. Pretend it's a color. What color is your faith, *m'hija*? Faith has colors, she says; otherwise those stained-glass windows in cathedrals would be as see-through as a horny man's promises. Was my faith a red-hot incandescence, fizzy as neon light that burned as bright but half as long? Or was it an ice cool ocean sunset blue, determined, immovable, but indifferent to compassion or suffering? I told her I couldn't see what she was talking about, so I guess my faith has no color. It's see-through, like glass.

What else can I tell you about Morrissey? He was born in Davy-hulme, England, but raised in Hulme, Manchester, is a strict vegan who fires any of his roadies if they eat meat, and sings his "love never lost 'cause it was never found" lyrics as if his words were speeding along a treacherous mountain pass, curving and undulating his syllables into trills and yodels until they sound almost Spanish. When the albums I listened to came from England, and Manchester meant more to me than East Los Angeles, the images his words conjured up in my head were, and are, Californian. His dreary, wet Manchester sky above pelted my red-tiled and tar paper L.A. rooftops below, falling on a girl with a jet-black, slicked-back bob haircut, black eyeliner, pushup bra, denim jean shorts, fishnet tights, and ass-kicking Doc Martens. You can't help who, or what, you love.

There's a small, wet chill on my knee. Blackjack nuzzles this spot again with his nose, and I reach down to rub him behind his ears, careful not to leave my hand too close to his mouth. He looks appreciative and happy, but he is also my mother's dog, which means that he can be feisty and cruel, snapping at you when you are at your most comfortable and relaxed. This may be due to his breed, a border collie mix, born with the impulse to chase, bite, and corral sheep. A better explanation is my mother walking him on an irregular timetable that can span several weeks, leaving a four-year-old dog with an enormous amount of pent-up energy that has nowhere to go. Whenever she walks him, he rockets out the front door, strains at his leash, pulls my mother down the sidewalk, lunges at other dogs, bounds into the street at passing cars, and nips at kids who try to pet him because they find his distinctive Oreo-and-cream markings irresistible. This leads to fewer walks, which leads to more bad behavior. I offer to walk Blackjack whenever I stop by, but my mother says the dog and I don't understand each other, which some days feels truer than others.

I rub his neck and walk him back into the kitchen, where my mother is cleaning the floor. Her hunched back bobs and weaves like a boxer, her arms gliding a square-head mop in taut N-shaped strokes across the floor before dipping the worn head in a yellow pail of soapy black water. She motions with a quick wave for me to lead the dog to the opposite side of the kitchen, where a knee-high white plastic doggy fence is installed in the doorway to the laundry room. Blackjack walks across the wet floor and, catching the scent on his paws, stops moving. I nudge him by his collar and then give him a few taps on his backside. He won't budge.

"Lead him," she says. "Don't let him lead you."

"You can't see what I'm doing," I say, realizing that's a feeble comeback. My mother is the world's leading expert on knowing what I'm doing at any moment without being able to see me. "The dog does what he wants."

"He's never going to follow you if he doesn't believe you know where you're going," she says, dipping the mop head in the bucket.

"I don't need him to follow me," I say, pulling at his collar. Blackjack whimpers while I try to slide him across a floor my mother will have to wax again. "He's your dog. He should do what *you* want him to do."

"You're my daughter," she says. "Do you do what *I* want you to do?"

"I don't know," I say. "You never told me what that was."

My mother stands the mop handle next to the refrigerator and walks over to the doggy gate. She motions with a firm gesture that says "come," and a jab of her right hand. Blackjack trots over in an obedient path, his paws not leaving a single track on the waxed floor, and hops the fence onto his bed in one fluid movement. Mother picks up the mop and cleans over the streaked areas I'd dragged him across.

"I'm finished in the living room," I say.

"Kitchen's done," she says, cocking the mop handle in a corner. "Rest of the house, too."

"You cleaned the house by yourself?" I ask.

"Yeah, wouldn't be the first time. And I couldn't sleep again. I had the nightmares."

"You could talk to someone about them."

"Why? I talk about it to the dog, and he says, get up and feed me, or get up and walk me. I feed him, walk him, and I'm fine."

"Not sleeping's unhealthy. You'd have to have been up since five to clean everything."

"Four-thirty," she says. My mother doesn't enjoy when I get things right, even if it's by accident. If five is the exact time she woke up (and I think it is), she'd still have said "four-thirty."

"I don't mind rising early. I get the moon all to myself," she says. Picking up the water bucket, she empties it out in the kitchen sink, the sludgy water trickling down a rusty drain.

"So everything's done," I say, trying not to conceal my excitement.

"Yeah, everything's finished," she says, and my day opens before me like a blossoming African flower or a clear stretch of Highway 1: beautiful, precious, uncomplicated, a million miles away from here. And in this early morning moment of utter simplicity, with no blame or regret exchanged between us, through a window over my mother's shoulder I see a pure, aurulent glow, a light that fills me with such a sense of peace, love, and acceptance that I could forswear sex, alcohol, and music if I had the slightest faith this feeling would return. But how could it? This was a moment that bends like palm trees in a strong Santa Ana, an elastic piece of time that, without warning, breaks and snaps back out the window, leaving me again in my mother's old kitchen, her words piercing the soft yellow glow.

"Blackjack needs a walk," she says.

"Mom, the dog doesn't like me."

"*Mi luz,*" my mother says, granting me this term of endearment half the time when she wants something, then taking it back the other half, when I disappoint her, "I've been up since before dawn. My feet are blistered. It's so hard for me to get down the stairs. One quick walk around the block and you're done."

"The blocks are long here," I say. "That could take half an hour."

"You don't have half an hour for your mother?"

"For you, yes. That dog, no way. He doesn't stay when I tell him to stay. If he slipped out of his leash, he could run into traffic and be killed. Or get me killed. It's embarrassing," I drawl, my subdued Mexican accent lapping on my tongue, those last two syllables, *ass* and *ing,* hanging in the air like lazy curlicues of marijuana smoke.

Mother catches it. "You talking like you *live* here," she says, tugging on her own words like stale toffee. Once, this would have been an admonishment for turning my back on *mi barrio, mi casita.* But this 'hood, where my mother's derived her credibility for toughness and hard living, has become too expensive for me to buy a home in. You can walk by apartment buildings in Echo Park now and actually *hear* through the open windows the sound of forks and spoons scraping leftovers from china plates and bowls into plastic-bag-lined trash cans. The dogs never had it so good around here.

"Too rich for me, Mom. Your old clients bought their summer homes here so they don't have to fly to Acapulco."

She laughs, unaccustomed to me teasing her, and takes out a can of premium dog food, the kind she used to take two buses to buy but is now sold in a pet boutique around the corner. Popping the tab, she shakes the wet slabs of dog food into a monogrammed silver supper dish behind Blackjack's doggy gate. He gives it a round of suspicious sniffs.

"You always have a room here," my mother says. This is a comment that I call a "let," as in "let it lie there, let it go." I don't really have a room here, but why raise a fuss? I've had a great morning with my mother. Chores have been handled, and I've experienced some sort of vision that's left a blissful, unexplained feeling coursing through my body, the result no doubt of looking outside and seeing that one of those glorious, breathtaking Los Angeles days is waiting for me!—as soon as I walk the dog. I watch Blackjack ignore his pricey dog food, feel that flush of anger at how much attention my mother lavishes on him, and hear the words tripping out of my mouth so fast, there's no time to catch them before they fall.

"Isn't my bedroom where you store things you don't use but can't bring yourself to throw away?"

Mother's shoulders tense up. "You weren't here, and I needed the space," she says, busying herself rearranging dog food on a shelf for no reason except to occupy her hands. Blackjack looks at me with a quizzical head shake—I'm convinced the dog is using me as a ventriloquist's dummy to speak the words he knows will get me in the most trouble—hops over the fence, his food untouched, and trots past me. He has heard this argument one too many times before, too.

"Mom, you have the house to yourself," I say, feeling pulled into this maelstrom without any hope of pulling out of it.

"I have friends," Mother says. "I don't need to make anybody stay here."

"Mom, that's not what I meant," I say, and that euphoric feeling I had moments before is cooling in my veins, hardening into bitterness and resentment.

"I have my friends, my hobbies. I have a very busy day. And my dog," Mother says and glances over at Blackjack's empty bed. "Where is he?"

"Maybe his schedule's packed, too," I say, but my mother's stare stops me cold. "What?"

"Did you lock the door behind you?" she asks.

My eyelids blink twice, a fleshy, audible *pop!* both of us hear. Her expression bubbles and solidifies like metamorphic rock, a harshness pinching the edges of her lips and eyes, making her neck wrinkles oscillate. This is a look that's neither contemptuous nor sympathetic. It's a look I've seen a mere handful of times in my life, taking me back to a time in my childhood when closets and spaces under the bed were scary places. It's a look that says, I'm not in control of this situation.

"He's too small to push open the front gate by himself," I say, knowing this is some desperate stab to shift the burden away from me.

"He can tear apart a cable-knit sweater and chew through a mesh leash," my mother shouts, racing to the living room. "He can push open an unlocked door!"

Outside the kitchen window, the smog lifts on a lustrous morning sky polished smooth like a stone. That vision is almost impossible to reconcile with what I see when I walk out into the living room: a wide-open front door and security gate, jacaranda blossoms fluttering into the house and waltzing across the tile floor, and a sharp breeze snapping up the hill, puckering the air around us. It's like the scene of a crime where the oxygen's been sucked up into a vacuum, making it difficult to breathe, your light-headedness stopping you from coming to any sort of rational conclusion about your next move.

That's what I'm feeling. If this is my state, how will my mother react? In a fit of grotesque panic, flailing down the hill, screaming his name up and down the street?

No. She was on the porch gripping an iron railing with both hands, staring at the expanse of hill below us. In the damp morning breeze, away from the dust and balmy scent of ammonia, her thoughts and her breath came easy. Her mind was made up:

"Adéntrense en este mar que forcejearon con sus jóvenes brazadas y traigan la sabiduría de la corriente con ustedes."

In Spanish, she knew how to say beautiful things, as if she were quoting poetry. She could turn her anger into song. In English, she was brutal. If she had tried to say what she was feeling in English, it would have come out as, Go away and don't ever come back.

"Wade into this ocean you floundered in with youthful strokes," she said, "and bring your wisdom of the currents with you."

I grabbed my purse, nodded my head. "Thanks, Momma. It sounds much nicer in Spanish."

It was a cold and windy morning for July, a brisk (for L.A.) sixty-one degrees, and I didn't object to my mother asking me to take a midnight blue, fake-fur-collar, and chenille-lined coat she'd stored in my old closet and I hadn't worn since college. It was an expensive coat I'd begged my mother to buy. I was going to have someone sew a huge picture of Morrissey onto the back, with his name written underneath in gang-style calligraphy, but the estimates I got were in the hundreds of dollars and I didn't know anyone who could do it cheap. The coat didn't make sense without the Morrissey picture, so I tossed it into the closet and never wore it again.

My mother had calmed down enough to dig through my old Tupperware containers of clothes and find it. For being shelved in plastic over a decade, the coat was a great fit. Hoping to thaw out the tension over Blackjack, I teased her about how she was softening in years; I couldn't remember a time, ever, when my mother asked me to take a coat.

"Afraid of me catching a chill?" I laughed. "There are no 'chills' in East L.A."

"You're not going to joke your way out of trouble with me," she said. "Quit acting like a man."

She agreed to accompany me as far as Vince's place on Sutherland, a dead-end street one block over with many backyards that connected with ours. Vince Hernandez used to stop by in episodic bursts, making several visits one week, then vanishing for months. Now he enjoys taking Blackjack for long walks, culminating in an overnight pass at his place that sometimes includes my mother. He's in his thirty-something forties, runs an underground auto repair shop out of his garage, has most of his hair, and has never married, though he came closest with Mother (which is how she tells it). When she is in the mood to tell me more, she dangles a tantalizing story about how Vince is my real father, which aside from one "fact"—they're about the same age—has never been corroborated by anything else other than wistful glances between the two and an easy familiarity coupled with a savage bickering that comes natural to any man and woman who've been intimate over a period of many years. On summer evenings at Vince's place, I watched him fight his way through my mother's bizarre sense of "long-term girlfriend" entitlements (she honored no commitments yet insisted on the benefits of a wife), then carry those fights into his dreams. He slept in prize-fighter's poses, body coiled, fists clenched, his chest puffed out and bubbled like an unwatched omelet, attacking the inert mattress and pillows until their concave indentations sagged into permanence.

To his credit, Vince did his best to act as a father figure when he was around. When he was away, I conjured him into a famous explorer who would sail around the uncharted regions of the world for months and years at a time, reappearing with gold, spices, silks, and exotic tales of mermaids and sea monsters. Someone who'd disappear for long periods of time not for his benefit but for mine, returning with riches that would make his time away worthwhile. Age wore the spell off—his absences grew so lengthy, and what he returned with became so worthless, I declared him lost at sea and would tell any guy who asked me where my real father was to fuck off.

Vince's house is nestled next to a support post for one of those big billboards that you find up and down the Strip but that are a rarity on this stretch of Sunset. The access ladder could be reached by standing on someone's shoulders, making the billboard a favorite forty-ounce-drinking, weed-smoking, outdoor fucking spot for teenagers. Vince joked about how hard it was to see the stars at night under sudden downpours of Olde English or used condoms. The steady stream of billboard crashers became such a nuisance that he removed the access ladder and constructed a new series of interlocking ladders that, with the insertion of a special key he made himself from a bottle opener, could access the trellis and the accompanying advertisement for a cocky local weatherman named Sergeant Sunshine. He hasn't been on TV for several years—he was removed for making a racist on-air comment—but his fluorescent blue eyes remain on Sunset, peeking out over a pair of gigantic Ray-Ban Wayfarer sunglasses with silvery metallic lenses that "reflect" a painted-on Hollywood sign and a cluster of palm trees with five-point, gold-star-shaped fronds.

Those blue eyes fed my teenage dreams. Sometimes, when the weather or the shouting drove me out of Vince's house, I'd climb up eighty feet to the billboard catwalk with my sleeping bag and feel the city lights pulsate under my body as I gazed into a Hollywood caricature that promised spotlighted red carpet premieres, rides in the backs of limousines, and the kind of glamour and riches that to a teenage girl seemed inevitable, if not my birthright. Later, when I realized I wasn't going to be a movie star, or even live like one, the billboard became that one recognizable landmark you see after a long trip that smacks you in the face and says, Welcome home, nothing's changed.

The same sign could be affixed to Vince's front door. An unprimed car with black plumber's tape trim juts out of Vince's open garage door. An old transistor radio blares music in the sharp morning air from what must be the last surviving English oldies radio station in Los Angeles. Vince stands next to the car in an Army green T-shirt, baggy cargo pants, and his trademark steel-toe boots, shaking his head in frustrated disbelief.

"Lady," he says and kisses me on the cheek. *"Cómo está mi pequeña estrella?"*

"She left the front door open," Mother says, "and Blackjack ran out. Thought he might have come here. Have you seen him?"

"Dogs run away," he says, not answering and grabbing an open Heineken. "Then they come back. Hey, lady, you want something to eat? You're white-girl thin."

"I want to know how the car's coming," I say, and Vince lights up with equal doses of pleasure and dissatisfaction.

"I can't believe the people around here buy cars and know nothing about them," he says. "I'm rebuilding this one from scratch. It'll be a classic when I'm done."

"You're an Einstein with cars," I tease.

"Yeah, I *may* be a genius," Vince says.

"You want to see the genius of men in action?" Mother says to me. "See how fast he puts on his pants after sex."

"Listen to your mom," Vince says, taking a healthy swig of beer. "So what are you going to do today, lady? How about we go to the Lotus Festival tonight at the lake? I haven't taken you since you were singing *Fraggle Rock* songs."

"She's going to look for my dog," Mother says.

Vince cocks an eyebrow, takes another gulp, and finishes the bottle. He yanks out a brand-new bottle opener (he goes through bottle openers the way the Devil goes through souls) and opens a new beer. "Why?"

"Blackjack's a small dog. He could get hit by a car or a bus," Mother says.

"Dog's too fast to be hit. Or be caught. Let him come back on his own. He wants to go out and see the world, maybe change it for the better, get a bitch pregnant."

"Every man wants to change the world," Mother says. "How come so few of them do?"

Vince examines the car's body. "Lady, if you wait until lunchtime, I'll give you a ride. You won't have to walk in circles."

"She won't catch him driving in a car," Mother insists. "She has to be on foot."

"Lady has better things to do today. And she doesn't know the neighborhood anymore. She needs a few places to start," Vince says. He finishes his second beer and opens a third. "Check with the Catholic boys. They're training for some intercity competition and running throughout Echo Park. Bound to run into them, and you can tell them to keep an eye out. Oh, and you should ask the Lord."

"The Lord?" I laugh. "C'mon, I'm not gonna fall for that one anymore." The Lord was an Echo Park urban myth, a clairvoyant oracle who, depending on whom you believed, would answer any single question you asked him, grant your one deepest wish, and if this wasn't enough, change one person's opinion of you so you could start a new, positive relationship with them (keeping up the relationship was on you). This sounded very sixties-ish to me, and the catch, of course, was that nobody I trusted had seen the Lord; some drunks outside the local bars, kids who'd claimed they'd hiked up the tinder-dry hill of weeds he lived on and saw him feeding on dog carcasses, and, of course, Vince. After a poker game where he'd lost his life savings, Vince claims the three things the Lord gave him were granted in one moment—he met my mother the next day.

"I'm telling you, he's called the Lord for a reason," Vince insists. "He's a wise old man. He knows everything that goes on around here. These people buying houses for too much money? He predicted this years ago. I never believed in a god—but I always believed in the Lord."

"Vince, stop teasing her," my mother says.

Over the sound of a passing police helicopter and a doo-wop group on Vince's tinny radio speakers come the chiming of bells from what used to be the Ukrainian Orthodox church up the street. The first of three Spanish-language Sunday services has concluded. Whenever she hears the bells, Mother has bitter comments about her disbelieving churchgoing neighbors strung like arrows from a quiver, but she's also superstitious, and I can see she is restraining herself today, afraid that some obnoxious remark about how fraudulent most Mexican Catholics' faiths are might boomerang on her and end up flattening Blackjack on Sunset Boulevard.

"I think this Lord's telling me to get going," I say. "There's a lot of ground I need to cover."

"He'll hate you for chasing him," Vince says. "Men always do."

"He can't hate me more than he does now," I say. "At least he'll know I'm not afraid of him."

"He's a dog, sweetheart, not a wild bear," Vince says and digs into his pants pocket. He pulls out a set of gold keys attached to a paper clip key ring. "Lady, if you're walking down Sunset, do me a favor and drop these off at Lorenzo's. I've been meaning to give these to him, but I'm going to be stuck under this car today."

"Lorenzo? I haven't spoken to him in years."

"It'll be fine," Vince says. "I've kept him up-to-date on you."

"She shouldn't get sidetracked," Mother says. "She's anxious to get home."

"It's not a problem," I say and take the keys. "It's one stop. I can find Blackjack and be on the road before noon. Mom, let me walk you home."

"I'm fine. You should get going."

"Okay. I'll drop by here later this afternoon," I say.

"I won't be here later."

"Then I'll meet you back at the house."

"I won't be there, either," Mother says.

"Where do you think you're going to be?"

"I don't know."

"Then how am I supposed to return your dog when I find him?" I can hear the edge in my voice popping my words up and out of my throat, as if I were holding a blade against my own neck.

My mother lingers outside the garage. Vince stares at the ground. I realize they are planning to sleep together, which I find kind of charming this early in the morning, but I'm amazed at their inability to acknowledge lust. It's funny—the older and less impressionable I got, the more they tried to protect me from whatever truths they shared and were ashamed of. The time for this kind of discretion was when I was a young girl, who believed that every night we stayed over at Vince's would be the last night I'd have to unpack my Strawberry Shortcake travel bag. Now, this secrecy feels ridiculous.

"He'll lead you to me," she says. "Trust him."

Then she leaves me and marches over to Vince, pointing her fingers at his chest and speaking in a raised voice, saying either cruel or loving things she will deny saying later. Her pain rolls in and out like the tide, sometimes a patter on damp sand, other times a torrent that could knock grown men off their feet. It makes her forget who she is, but it never forgets *where* she is.

Vince pulls her close and folds her hair behind her ears. They embrace like two people trying to untangle themselves from a collision, something I can see only from a distance, as I'm walking away.

It's 10:00 A.M. on Sunset Boulevard. I can hear the neighborhood waking up, a phlegmatic reveille played on collapsing metal bars and security shutters, with a gathering army of grandmothers pulling wheezy basket carts to the supermarket for their Sunday shopping trips and their old husbands shuffling behind them and spitting on the sidewalks, their expectorations horns heralding the arrival of some urban, impoverished sun king.

This much is familiar to me. Except for the Sergeant Sunshine billboard, though, the physical reference points from my youth appear skewed or rearranged. The vacant lots I played hide-and-seek in; the ninety-nine-cent stores where my mother and I shopped for wispy matching sundresses that, if we were lucky, lasted three or four washes; Pilgrim's supermarket, where I used to go after school and stare at my father's light-skinned mistress, seething over her flirtatious behavior yet in total admiration of her makeup and hairdo: these places are gone, replaced with unfamiliar stores and people I don't recognize, walking through the ghosts of memories I alone can see. Bizarre "gentrified" color schemes—pastel salmons and electric tangerines—coat the outlines of buildings whose shapes are recognizable but whose occupants and appearances are not. I caress the fresh coats of paint and stucco on these buildings, looking for the cracks and bullet holes I ran my fingers along on my way to school, but smooth, patched surfaces betray none of these former imperfections.

I'd driven this stretch of boulevard hundreds of times, including this morning when I went to my mother's house. Why do things appear so different out of my car? Where are the battered houses and dilapidated stores with Spanglishized names? Where are *los borrachos* and the wandering covens of Watchtower *señoras,* holding their flimsy magazines against their breasts like medieval shields and searching for fresh souls to convert? It is as if an antimatter explosion had detonated high above Echo Park, reconstructing decay into a glittering faux affluence, a Willy Wonka neutron bomb coating the landscape in radioactive smiley face yellows and Wellbutrin blues.

Lorenzo's Furniture Store staggers between two renovated storefronts, a hobo being helped to his feet by two well-dressed businessmen. Its fifteen-foot, street-to-roof windows are coated in that same healthy layer of dust I remember, displaying what could be the same exact eighties-style recliners and dinette sets that were for sale when I was in grade school. Inside, the light is from a late winter afternoon, settling its shadows on plastic sofa cushions and a maze of dressers, shelves, and entertainment centers. When I was in elementary school and my mother worked late nights cleaning offices in Universal City, I came here and played house.

Lorenzo set up my own model "room" near the back of the store, including a four-poster bed whose upper canopy panel he covered with rolls of glow-in-the-dark star stickers. "It's just like the stars outside," he said, "but you can't see them cause the lights here are too bright. Maybe one day you'll go somewhere where you can see them for real. Remember this star," he said, pointing to Sirius, the Dog Star. "It's the brightest in the sky. So even when you're in the dark you can find your way home. Just follow the dog," he said, and we howled like mutts until one of his workers caught us and he shouted at them to get back to work.

Mother put the bed on layaway, but there was a dispute over the price, and Lorenzo was excommunicated from her circle of friends. Both items were sold (a worn-out mattress and a used dresser covered with stickers—on discount—are an excellent deal to a family stretching its money), and I went back to waiting for my mother at home eating Hot Pockets on my flimsy twin bed. When it came time to buy my own furniture, instead of offering Lorenzo an olive branch, I bought cheap particleboard bookcases that required an unwieldy Allen wrench and an instruction sheet in Swedish for assembly.

There's raucous laughter coming from a side doorway. Four men are sitting around a mirrored dining table playing poker. Lorenzo's black, curly hair is now a greasy dishwater white, his broad shoulders pinched together like a clothespin. He peers over a set of thick bifocals when he sees me.

"We're closed, miss. Come back in an hour."

"Vince asked me to drop off some car keys."

"Oh, you see Vince?" Lorenzo asks. The other guys perk up, speaking Spanish in quick, poking thrusts as their eyes drift from their tightly clutched spreads of cards to my breasts and hips. Vince's name on the lips of a woman is some sort of seal of approval for these men, and I can't decide what appalls me more, the fact these men are leering at my body in front of a man who was a kind of paternal figure, or Vince's name being synonymous with attractive women who may or may not include my mother. I fold my arms across my breasts, ready to drop Lorenzo's keys in the middle of their pot of cigarettes and dollar bills and leave.

"I don't see him," I say. At school, I used to introduce Vince as my father, then my stepfather, then my mother's boyfriend, each downgrading based on my evolving feelings. "We're friends," I say.

Lorenzo stands up from the table. "How do you know him?"

"He hangs out with my mother sometimes," I say, surprised how vapid and adolescent that sounds, and hand Lorenzo the keys. The tips of my lacquered black nails graze his palm's love line, and I see that flicker of recognition, followed by a fervent expression of disbelief on his face reserved for courtrooms or church. He *knows* me, and while there is a part of me that wants him to cut across these many years with a simple gesture, a sweet, graceful movement, perhaps brushing a stray hair from my face, or clenching my hand, he lacks the faith to act on these feelings and will instead ask another question to confirm his suspicions, keep his distance, and refrain from slipping back into a late afternoon years ago when he was a man who believed that finding joy and beauty in life were as simple as watching a child jumping on a bed.

"He must trust you. He never lets anyone handle his keys," Lorenzo says. He sets his cards faceup on the table. *"Se acabó el juego!"* he shouts. *"Dejad de mirar y empezad a trabajar."* The three men strap hernia belts around their waists, hitch the connected suspenders up over their shoulders, and move the table and chairs back out on the showroom floor.

"Vince needs someone he can count on," and this comes out as a dig at my mother, though it's not meant to.

"I'm glad you said that. That means I can give you the chair."

"The chair?" I ask.

Lorenzo leads me back through the maze of bookshelves and dressers to a waist-high oak chair with intricate grapevine spirals etched into its legs and arms, a green cashmere seat cushion with a sunrise stitched into it, and an inlaid brass back spread with a pair of golden lions encircling a silver *E*. It is the sort of chair you'd expect to find in the smoking room of a movie palace, and there is something beautiful, almost haunting, about this kind of attention to detail.

"Vince did some work on a classic car for Father Alemencio. He caught up with Father checking in with this crazy old woman who lives up in the Heights," Lorenzo says, "and while Vince was there she asked him to drop off this chair to be refurbished. Vince can never say no to a lady."

"He's capable," I say.

"I've fixed up the chair," Lorenzo continues, "and Father paid for the bill, but she's never come to collect. Vince said he'd drop it off, but he never got around to it. He told me when he dropped off these keys, he'd take the chair. You dropped them off; now you can take it."

"No, I can't. Not today."

"Why not?" Lorenzo asks. "You said you were Vince's friend, right? You said he could count on you, right?"

"I don't have time for this. I've lost my mother's dog and I have to find it. And my car's parked, like, four blocks away from here." I can't believe how spoiled that sounds.

"It's not far if you know your way around here," Lorenzo says. "Go past the lake, up a couple blocks, then straight ahead until you hit Kensington, where the old Victorian houses are."

"No, no, no," I stammer. "I have to be out of here by noon. I have things to do. I have my day planned out," I lie.

"You could call Vince," Lorenzo says, and the thought of interrupting him and my mother having sex makes me shudder.

"No, I can't do that, either," I say.

"Or you can take it yourself," he says. "If it doesn't get done today, I have to charge him for keeping this here."

"Why did Vince offer to deliver this chair?" I ask. "Why don't *you* deliver it?"

"Because the Coat Queen's crazy."

"The Coat Queen?" I ask. The mere idea of learning there's someone who lives around here called the Coat Queen, and knowing that I'm being sent on an errand to meet her while looking for my mother's dog, explodes that pristine image I had earlier of an unspoiled, unhurried day. How did such a simple day get so complicated so fast?

"You should know this in advance," Lorenzo says, tearing a sheet of protective plastic from a large roll to wrap the chair in. "Lady's always got these old coats on, and always wears more than one. Hot, cold, don't matter. She has thousands of 'em."

"And an old woman who's always cold scares you," I say, then mutter, "Hope your wife never turns fifty."

Lorenzo ties down the plastic with twine. He stands back, checks that the fit is snug. "I don't like confrontations," he says.

Was this the reason he and my mother never reconciled? Was this his way of making me do penance for my mother's grudge? I am afraid to ask, but more afraid to refuse.

"Give me the address," I sigh.

Lorenzo disappears in the back and returns with a crude line map. Then he offers his hand and we shake. He's waiting for me to offer my name, which I don't. He knows who I am. Why say anything? Isn't it better this way? That wonderful feeling of seeing someone after a long time has for me always been replaced by a sinking, uncomfortable dread, a silence that says there isn't one way to reestablish that connection we once shared and will never share again.

"I wish I had cash on hand to pay you for helping out," he says. "Why don't you take these?"

He pulls a crusty roll of star stickers from his pocket. "They don't stick too well. You could tape 'em up, though." The stickers are moist in his hand. One peels off the roll and sticks to my palm.

"Okay, well, thanks," I say, more dismissive than I need to be. I mean, *really*—stickers? Didn't time move at all in this neighborhood? The chair is an awkward weight, so before long I set it down to readjust my grip. The sticker is still affixed to my hand.

It was Sirius, the Dog Star. In a rush I'm misty-eyed. How many nights did I fall asleep in that cheap four-poster bed staring up at and trying to reach my brilliant glow-in-the-dark sky, dreaming of a life that was elsewhere, then woke up in my old, darkened bedroom? How many times had I left Echo Park only to end up back here? What was I searching for? My hope? My faith? The light to find my way home?

A blast of air from a passing bus, carrying one man sitting in the back, lifts the star off my hand. Follow me, the star seems to say, as it corkscrew whips in the air, fluttering like a phosphorescent butterfly down the street until it plops into the waters of Echo Park Lake.

If Chavez Ravine is where God's hands touched the ground, Echo Park Lake is where God stood while doing so. It's an enormous half-mile-long footprint in the center of Echo Park, sandwiched between Sunset Boulevard and the Hollywood Freeway, those twin arteries of Los Angeles's bloodstream. The lake itself has evaded progress for over one hundred years as the land around it metamorphosed from rolling dirt trails into interlocking sections of houses, apartment buildings, and condos. It's survived an oil spill in which it was set ablaze, been dragged hundreds of times for missing children or heartbroken lovers, fished in for city-water catfish, dredged to its floor and converted for a short time into an unofficial neighborhood garbage pit, been home to numerous movie and video shoots (my favorites are Jack Nicholson floating on a boat as he spies on a couple having a secret tryst in *Chinatown,* and the Bangles dancing around the lake in a video for "Manic Monday"), been skimmed across by a multitude of paddleboat rentals, played host to frequent ghost sighting, including the Lady of the Lake, a woman in a blue dress who has appeared hundreds of times walking across the water and whom my mother tried to convince me for years was my great-grandmother, and is home this weekend to the Lotus Festival, which happens every July.

Its name comes from the hundreds of cucumber green lotus pads that sprout large, starry pink and white fronds this time of year. A cornucopia of food stands selling barbecued meats prepared in methods and styles from around the world are set up around the lake, along with arts and crafts booths, palm-reading tables, inflatable bounce houses, collapsible carnival rides, a miniature Ferris wheel. Later there will be dragon boat races across the lake's murky toilet green water and a large fireworks display at the end of the night, launched from a platform attached to three large permanent fountains that shoot continuous jets of water fifty feet into the air throughout the year.

And here *I* am, amid the sounds of locking metal pins, grilling meat, and hammering nails, sitting next to a palm tree carved up with English graffiti on an ornate movie palace throne. Crescents of fountain mist drizzle over me while I watch families of ducks waddle into the lake, their feet creating delicate ripples of water that swirl together into dizzying, hypnotic patterns. This is the first chance I've had to sit down this morning and *think,* think about whether there's any way out of delivering this chair, or finding my mother's dog. There's a sense of deflated tranquillity and acceptance, the calm that comes right before tackling an impossible problem you know has one painful solution.

Across the lake, what appears to be a trail of floating white dots, the bouncy kind you see on kids' shows that follow in time the words of a song, drift along the water's edge. The glare's too strong through the fountain mist to see what the dots are, but there's a musicality to their movement, a slapping of the pavement in time to their own percussive beat. They're runners, a graceful, fluid caravan of young boys, jogging around the lake, stretching their legs back and forth in place, bodies standing still on a long conveyor belt, yet moving closer. They're shouting a call-and-response chant between themselves and an older voice that's leading the way, set to the tune of a popular rap song, whose tune itself was borrowed from another song:

Tally ho! Tally ho!
Shit!
Tally, tally ho!
Bullshit!

Approaching the boathouse, the boys slow down in unison, like a train edging to a stop at a platform. Their crisp white-collared, short-sleeve shirts have a red-stitched insignia that says ST. GOTTESCHALK'S. The leader, a rangy man with a military crew cut and gray stubble poking through his four o'clock shadow, yanks off a pair of aviator sunglasses and makes a whirring motion with his hand.

"Take five, boys," he says and lights up a cigarette.

The boys yell and shout while they bend, flex, and stretch in tight clusters. They ignore me; a woman sitting next to the lake in a gilded throne chair doesn't seem out of the ordinary to them.

The older man walks over and stares at me in the chair.

"Hope?" he asks.

Mr. Charles MacArthur, or Crazy Mac, the track coach at Downtown High, where I was on the varsity squad, is now the coach at St. Gotteschalk's, an old Catholic school built over a razed convent and located next to the expanded freeway off-ramp and a strip of renovated luxury condominiums. Crazy Mac had an incandescent reputation in school. His jogging songs were littered with obscenities, he drank and smoked on campus, drove an expensive sports car no teacher could afford on their salary, and because of his long, unex-plained absences, was rumored to be a government spook.

"Like a queen on her throne. Glad to see nothing's changed, Hope," he says, calling me by my nickname. "Bet you still remember how orgasmic a smoke is after running. Want one?"

"I don't smoke anymore."

"Ah, so you don't run anymore," he says.

I flinch because he's right. It was the one thing that brought me joy in high school.

"How's life at St. G's?" I ask.

"Less bullshit than the public schools, at least until they get shut down and turned into condos. I've brushed up on my Bible. 'In our hearts, we seek compassion. In our souls, we look for grace,'" MacAr-thur says.

"That's pretty," I say.

"It's a load of shit," he says. "But God keeps the alimony pay-ments on time."

"Another divorce?"

"When it comes to relationships, women are chess players," he says. "They see several moves ahead. Men are playing checkers—jump, jump, jump, king me." He motions to the chair. "So this is what happens when you quit running. You become so lazy you need to carry your own chair around."

"It's not mine." I laugh. "It's for someone called the 'Coat Queen.'"

"Have fun," MacArthur says. "She soaks us with a garden hose whenever we jog by her house. Two minutes, guys!" he screams over his shoulder, and the boys dissolve back into a pair of straight, ordered lines.

"We gotta move, Esperanza. In training for the fall invitational. You're welcome to join us. You could show these plebes what a runner looks like."

"I can't," I say. "I'm looking for my mother's dog. Have you seen him? Small, fast border collie? Jesus, he's not even *my* dog."

"Can't help you. And knock off the blasphemy," MacArthur says, "or you'll have to answer to the Lord."

"You're crazy, Mac." (This is what *anyone* would say to MacArthur after talking to him, hence his nickname.)

"Not about this. The Lord's for real," he says, and I can't tell if we're talking about the Lord from Echo Park or the Good Lord Above. "But it's a good thing you're looking for a dog," Mac says and stubs out his cigarette. "Dog's a symbol for envy, one of the seven deadly sins. Okay, boys, mount up!"

The boys walk up a sloping path, waiting for Mac to take the lead. They break into a synchronized jog, floating dots once again, singing a brand-new song:

> *In heaven, they don't serve beer up there!*
> *That's why we're fuckin' drinkin' here!*

When I'm sure Crazy Mac's out of sight, I do a short jog carrying the chair. Twenty steps later, I'm winded. I follow the ducks' example and waddle up the hill to Kensington Road.

On a street that borders Angelino Heights lies the Coat Queen's magnificent three-story emerald green and candy-cane red Victorian mansion, one in a row of over two dozen magnificent Victorian mansions lined up next to one another like a storybook lane. Her house sits on a corner that intersects with a street that dead-ends in an open field enclosed with a chain-link fence where *trabajadores* are working and dotted with surveyors' flags and colorful banners announcing the construction of a new housing development.

The sky above her home, punctured by an intricate weather vane, is as blue as the waters off a Caribbean island. A wrought-iron fence guards a razor-sharp front lawn and a wall of immaculately trimmed twenty-foot hedges. Chrysanthemum, bluebell, and lily flower beds, with birds of paradise peeking out from underneath an overgrowth of trumpet vines, grow alongside a cobblestone walkway. On the front porch is an antique bench swing, swinging in the breeze over elaborate marble tile arranged in a Spanish-style mosaic. It is difficult to imagine this house looking any different at the turn of the twentieth century. Could this be the home of an antisocial lunatic?

I knock on the door and set the chair on the porch next to a row of potted strawberry plants. Their scent makes me think of Gerald. He was sweet to me in ways that I appreciated—like taking me on picnics and bringing me baskets of fresh strawberries because he knew they were my favorite—but that also left me feeling vulnerable, dependent, and conceited, like making me mix tapes with "love" songs from bands that made him want to drink all day (the Replacements, the Clash, and Bob Marley & the Wailers). When he proposed to me, with a mix tape of course (U2's "All I Want Is You"), he said he wanted children. Lots of children. And for a moment I saw them—a beautiful but ragtag band of mixed children, struggling to find an identity between Mexican and American. I was trying to find a way to do it, and not feeling very successful. If their mother couldn't find a way to do it, what hope was there for them?

I told Gerald to get up and go so many times, when he got up and left for good, I felt stunned and heartbroken. When I found my courage late one night in a wine bottle to get back in touch, I saw a photo online of Gerald posing with his fit, athletic wife sitting on his lap at a company picnic, a baby in her arms. I drank several more glasses and dreamt of running my hands through his blond hair as the smell of strawberries filled the room.

I knock on the door again. No one answers. After I left Echo Park, I lost my impulsiveness, the need to answer questions, the ability to not take no for an answer. The instinct to push open closed doors without knocking. But now I have no fear or compunction. Something speaks to me in a whisper, and had there not been a breeze carrying away the street noise—the sounds of cars, buses, construction, machinery; neighborhood progress—with it down the block, I might never have heard it.

It says, "You belong here." I bring the chair inside.

The floor-to-ceiling double front doors with carved angels, pineapples, and frosted glass, several inches thick, open onto a parlor with a brass and ivory-cushioned sitting bench, a pair of thick oak end tables, and a miniature glass chandelier hanging low over a stairway with a grooved balustrade, channeling running water down into an iron chalice littered with fresh rose petals. I've walked into the lobby of a grand movie palace from the 1920s, a meticulous construction that is a seamless illusion of a separate and more opulent life. Had I missed a split in a dividing wall, I'd have set down the chair and walked out. Instead, I place it next to a velvet sitting bench, pull the sliding doors apart, and wander into a shapeless room without windows.

A crack from the door spills light in like flames itching the corners of the darkness, eating away at its edges. Stuffed onto a maze of conjoined rolling chrome coat racks are overcoats and cutaways, box coats and mackinaws, maxi coats and morning coats, shrugs, basques, and frocks, along with a panoply of wraps, tunics, ulsters, toppers, manteaus, and stoles. Layers upon layers of coats, arranged in unsteady, vertiginous stacks, threaten to topple over and crush anyone reckless enough to pull a garment from its Byzantine placement to try on. It's summer, so the temptation is small, but in this black, airless room, a sweaty chill flutters across my back and scampers down my forearms. I shiver while I finger textures both rough and soft through sheets of protective plastic.

"Who are you?" she asks. In a far corner of the room, a woman silhouetted in an ankle-length evening coat stands by a doorway.

"I'm sorry," I say. "I delivered your chair. From Lorenzo's? I left it out in your front parlor."

"Do you expect me to believe that?" she asks.

"I'm sorry," I stammer. "I'll leave."

"Come out of the dark," she says.

I sidestep through the room, following her as she sweeps into a large formal room like a movie star at a red carpet premiere. Her chocolate-trim fur coat ripples as she makes sweeping arm gestures. She ushers me into a dining room with a grand table that has twelve chairs and thirteen place settings. Disappearing behind another "fake" split wall, she returns with Lorenzo's chair and slides it in at the head of the table.

"Thirteen chairs. Now I can use this table again," she says. Dust coats my finger as I run it across the tarnished silverware. "Oh, but I haven't had guests in years." Her laugh makes me shudder.

"Are you cold, dear?" she asks.

"No, I'm fine," I say. "My mother made me bring a coat. She's crazy . . . um, I mean, she worries too much."

"She made you wear it this morning?"

"Mothers do that kind of thing."

"Not all mothers," she says and reaches out to brush my fur collar. "This is a beautiful coat," she says.

"Thanks," I say. It feels like time is creeping away from me in this house.

"You carry your mother's warmth wherever you go," she says.

"Um, I guess?"

"That's so lovely. I'm very happy for you," she says and starts to cry.

"Oh," I say. I'm anxious to find a way out of here. Then it hits me. "Would you . . . like it?"

"You would give me your coat?"

"Uh, sure," I say, sliding it off. "It's been sitting in a closet."

"You would give the coat off your back to a complete stranger?"

"Yeah," I say and hand it to her.

"Why would you do this?"

"I don't know. I never wear it. I don't need it. And you're letting me give it to you."

She weighs the coat in her hands. "I . . . don't know what to say."

"Well, enjoy it. I have to go now. I'm looking for my mother's dog," I say and walk to the front door.

On the front porch, I hear Crazy Mac's runners in the distance. The Coat Queen touches my shoulder. "I want to thank you. But I don't know your name."

"Aurora. Aurora Esperanza."

"Esperanza?" she says. "That's a beautiful name. It means 'hope.'"

"Yeah, I know."

"Esperanza is my last name, too," she says.

"Really? That's . . . neat," I say. "It's a common name."

"There's nothing common about hope."

"No, I meant—"

"I understand what you meant."

"Hey, maybe we're related." I shrug.

"That would be something, wouldn't it?" she says and touches my cheek. "The Lord does indeed work in mysterious ways," she says and closes the door behind me.

That name again. Am I hearing things that aren't there?

I walk across the street in a daze to the now deserted construction site, where I hear a radio play an old Spanish *ranchera.* The workers are gone. How long had I been in the Coat Queen's house? The song drifts above a barley sea of weeds, dead brush, and garbage, an unfamiliar melody paired with a recognizable voice. I can't place it, though. There's a plaintive loss I feel whenever I walk past a construction site, or a kitchen in a restaurant, and overhear one of those ancient Spanish songs playing through a pair of cheap transistor radio speakers. The pain in the balladeers' voices in those songs; it's like picking up an emergency broadcast from a world that exists only in my peripheral vision.

The fence is too high to scale, and its support posts have been sunk deep, but there's a part of the chain link that hasn't been secured to the posts. A section of metal peels back like the lid of a pull-top can, and I crouch in underneath. On the ground are scattered broken bottles, small but deep holes, and concrete blocks with plastic bottles and take-out boxes laid out on top of them as if they were makeshift dinner tables.

The voice sounds stronger here, as if growing in confidence the farther I tread in. The fence's boundaries dissolve into the glint of a past midday sun, a taut metal wire receding into that graying horizon line of smog that makes Los Angeles appear to be under a perpetual smoldering cloud from an extinguished fire. The field expands beneath my feet, sprawling up to and over the lip of a steep dirt hillside. From the tip of the ledge is a locked-in-a-tower's-eye view of Echo Park. This view will become the sole possession of whoever's house is built here, and they will see every day what I may never see again: cottages and bungalows spread across these hills— these glorious mounds and valleys my mother told me about—like tar paper jam, streets stitched together in Spirograph patterns, and God's footprint, Echo Park Lake. Her geysers rise up like hot sewing needles piercing the smoggy air, and her big toe sprouts a boutonniere of fiery pink lotus blossoms. Boats float in lazy curlicues across her waters while the Ferris wheel's screams and laughter are a collective, buzzy hum, the sound you hear when your ears ring. The din and shuffle of several thousand people down below walking at a window shopper's pace blend in with the faint chanting from Crazy Mac's running school battalion off in the hills.

The song I've followed to the edge of this hill rises in both pitch and volume. It's not coming from a radio, and it's not a *ranchera*. A man's singing in a trilling, echoing yodel, filtered through a crackling PA system, a voice much like . . . Morrissey's! But . . . he's singing in Spanish. It can't be him, then. I've never heard Morrissey sing in Spanish; if he had, I'd have heard it online, or on the radio after midnight, when they play ironic, novelty, or "joke" records (songs sung by popular musicians in Spanish). Is there a Mexican Morrissey imitator who has mastered mimicking his appearance (the easy part) and his singing ability? Impossible. Where is the song coming from?

Rocks scatter down the hillside as I step on a firm mount on the cliff's edge that juts out over the chasm. As I move onto the lip, a hot, reflective light shimmers in my eyes, making me squint. From what must be over a mile away, I am blinded with a powerful brightness, a brightness so white it turns everything black. Here in this darkness comes that feeling I had in my mother's kitchen when that blond morning glow came through her window, more intense and warm than before. There is a complete and overwhelming feeling of love and acceptance; no sensation of hot or cold, no fatigue or exasperation, no embarrassment or hate. And no fear. I'm blind, standing on a slender mount jutting over a sheer drop, and I have no fear.

In this brief moment, I have faith that I will not fall.

The song, then the light, dissolves into the sound of barking and another vision too miraculous to be believed. Blackjack is sitting behind me, panting with a happy grin, small dirt splotches on his fur the one clue to his day's adventures. Taking his leash out of my purse, I kneel to his level. Why didn't I bring doggy treats with me?

Stepping off the ledge, I whisper his name and edge my hand around to his collar. Blackjack cocks his head, studying me, trying to judge my intentions while I jabber in what I hope is soothing baby talk that will calm him long enough for me to leash him. My fingers graze the back of his neck to grip his collar and attach the leash's metal pull tab to it.

That's when he rears back. I scuttle a few inches on my knees over to him.

Back again he goes. Seeing the leash dangle by my side, Blackjack crouches into a sprint stance, ready to play a game of chase.

I take one step forward, and he's off, running back across the field. Damp clouds of pollen clot my lungs as I pop up and down behind him like grease on a hot frying pan, trying not to step into one of the many holes that could snap my ankle in two.

Blackjack sprints around the lip of the ledge to the far side of the cliff, reaching a fence surrounded by thick brambles and dead bushes that trap him. He's got nowhere to go.

I lunge at him, but slip on a loose clod of soil, buckling my legs. Blackjack wiggles his body through a narrow opening under the chain-link fence. My body's braided on the ground like rope when I get a whiff of powerful, insouciant, protest excrement covering the plastic soles of my now cracked shoes.

"Dog shit." I laugh. My exhaustion turns my laughs to tears, and the sound I make rolls down the hillside like the noise of box-sledding kids screaming for their lives in terror and in joy.

A sharp pain in my ankle—stronger than a sprain but not a broken bone—keeps me from squirming under the fence. Lying on my back and using my hands and one good leg for support, I crab-crawl down the hill to where the fence drops off and ends in piles of rolled-up mesh wire clustered around a large hump in the ground, then claw my way back up the hill on the opposite side of the fence. When I reach the top of the cliff, my hands are covered with scratches and cuts, my pants and blouse are filthy, and my purse has large clumps of dirt in it. I'm dirty and exhausted in a way I haven't been since I used to play outdoors.

It's late in the day. The sky's lost a fight with the sun, beaten to a black, blue, and purplish hue with a thin, smoggy gauze acting as a dressing. On this side of the hill are pockets of run-down bungalows hosting barbecues complete with loud Spanish *rancheras,* racks of meat cooking over tinfoil-wrapped grills perched atop blackened hibachi tubs, large beat-up Igloo coolers stocked to the brim with ice-cold beer and *paleta* ice cream bars, and rows of folding patio chairs where *hijos* and *hijas, abuelitos* and *abuelitas* sit, laugh, drink, and eat from paper plates balanced in their laps. On both sides of this gully are developers' flags and markings cutting a rough perimeter across the hillside and intersecting at a construction site for a condominium complex to be built next year.

Leading from the spot where Blackjack nudged his way through a dense layer of brush are his paw prints, tracking over a muddy knoll and onto a barren field where, situated like a cross atop a mountain, there is a large shack blaring a Spanish *telenovela.* Through an open door I see a pair of white dress shoes facing a television, with who- ever's watching it hidden behind a sheet of compressed aluminum siding. A teenage boy in a baggy white shirt and long khaki shorts with a pockmarked face waves me away.

"You can't cross here," he says.

"I'm not crossing. I'm looking for my dog."

"There's no dogs here," he says and walks right up to me, trying to press me back.

"He came in through the brush," I say, standing my ground. "I need to check if he's here."

"There's no dogs here," he says, louder, more threatening. He stands right up to me, his height bringing him up to around my shoulders.

"I'm not leaving until I check on my own."

The boy sighs in my face. "You're gonna have to ask the Lord for permission."

Is it him at last? Is the neighborhood's miracle worker a destitute hermit who has a satellite dish hookup to his tin can of a house in the middle of a barren field so he can watch *telenovelas*? Any faith I'd built up about my experience in meeting the Lord disappears. This is no benevolent spirit. This is an old man with a punk kid for a son.

"I think 'God's' got better things to do than help me find my dog," I say.

"I didn't say 'God.' I said the Lord. The Lord knows. He knows where the dog is."

"I thought you said he wasn't here."

"He's not," the boy says, "but the Lord knows where he is."

"He does? Okay," I say, willing to play along if doing so will give me a chance to check the shack. "Let me speak to . . . the *Lord.*"

"The Lord's busy right now," he says.

"Why did you tell me I had to meet with him, then?" I ask.

"I didn't say you had to meet with him," he says. "I said he knew where the dog was."

"So why can't I speak with him?"

"The Lord's busy," he says.

"Is that the Lord right there?" I ask, pointing to the pair of shoes, which haven't moved since I set foot here. "Is that him, sitting in a chair watching *novelas?*"

"I don't make the rules."

"Why can't he see me?" I shout. "I need to see if my dog's in there!"

"But it's not your dog," the boy says and starts walking back to the shack. "And I told you, the Lord's busy." He pulls out the back of his shirt, flashing the taped butt of what could be a snub-nosed pistol. I back away, unwilling to press further and cursing myself for my cowardice.

"Why are you doing this? Why can't I talk to him?" I shout at the boy, surprised at how the pain in my ankle, and the deliriousness from a daylong, fruitless search, has made me hysterical.

The boy turns and says, "Because the Lord works in mysterious ways. Don't you know that?"

The way back to the cliff is, for some reason, much longer than the way to the shack, and when I reach the ledge, it's black out. Not night. Black—that brief, eerie time right after dusk but before the streetlights and car headlights blink on. How did it get so late? Where did my glorious, unspoiled free day go? How could I have been so wasteful with one when there are so few to be had at my age? There's chatter and laughter from the several thousand people at the festival, an ominous sound, like approaching thunder. Dim, undulating grill fires dot the hillside below, but the steepness of the climb means there's no way I can walk or crawl back down without a flashlight. Heading to where I think the street is, I wander into a maze of brambles, weed stalks, and eight-foot-high brush. There are no revving engines from drag-racing cars or bass-booming radios to lead me out, no televisions screaming from open windows, no kids yelling down the block to ask their parents if they can stay out five more minutes. With the layer of dirt and sweat caking my body, the exhaustion I feel from walking around without any sense of direction, and the dread at returning to my mother's without Blackjack, it takes my remaining strength not to collapse on my knees and cry.

Yet when this one thought—me buckled over in an emotional meltdown—enters my head, a light cleaves the thick brush, leading me through a jagged thicket of thorns and weeds scratching my bare forearms, digging their way into my jeans. I slash my body forward and follow the light out of the brush and onto another construction site, this one connected to a street that intersects Sunset Boulevard. The light that led me out of the thicket is the familiar and now comforting gaze of Sergeant Sunshine, his sunglasses illuminated by a row of spotlights from the street announcing the opening of a new "space" for artists and musicians in what used to be a drinking bar for off-duty police officers. Was this where the bright light I saw on the ledge was coming from? Was it a billboard advertisement that rekindled my faith?

The streets are jammed with double-parked cars and revelers headed to and from the festival. Wading through the crowd, I'm pushed aside by a mother with her young daughter walking in the opposite direction. Her daughter is wearing red satiny pajama pants, Hello Kitty clogs, and a leopard-print jumper with triangle cat ears on the head; on each of her sleeves is the word *Gwen* in Low Rider calligraphy script. She's got so much fancy gear on her I can hardly see her face. Attached to her wrist is a purple balloon that, caught on a breeze, flies into a crisscross pattern of low-lying Chinese lantern decorations and tangles around my arm.

"I'm sorry," the mother says. "She doesn't watch where she's going." The mother kneels down, working with the girl to free the balloon.

"Here, let me help you," I say. "Tangled up pretty good, isn't it?"

"Yeah, sure is." She jiggers the girl's wrist like a broken toilet handle, ensnaring it amid the strings above.

"Ouch, Mommy," her daughter says.

"Hang on, Maria," she says. "Mommy's doing her best."

"It's tied up in a big knot," I say.

"Sorry, this is a pain in the you know what."

"It's okay. I think untying this knot is a two-person job."

"Do you live around here?" she asks.

"No. Um, I mean, yeah, I . . . I know the area."

The mother stands up, holding the girl's hand tight to get a better handle on the knot. "Lots of changes," she says. "About time, too."

"I feel kind of lost," I say. "I guess it's good for the neighborhood."

"I love it," she says. "So many new people to meet and things to do. You should've seen the way it used to be."

"No, I remember. I remember the way it was."

"Oh, did you grow up around here too?" she asks.

"I've been in and out. Mostly out."

" 'No place like home,' though, right?"

"I . . . don't know," I murmur.

"What was that?"

"I think I can see what the problem is," I say. "Here, you hold one end, and I'll pull it loose from the other."

Untying the knot like a bow, we pry the balloon loose. "Wow, that was a workout," she says. "Thanks a lot. I'm sorry, what's your name?"

"Aurora."

"Angie. And this is Maria. Say 'thank you,' Maria."

"Thank you, Maria," the girl says.

We laugh. Angie offers her hand. I shake it, then out of sheer exhaustion, lean in and give her a hug. She strains against my caress, out of genuine concern or apprehension, I'm not sure which.

As they walk away, she waves Maria's hand at me, which entangles the balloon again. Instead of untangling it, Angie kneels down and shouts at Maria about her carelessness, her voice loud enough for me to hear over the din of the crowd. Maria shakes her head no, dabbing tears from her eyes, inhaling her sobs in large gulps. Angie scolds Maria as they blend into an anonymous crowd on the corner of Sunset Boulevard, the balloon a drifting, floating violet drop on the horizon that dissolves into the fixed background, a small detail on a massive landscape painting.

The Ferris wheel's lights snap on, etching fluid red and yellow neon circles in the sky. A quicksilver group of bodies congeal around me, eager for a closer look. It's a tense, excited crowd, open to the possibility of both happiness and joy at partying late into the night, or disappointment and anger at being turned away from an over-crowded gathering. In the air are the smells of baked breads and skunk, belligerent shouting into cell phones and parents disciplining overstimulated children, raucous laughter and lovers recounting their day's banal events to each other in exaggerated tones of excitement, a fierce blend of Spanish, Chinese, and English speakers vying to be the loudest.

Angie's question—no place like home, right?—sticks in my head. Is this still my home? Do I even belong here anymore? My exhaustion tricks me into seeing old faces amid these strangers. Boys I went to school with that I liked, or who may have liked me, now men with faces like sun-dried apricots. There's Lorenzo bargaining with a game operator for another batch of plastic rings to toss. Crazy Mac cuts a swath with his boys in tow through the crowd to the Budweiser booth. A *trabajador* around my father's age wanders around in a circle carrying a large yellow mallet. Vince is walking hand in hand with a woman who could be my mother save for the confidence and poise she stands with. But none of them see me, and they probably aren't the people I think they are; everyone's too lost in their own thoughts. Walking around the lake, searching piles of garbage for Blackjack, I'm back to being a stranger in my own neighborhood, in my own home.

I'm standing by a carpet of blossoming lotus flowers when I see a body floating toward the fountains. It drifts facedown like a crumpled leaf, its sleeves and upper body visible, its hands and legs submerged. A second body, this one with a fur collar, spins in a lazy circle behind it, again without hands or legs. Then a third one, a peacoat. Dozens of coats, like broken starfish floating out across the water, flutter into the lake from a red Japanese footbridge and drift into a misty wall of fountain spray. They twist and swirl as they fall, their arms flapping like wings about to take flight.

The Coat Queen stands on the middle of the bridge wearing the coat I gave her, several large boxes by her side. Nodding her head, in conversation with no one I can see, she dumps another coat over the railing.

"What are you doing?" I ask.

"I don't need these anymore."

"My coat worked? You're warm at last?"

"No," she says, "it did not work." She drops another coat over the bridge, and it plops onto the water, a plush suede lily pad.

"I . . . I don't understand. You're wearing my coat."

"It's not your coat that worked," she says.

"Then why you are throwing these away?"

"Aurora Esperanza," she says. *"¿No crees en milagros?"*

A coarse, hungry tongue laps at my fingers. A wet nose burrows itself in my palm. I crouch down and hug Blackjack, who jumps onto my shoulders, licking my ears and neck, and buries his head in my armpit. Grabbing his leash, I attach it to his collar, and lead him off the bridge.

Underneath the shadow of the Ferris wheel, on an uncrowded part of Echo Park Avenue appears a hunched man with brown hair down to his shoulders, a malnourished beard, wearing a shabby linen suit and the same shoes I saw sticking out of the Lord's shack. A weird, glossy fuzziness fleshes out the edges of his body, an aura of what must be Ferris wheel light that gives him a dazzling carbonated glow. He looks like the cardboard cutout that stands next to amusement park rides, telling you how big children must be before they can ride. Beside him are the teenage boy I spoke to and three men, larger, older, and more intimidating in appearance.

"I'm not here to cause trouble," the Lord says.

Sensing my discomfort, Blackjack pulls the leash taut. "I have to get home," I say. "Please let me by."

"He's not ready to go home with you yet," the Lord says. "I must take care of him until you're ready."

"I don't believe in you," I say. "Stay away from my dog."

"He's not your dog," the Lord says.

"And you don't belong here," the teenage boy says. "You're not foolin' nobody. You don't belong here."

"Leave me alone," I say and take several tightrope steps back.

"I can't let you leave here with him," the Lord says.

His men move on me. Blackjack's confused, growling at the approaching men but making no effort to run away. One of the men lunges for the leash, and I jerk it back, choking Blackjack, who yelps. Another man tries to snap my free arm away from the leash to knock me off balance. I scratch his forearm, drawing blood. A third man rushes at my arms while the boy wrestles the leash from my hands. He yanks the butt of his pistol from his pants, revealing the taped-up grip of a coiled dog leash. He fastens it to Blackjack's collar and leads him, without struggle or complaint, to the Lord.

I'm overwhelmed with a new and conflicting sensation of protectiveness for Blackjack. I flail against the boy and the men gripping my forearms, stomping on their feet while the third man leans down and tries to grab my legs. I kick him in the jaw with the foot whose ankle I twisted and hear a meaty snap. The man I scratched grabs my free leg and tries to wrestle it underneath his arm. They're taking away my mother's dog by dragging me to the ground, each man trying to suffocate my body by throwing his weight on top of me. I can feel their breath on my neck, their sweat on my legs and forearms. I shout for someone, anyone, to help me, but the crowd is applauding the fireworks, fleeting gardens of fiery pink, green, and red blossoms booming and shaking the ground.

Four men grab my arms and legs, tearing at parts of my body, trying to pull me to the ground—but I am still standing.

"My dog!" I scream. "Give me back my dog!"

The Lord says, "He's not your dog yet." Then he disappears into the crowd.

I lunge in his direction by grinding both my feet into two of the men's shins and, leaning my weight forward, trip the men off balance. The five of us wobble like a top losing momentum and then, in one tangled heap, slam onto the ground. I wriggle out from under the teenage boy, who has fallen on my lower back, and crawl on my hands and knees up a grassy hill, rising to my feet to the roar of *oohs*! and *ahhs*!, the crowd entranced with the pyrotechnic display.

Blackjack's being led into a doggy crate in a large white van. I pump my legs in time to Crazy Mac's rhythmic chants, which I hear in my head, running, then running faster, feel the satisfying solidness of pavement slapping under my feet and the wind rushing through my hair, a thrill I haven't experienced in years, running faster, a euphoria that keeps me running, down the street as the van pulls away, out of reach, running to the opposite side of the lake, where a man is striding through the crowd, oblivious to his presence, their heads craned to see the fireworks reach their crescendo, a cataclysmic barrage of seismic booms and blinding flashes that light up the fan-shaped geysers and the lake underneath. The man's salt-sprinkled black hair is coiffed in a fifties-style pompadour, his silky Egyptian blue shirt glitters under a shower of mist, and his jeans are cuffed atop a pair of expensive-looking boots. He walks up to the curb and disalarms his Porsche, a glistening metallic silver.

He mouths the words, "You belong."

This is the color of my faith.

Morrissey stands up on the car's doorframe, aware that I and I alone see him and know who he is, and waves, a gesture neither dismissive nor inviting but a simple acknowledgment that we have made contact in this brief moment that doesn't need to be shared or verified by anyone else. It's a beautiful secret, which is rare as so many secrets in my life are ugly, and it fills me with an overwhelming sense of peace and accomplishment as I close my eyes and pass out on the lawn of Echo Park Lake.

The next morning, under a hangover sky, I kick my way off the corduroy side of my mother's couch and thump onto a cold linoleum floor. My face is scored from the corduroy, and my ankle's wrapped in an Ace bandage. I limp to the dining room table, where Vince is drinking tea with lemon from a cracked coffee mug.

"How you doing this morning?" he asks, monotone.

I'm unsure how much to share with Vince. How much does he know? If he wrapped the bandage around my ankle, he must know enough, but how much comfort should I expect from him? I'm in a lot of pain, but does he want a daughter today, or an acquaintance? I decide to play it somewhere in the middle.

"What time is it?"

"It's Monday. You've been out solid for almost twelve hours," Vince says.

"Shit, I need to get out of here," I say. "I could use a ride. I don't think I can drive."

His shoulders stiffen up. He takes his cup to the sink, turns on the water full blast, and washes it out. "You should call a cab. I'll pay for it."

"Forty dollars to get across town?" I say. "I'd rather walk on my one good foot."

"I'm really busy today, Aurora," he says, reverting to my name. Vince is back in "detached" mode, which always follows when he sleeps with my mother. When I was younger, this first confused me, then made me cry, then angry, then exhausted, and now accepting. There's nothing left here for me to do or say except to say good-bye.

"Where's Momma?" I ask.

"Outside," he says.

She's sitting on the porch with her own mug of tea, Blackjack resting at her feet. He's licking her fingers clean of wet dog chow, which she dips her hand into from a bowl and nurses under his mouth.

"Vince is going to bail again," I say, sitting by my mother's side.

"He's a good man," she says.

"Of course he's a good man," I say. "But he's still going to take off."

"You don't know that," she says.

I watch Blackjack nurse from my mother's fingers. "When did he show up?"

"Last night, after the festival," my mother says.

"How did you find him?"

"Jesús brought him over," she says.

"Jesús?"

"Yeah, Jesús. You know, the Lord?"

"His name's Jesús? That's why they call him the Lord? He's . . . real?" I ask.

"Of course he is," she says.

"But . . . what did he want with the dog?"

"What did he want? He's the trainer."

"A dog trainer? But Vince said those things about the Lord . . ."

"I told Vince he shouldn't tease you. Jesús lives out in a field all by himself, and everyone around here makes up these crazy stories about him. He's not crazy. He needs a big space to train his dogs. This neighborhood's getting too crowded for the hermits. They're turning his land into condos. Anyway, he was part of the surprise. I may be leaving town for a while."

"Where? And why?"

"Vince's thinking about San Diego, and I'm thinking I might join him. I can't take Blackjack with me. This is his home. I was going to give him to you, but I needed someone to train him to be a calmer dog."

"Mom, I told you, I don't—"

"Like him. Right, got that. But I don't trust anyone else. And I thought if he calmed down, you'd meet him halfway."

I dip my hand in the wet dog chow and hold my fingers under Blackjack's mouth. "Why didn't you tell me any of this yesterday?"

"The dog got out. Didn't make sense to tell you anything if he didn't come back."

"Christ, Mom," I say. "Those men tried to beat me up."

"They thought you were trying to steal the dog. They protect what's theirs."

"I do, too," I say, defensive.

"*Yo vi, yo vi.* Vince came running over when he saw the scuffle, caught you when you ran after their van and passed out. It took four men to drag you down," my mother says, her voice cracking with a hint of pride. "I didn't know you cared about the dog that much."

"I care because he's *your* dog, Mom."

"*Was* my dog."

"Does Vince know you're going with him?"

"He knows he can't live without me for long."

"Mom, maybe you should let Vince live on his own for a while," I say. "I need you here. Blackjack needs you."

"You two took care of yourselves yesterday."

"I can't take care of a dog. I wouldn't know where to begin."

"You could start with a walk," my mother says.

"A *walk*," I say and laugh until the pain in my ankle makes me wince. My mother stands up and stretches, her body firm and taut, like that of the woman I saw Vince talking to last night. It *was* my mother.

"How about a game of fetch?" I say, picking up a yellow chewed up Frisbee in my mother's front yard and tossing it. Blackjack scampers over, eager to play.

"You want to play fetch with us, Momma? Up in Elysian Park?" I ask, my voice cracking. I want nothing more in this moment than for her to join us, to choose me over Vince.

She sees the confident grip I have on Blackjack's leash and shrugs her shoulders. "I'm too old to chase things that don't belong to me," she says.

I leave the Frisbee on the steps and walk Blackjack to Elysian Park. On the way there, we make a brief detour to a *mercado* where, many years ago, a young girl was shot and killed while dancing on a corner. Blackjack sniffs at the remnants of a shrine attached to the back of a squat utility box that is to this day replenished every few weeks with fresh flowers, candles, drawings of the Virgin Mary, and a mosaic of Xerox copies of a group photograph of mothers and their young girls, standing and crouching in two neat rows, everyone following the rules except Mother and me. I take out Lorenzo's sticker roll and spell out ALMA on the utility box in rows of sparkly stars and hearts, the only graffiti "tag" I've ever drawn.

For years afterward I knew when we looked at that picture, my mother and I saw different things, though we never talked about it. It was so crucial to the police that they figure out whether I was standing or falling (my mom says white people always have to know all the details), and that photo was analyzed by almost everyone in the city to figure out what the real answer was. I don't remember whether I was rising or falling, but that didn't matter. I was in motion, and I lived. What I saw in that photo was my mother staring in disbelief that my body had the audacity to rise up to her height. She wasn't looking at my head and my mouth. Where the trouble began, she liked to say. What she saw was a tough-looking girl in baggy clothes, trying to pretend I didn't have a body that was starting to resemble a woman's and a face that resembled her own. I'm my own way, I liked to say then. I don't say that much anymore.

The one difference between an accident of chance and a miracle is faith. The truth is that everyone who looks at that photo sees what they want to see, in much the same way everyone looks at an oil stain under a freeway overpass and sees what they want to see, be it a puddle of ooze or the Virgin Mary. People claimed to see the Virgin Mary in our photo, standing between me and my mother. For years I thought back to that moment and realized that, if I'd listened to my mother, I'd be dead. That gave me a reason to ignore everything she said, including her good advice. But I realize two things died that day: Alma, and my connection with my mother. I have waited years to reestablish that connection, to feel for her the way I used to when I hugged her close to breathe in her perfumed neck, or when I spotted her returning from the supermarket from my bedroom window and ran down the street to carry as many grocery bags as I could loop around my fingers, or the way I clutched her waist at the sight of a strange dog. The Lord had, in this absurd way, granted my wish to get back my mother's dog. Why couldn't he give me my love for my mother back, too?

Elysian Park sits underneath Dodger Stadium, the former home of Chavez Ravine, and of Aurora Salazar, the last woman to be taken from the land that once was hers. Heading down Scott Avenue to Elysian Park Drive, Blackjack and I walk amid verdant meadows, plump trees, picnic tables, and large patches of grass rolling around the hills in sea green waves. We sidle up to a pickup baseball game and lie behind the backstop on a splintered bench. Blackjack's itching to chase the ball each time it's hit, but he stays by my side.

A bright yellow Frisbee sails over me, as if suspended from strings, a lost UFO from one of those old black-and-white sci-fi movies I loved watching on Saturday mornings in my pajamas. Blackjack takes off and catches the wayward satellite before it slams into a steel-drum trash can. Racing back, he leaps right past me and returns the Frisbee to my mother.

She walks over, holding the Frisbee out to me. Our fingers interlace and lock in the exchange. She lets them linger there, then pulls the Frisbee away. The whip-snatch motion sends both our hands upward, sailing the disk in a clear, uninterrupted trajectory. I watch Blackjack take off in haste as it soars high above the ground, where the ghosts of Chavez Ravine walk side by side with the souls of the bereaved, through the sun-dappled leaves of the walnut trees, across the thickets of dusty chaparral, down a plain dirt road lined with Mexican fan palms, to an amaranthine valley of orange groves that bloom from here to the ocean, a land rich with roots that grow, thrive, burn, are razed, heal, then grow again, deeper and stronger than before.

This is the land we dream of, the land that belongs to us again.

Gracias

Teachers—Howard J. Shorr, Jon Reider, John L'Heureux,
Susan Weinberg, Angela Hassall,
Judith Grossman, Wilton Barnhardt, Geoffrey Wolff, Nick Lyons,
Randall Sullivan, William J. Bernstein, Margot Livesey

& every author it was my privilege to work with in publishing.

Family—Amy Hundley, Sophoat Lim, Jeff Lytle, Daniel Maurer,
John Reed, Jason Wishnow

For "yes"—Susan Golomb

For the golden opportunity—Amber Qureshi, Martha Levin,
Dominick Anfuso, & everyone at Free Press

Wherever you are—Frank Zamora

For turning over a new leaf—Alaina Sudeith

"Pattie Boyd"—Kitt Allan, who's on every page

Thank you for spending some time in Echo Park.

About the Author

Born and raised in Echo Park, California, Brando Skyhorse is a graduate of Stanford University and the MFA Writers' Workshop program at UC Irvine. For the past ten years he has worked in New York as a book editor. He's currently writing a memoir about growing up with five stepfathers.

The Madonnas of Echo Park

A Novel

Brando Skyhorse

Reading Group Guide

ABOUT THIS GUIDE

The following reading group guide is intended to help you find
interesting and rewarding approaches to your reading of *The
Madonnas of Echo Park*. We hope these enhance your enjoy-
ment and appreciation of the book. For a complete listing of
reading group guides from Simon & Schuster, visit
BookClubReader.com.

SUMMARY

The Madonnas of Echo Park follows the lives of Mexican Americans in the shifting landscape of Los Angeles's Echo Park neighborhood, highlighting the intersections and collisions of American and Mexican culture. Felicia, a housekeeper, and her daughter, Aurora, weave in and out of each others' lives, struggling to find a common ground on which to relate. Aurora's estranged father, Hector, finds himself a witness to a murder and must choose between deportation and complicity. Aurora's former classmates Duchess and Angie, steeped in American culture, drift apart as they choose different paths in life, each looking for a place to fit in. Felicia's aging mother, Beatriz, who gave Felicia up as a baby, is torn between guilt and nostalgia and her own driving self-interest. As their lives tangle together and bounce apart, each is given the opportunity to decide what is truly important to them.

QUESTIONS FOR DISCUSSION

1. The first chapter of *The Madonnas of Echo Park* is actually a fictional Author's Note, telling the story of the real Aurora Esperanza and the inspiration for the novel. Did you read the Author's Note before starting the novel? Did you realize it was fictional? Do you prefer to know an author's thoughts about their book before you start, or formulate your own thoughts about it first?

2. The reporters that cover the drive-by shooting raise questions about the positioning that saved Aurora and placed Alma Guerrero in the path of the bullet. Felicia seems doubtful herself

about what actually happened during the shooting. Was it just a mother-daughter spat, or did survival instincts kick in and shape the incident?

3. "Tall poppy syndrome" or "crab mentality" is often pointed out by observers of minority cultures, when a member of the community achieves, or has goals, outside of the average and is dragged down or derided by others. Do you see this at work in any of the characters' lives?

4. The incident on Efren Mendoza's bus highlights the racial tensions simmering below the surface of everyday L.A. Was the bus driver trying to manage an unmanageable situation or acting out of his own prejudices?

5. Aurora, speaking of her obsession with Morrissey, says, "You can't help who, or what, you love." Is she speaking solely about music, or is there a broader context for her statement? Do you agree with her?

6. Felicia works for wealthy white people cleaning their homes; Hector and Diego do construction work off the books. Are these genuine opportunities, or are they examples of immigrants being taken advantage of?

7. Beatriz (Felicia's mother, Aurora's grandmother) believes she has been visited by Our Lady of Guadalupe at a bus stop on Sunset Boulevard. Do you believe in religious visions, or is this simply a hallucination brought on by age and guilt?

8. Juan's father, Manny, is an ex-gangster. What purpose do gangs serve for their neighborhoods? Are they the only option available for many teens, or are they an actual choice on the part of their

members? Can people truly change after being involved in that kind of violence?

9. Felicia knows her employers as Rick and Mrs. Calhoun, despite the fact that she becomes much closer to Mrs. Calhoun than to Rick. Is the way she refers to them indicative of their relationships? Why doesn't it change with the changing circumstances?

10. Are the Calhouns camouflaging their dysfunction with charitable acts, or are they genuinely sympathetic to Felicia? Is this an accurate portrait of their society/demographic? Are the Calhouns' dark secrets the exception or the rule?

11. Which character was your favorite, and which was your least favorite? Which one did you identify with the most?

12. *The Madonnas of Echo Park* has many points of view and many connections that are often revealed slowly. Did the structure of the novel enhance or detract from the reading experience? Would you change it? If so, how?

TIPS TO ENHANCE YOUR BOOK CLUB

1. *The Madonnas of Echo Park* is inspired by a childhood incident that the author can't let go of, as told in the Author's Note. Consider it from the real Aurora's perspective and ask members to share a formative moment from their own childhood, in which they were refused something because of who they were or how they were perceived.

2. Several of the characters mention favorite musicians from their teen years—Aurora was obsessed with Morrissey, Angie loved

Gwen Stefani and No Doubt, and Alma enjoyed Madonna. Ask members to pick an artist who was essential to their teen years and bring their favorite song by that musician to the meeting.

3. Immigration reform is a perennial topic in American politics, with many calling for more aggressive laws while others believe that more leeway should be allowed. Have members vote anonymously on immigration reform—stricter or more relaxed—and discuss the results.

4. Have a book club movie night: watch *A Day Without a Mexican,* in which the entire Hispanic population of California disappears. How does the portrayal of Angelinos, both white and Hispanic, compare with *The Madonnas of Echo Park*?

5. Ask each member to select their own Echo Park, a real place that they would write about, to discuss with the group.

AUTHOR Q&A

1. **_The Madonnas of Echo Park_ opens with a fictional Author's Note, recounting an invented childhood incident that is the inspiration for the novel and is a story in itself. Why did you choose to open with a fictionalized Author's Note?**

I'm fascinated by books where the author inserts himself into the narrative. Less fascinating, though, are the results, which often reduce the potential of an intriguing idea down to something that seems artificial. What's missing in many of these attempts is a sense of urgency or actual risk. Why is the author putting themselves into their own book? What do they gain as a writer, and what do we gain as readers from the experience?

For years I lived a life in which I unknowingly—then knowingly—denied my Mexican heritage. When I was writing the book, I assumed there would be questions about why someone named Brando Skyhorse would write about Mexican Americans in East Los Angeles. They were questions I had myself and part of the reason my next book is a memoir. The risk, then, was to acknowledge that part of my life in this book in some way. The best place to do that was, it turned out, in a fictional Author's Note. The Author's Note is often considered the one unshakable pillar of truth in a book and has been used in recent years as a venue for full-length disclaimers for memoirs that may stray too deep into fiction. What better place, then, to create a fictionalized reality for my experiences, and what better signature to attach to such a piece than B.S.?

2. Who are your influences as an author?

During my early apprenticeship learning to write, I overdosed on William Faulkner (*Absalom, Absalom!* is my favorite novel), Virginia Woolf, and George Orwell. I then wrote many poor imitations of each. Over time, I learned how to glean important writing lessons from a variety of books. On that instructional bookshelf: Raymond Chandler's *The Big Sleep,* Nick Hornby's *High Fidelity,* Stephen King's *The Stand,* Michael Cunningham's *The Hours,* Kazuo Ishiguro's *The Remains of the Day,* and many others. And that's just the fiction collection!

I think writers can pull influences from everywhere. I'm a huge fan of Charles M. Schultz's *Peanuts* strips. They're probably the first thing I remember reading and savoring. When I had enough pocket money, I'd buy as many used collections of his strips at garage sales as I could find. I'm sure I pulled some subconscious writing lessons from them as well. At least I hope I did, as the strips from 1950–1970 were brilliant examples of economic yet heart-wrenching storytelling. And while we're talking about illustrated storytelling, might I add that Marjane Satrapi's *Persepolis* is one of my all-time favorite books?

3. **The Madonnas has an ensemble cast of characters, all connected to one another in a tangled web. Did this complicate the writing process? How did you decide on the structure of the novel and keep track of the intersecting storylines?**

The idea for *Madonnas* came quickly in an outline form of about fifteen to twenty vignettes all connected by one word, *Amexicans,* which was the book's original title. Each vignette had a character dealing with a central conflict, and as I wrote them, some grew in importance while other vignettes didn't prove strong enough to be anything more than an idea or a few sentences in an abandoned Word file. I knew the characters all inhabited the same area, Echo Park, and were living in the same time period (from the 1980s to today), but their connections only surfaced as I wrote my way through the book. It did take some figuring out on scratch paper as to which characters were connected to whom, but no longer than it takes me to figure out a tip in a restaurant (that is to say, a very long time).

4. **In some ways The Madonnas resembles a collection of short stories. Which character did you start with? Which was the most difficult to write? The easiest?**

I didn't worry too much about the form of what I was writing because I wanted to get everything down on paper first. I'd already written a long novel that had some sections that I enjoyed but was a disaster in every other way and didn't find publication for good reason. (Of course I can laugh about it now!) An early draft of *Madonnas* did indeed resemble a story collection but, like mercury, the chapters kept congealing to one another and the characters kept revealing connections among themselves so I decided to pursue them.

Aurora revealed herself to be a central character early on, and I knew that the entire book would pivot around her journey, whatever it turned out to be. Her beginnings were humble—she was chasing a dog around Echo Park. That was all I knew. Yet the more time I spent with her, the more she became her own woman with her own energy, vivaciousness, and passions. At a certain point, I stopped trying to lead her and just followed along, which proved to be a wise move as she led me to a majority of the book's other characters.

Her connection with Felicia, though, was where I had the greatest challenge, and in a sense they are related much more than just being mother and daughter. Felicia was just as headstrong as Aurora and her chapter, "The Blossoms of Los Feliz," was an enormous challenge in that I wanted to make Felicia's voice and experiences as honest as possible. My editor, Amber Qureshi, was crucial in helping me work my way through the several drafts of Felicia's story and in fleshing out the various connections among the other characters.

It's true that you remember the most difficult characters but you also remember the characters that have a lot to say and a seemingly effortless way of saying them. Efren Mendoza, the bus driver, was probably the easiest character to write because his anger and obsession with rules and regulations gave me a built-in conflict that I simply had to write toward. He represents that fierce, aggressive side each of us are capable of expressing—in an email, driving on the freeway, waiting in line at the supermarket—but says things in such a pure and true way that it's hard not to be seduced by his voice, even though you may disagree with what he's saying.

5. **The geography of Los Angeles, specifically the Echo Park**

neighborhood, is intrinsic to the storyline. Was it a challenge to stay faithful to the geography, and did you worry about making mistakes? Do you think you could have told the same story in a place that resembles, but isn't, Echo Park?

I wrote about the landscape in *Madonnas* from memory. I haven't been to Echo Park in twelve years. Yet what amazes me most is that seeing the neighborhood depicted in movies, or getting reports from friends who have just visited the area, and also using Google maps, I can tell that the geography is almost unchanged. One of my former stepfathers told me in an email that when he recently visited Echo Park after being away for many years, "the people have changed but the place is still a dump."

There were minor geographic tweaks I made to facilitate connecting the various characters but the book makes a faithful effort to render it just as I remembered it. Like my stepfather noted, some of the people have changed, and I made an effort to represent that oncoming feeling of a neighborhood that's in the process of gentrification, but what you read is, I hope, what you get.

I couldn't have told this story anywhere but in Echo Park, and it had to be the Echo Park I remembered from my youth to address the various things I wanted to say in the book. It wouldn't have worked where I live now, in New Jersey, because the way a transplant looks at a place is invariably different than the way someone who was born and raised there looks at it. My memoir will likewise be set in Echo Park, but Book #3 (of which I have a vague idea for now) is telling me it's time to explore other territory, and I'm looking forward to having the opportunity to do that when the memoir is done.

6. Music is important to your characters—from Madonna to Morrissey, many have a musician that is essential to their lives. Who is your essential musician? What did you listen to during the writing process?

Anyone taking a cursory glance through the book will see that I wear my eighties childhood on my rayon print shirt sleeves. Looking through my CD (yep, still have those) collection, it's astonishing how many eighties artists there are and how many albums and singles (remember those?) I bought from certain bands. I tend to play songs on repeat when I'm writing because it helps me zone into the work, but much like the character Rob from *High Fidelity* I can't give you one essential musician because I couldn't limit myself to just naming one. The characters themselves, though, do a good job of explaining what I was listening to throughout the book's writing. "Cool Kids" required a steady diet of Gwen Stefani solo/No Doubt. Aurora would only let me listen to The Smiths, Morrissey, Depeche Mode, and the occasional eighties one-hit wonder song. (Also note that her story is the book's longest). "The Hustler" came alive when I played Los Lobos, while Felicia was a big eighties-era Madonna fan. And surprisingly, the bus driver in "Rules of the Road" thrived when I played Kanye West.

7. **In L.A., Mexican and American cultures meet—sometimes they mingle, sometimes they clash. Just in the span of *The Madonnas*, Echo Park undergoes a cultural shift. What do you believe is the future of the neighborhood? Of the city?**

When I was growing up, I remember watching a documentary about Sunset Boulevard, which runs right through the neighborhood, and the narrator said, "Echo Park is the most beautiful ghetto in America." It didn't start out that way. It was once a secluded enclave for Hollywood's silent-film-era movie stars. Charlie Chaplin lived in a large Victorian mansion that overlooked Echo Park Lake; Tom Mix helped form the first Los Angeles movie studio there. Nearby is Dodger Stadium, which was built upon an old Mexican neighborhood called Chavez Ravine that was demolished by the city in order to lure the Dodgers from Brooklyn. Today, Latinos (largely Mexican), Vietnamese, and an influx of young urban gentrifiers live together in an area that is a mix of different cultures and identities, something that, for me, feels unique in a city like Los Angeles, where so many neighborhoods have stricter ethnic boundaries. I can't predict what's next for Echo Park or Los Angeles but I do know that transition comes in waves. Whatever that next wave is, Echo Park will maintain that aura of imperviousness to time that makes it so special for me.

8. **There are several single mothers in the book—Felicia, Christina, and Angie—as well as many strong female characters. Are they reflections of women in your own life? What was it like to write from the female point of view?**

Writing this book would have been lopsided and incomplete without the womens' stories of Echo Park. Along with a rotating cast of stepfathers, I was raised by my mother and grandmother, two strong, opinionated women. Growing up in that environment made me more attuned and probably more sympathetic to a woman's outlook on life and the various trials they face in a day. Whenever I write, the female characters often have a stronger and more assertive sense of who they are and where they want to go, two things that as a writer you always want your characters to have, and as a result I tend to enjoy writing from a woman's perspective more. I didn't plan for *Madonnas'* two central characters (Aurora and Felicia) to be women but looking at the finished result, I don't see any other way the book could have been structured.

9. **How long did *The Madonnas* take to write? What was the hardest part? The easiest, or your favorite?**

Writing the book took about nine months. Thinking beforehand about writing the book, and revising what I'd written after, took another three years. What I write evolves every day because the way I look at my work is different today from the way I looked at it yesterday. It's having different perspectives on a piece of writing that allows the most beneficial work—revision—to take place. Revision is both the hardest and my most favorite part of the process, depending on the results I have to read at the end of the day.

10. **In the Author's Note, you state that in the early 1980s, you didn't know you were Mexican. This is actually true. How did writing the fictional Author's Note compare to writing your next book, which is a memoir about growing up with five stepfathers and being raised as a Native American? Do you identify yourself as Mexican now? How has your awareness of your heritage shifted over the years?**

In memoir, the risk for a writer comes in daring not to lapse into lying or exaggeration to tell a more exciting story. The temptation is great when your facts may not adhere to a neat, fictional symmetry and memories can be as fleeting as vapor. The goal in my writing a memoir is not to exaggerate or sensationalize my experiences but to uncover as many truths as I can about my upbringing. What actions led to my having five stepfathers? Was it my mother's intent to have such a disordered personal life? You must understand that for a number of years, many of my mother's closest friends (and ex-boyfriends) had no idea she was Mexican and believed her when she said she was Native American. Also, can a reader who may have had their own dysfunctional home life find some solace or encouragement in reading about my own experiences? I want to write an engaging and entertaining book but not at the expense of discovering my own truths. To do otherwise would put me in the position of selling out my own creation and I have no interest in doing that.

When I was three years old, my Mexican father abandoned me. My mother decided to raise me as the biological son of another boyfriend/husband, an Indian in prison named Paul Skyhorse. As for "Brando," my mother liked to joke that she was so enamored with the movie *The Godfather* she decided to name her unborn child Brando or Pacino. Pacino Skyhorse? I think she made the right call.

For many years, I didn't know the truth about my past. I was raised as an Indian and was introduced to Indians who were part of the American Indian Movement in Los Angeles in the 1970s. My mother told people she was Indian even though she was Mexican. Then when I did know the truth, I lied about it because my mother felt it wasn't anyone's business. After she died, I kept up the lie because it was easier than a long-winded explanation of what the truth was. Now I embrace both Mexican and Indian identities as if I were an immigrant, someone who moves between the worlds of Indian and Mexican culture, but into the "American" world, too.